in **Numbers**

By

Jeanine Hoffman

ePublisher

book

http://L-Book.com

Strength in Numbers
Lesbian Fiction: Romance

Copyright © 2007 by Jeanine Hoffman
All rights reserved.

eBook ISBN: 978-1-934889-50-3
Printed ISBN: 978-1-934889-51-0
Audio eBook ISBN: 978-1-934889-52-7
(Audio sold only at http://L-Book.com)

First Edition
eBook, Print, Audio Format
Published: April 2010

This book is Published by
L-Book ePublisher, LLC
La Quinta, Ca. USA
Email: info@L-Book.com
Web Site: http://L-Book.com

Editor: Judy Underwood

Cover Design by Sheri
graphicartist2020@hotmail.com

Visit Our Web Site at

http://L-Book.com

Author's Note

In the course of writing this novel I was reminded of how much enjoyment some people receive from doing little things for their partners, friends, and family. Once upon a time, a long time ago, I was taught that lesson from my grandmother in the form of culinary joy. We would cook together and for each other and enjoyed sharing the kitchen as well as the end product of our endeavors.

I've found throughout my life that the way to some women's hearts is through their stomachs as well as the act of showing you care enough to prepare a meal for them. I've also found a simple joy in being able to share a kitchen with a close friend or partner. Done well, we can almost dance our way through the preparation of a very enjoyable meal. Most of all, I enjoy the simple pleasure of cooking for my friends and family. It is a way for me to express my love and friendship in a quiet way.

In the original draft of this book, there were extensive (and I do mean extensive) cooking scenes because a few of the characters share a love of cooking in the same way that I do. Instead of forcing the non-cooks among us to go through a verbal recipe of sorts, my wonderful publisher and I came up with another idea.

At the end of the book I have included the basic recipes from the story line. The measurements may not be precise but I encourage you to fiddle with them and make them your own. As one of my favorite women would say: Bon Appétit!

Acknowledgments

So many people to thank and so little space! First and foremost, my thanks to the amazing people at Fox Chase Cancer Center without whom there would be no author and therefore no book.

Also much thanks goes out to the members of the Virtual Living Room – you women ROCK! I would be remiss if I didn't thank MJ, JD, CP, DK, (Do I know people with names and not initials? YES!), Rrrose, Cheri, Rachel, Vic, Jae, and Fran. Thank you all for the help, support, and belief in me when I had very little left.

The Royal Academy of Bards must also be thanked for providing so many of us a chance to see what others think of our work before taking it any further.

A huge thank you to Roxanne for taking a chance on me, and Judy for turning my thoughts into something eminently more enjoyable to read. She has been wonderful! Sheri for what is always going to be an amazing cover if she works on it, and of course, you! Whoever you are that took a chance to read this book. I hope you enjoy reading it as much as I did writing it.

Thank you!

Dedication

To the medical personnel that care for us when we can't, – I thank you.

To Sue – without you, there is simply no point.

And Parker – you are too young to read past this point – but thank you for accepting my need to take time away and write.

Strength in Numbers

CHAPTER 1

"*D*AD, PUT ME DOWN – you're crushing me!" Jay teased her father with a smile.

At six-seven, Jay's father was a big man by anyone's standards. He had a significant amount of grey in his once black hair and was built like the construction worker he'd been before he started his own contracting company.

"My daughter, the banker," he teased back. "So busy that we don't see you nearly enough." His big brown eyes twinkled at her. She got her five-foot-nine inches from him but her lithe build and hair color came from her mother. Steven Conway took a second look at his daughter, taking in the shadows under her brown eyes, the slight dishevelment of her honey blond hair as it fought to escape from the French braid she'd worn to work. He worried about the long hours Jay put in, but he was proud of her and all that she had accomplished in the financial world. At thirty-five, she was one of the youngest senior lenders in a successful regional banking firm in Philadelphia, but her long hours were relentless and she looked tired.

He gave her another quick one-armed hug. "Can you be social for a little while, or are you as worn out as you look? Your mom invited the neighbors over at the last minute."

"I'm good, Dad. It was just a long week. I'll be fine once I get some of Mom's great cooking in me."

"Who's coming over?" she asked.

"Well, it is a bit of a surprise," he said, stopping. "The McIntyres and..."

Jay turned quickly. "Not Bailey?"

He nodded. "I knew you'd be surprised."

"I just saw her at work. She's applying for a lending position."

His face mirrored the shock she felt. "And will she be offered the post?"

"Looks that way. Sharon is having HR run the screens and assuming she passes an offer will be made."

He exhaled and gave her a supportive smile. "Okay, kiddo, we can do this. Let's go break bread with the neighbors and their wayward daughter. You are spending the night, right?"

Jay nodded. "Brunch tomorrow and a round of golf before I head back into the city?"

"Sounds like a plan! Let's go join everyone." Her father took her bag and opened the back door, letting her enter first.

Jay's mom, Laura, gave her a hug and kiss on the cheek as Bailey's parents rose to greet her. Just then Bailey stepped into the room, carrying a drink in one hand and a bowl of mixed nuts in the other. She smiled at Jay shyly and said a soft hello.

Jay smiled stiffly and turned to her mother. "I'm going to run upstairs and change. How much time do I have?"

"We have about twenty minutes before dinner is ready. You made better time than I thought you would."

"Guess I got lucky. All the traffic was coming into the city by the time I left work. See, Mom, working late has its perks!" It was a never-ending debate between her and her mother.

* * *

Jay dropped her bag on her childhood bed and sat down to take off her shoes. She pondered the strange course her life was taking these days. She stared into space, too tired to be angry. What was Bailey doing back here? She collapsed back on her bed and thought about their unexpected meeting last week.

She had agreed to meet the new candidate for her section, grateful that she might finally have some help with her workload. As she walked to her boss's office, she noticed the dark haired woman in the reception area and stopped, frozen in place. It can't be... she's in Florida. What is she doing here?

The dark haired woman looked up, caught sight of Jay, and smiled warmly.

"Jay, I didn't realize you worked here."

"Bailey?" Jay gathered her thoughts and replied in the most professional tone she could manage. "What are you doing here?"

"I'm applying for a position in lending. I've decided to move back home."

Before Jay could respond, Sharon's door opened and her assistant stuck his head out. He smiled and motioned her inside. "She's ready for you now, Jay."

"If you'll excuse me," Jay nodded coolly to Bailey, squared her shoulders and headed into Sharon's office. Once inside she shut the door firmly and confronted her boss. "That's the woman you want me to meet?" She pointed at the door and the lobby.

Sharon looked startled. "Bailey McIntyre? You know her?"

"I grew up down the street from her. Our families are friends."

"Why didn't she use you as a reference?" Sharon asked, standing. "Jay, is this going to be a problem? Anything that I should know?" She stared at Jay. "Is she an ex?" she asked in a strangled whisper.

"As a matter of fact, I haven't spoken to her in years, long before I came on board here." Jay couldn't help thinking that if Sharon didn't know she was gay then this issue wouldn't have come up at all. On the other hand, if Sharon would loosen up about being openly gay, both of their lives would be easier.

"Let's meet with her and see what I think. I've heard good things about her career from our parents but we've never worked together. Actually, I haven't seen her since sometime during our first summer break from college." Jay took a moment to calm her breathing before nodding to Sharon that she was ready.

Jay snapped back to the moment and decided it was time to get changed before her mother came looking for her. Suddenly her past was back in her present, and she wasn't sure what do with the feelings brought by that situation. It had been years since they had spoken and now they might work together. Life was ironic to say the very least.

With a sigh, she forced herself to get up and change her clothes. She made a quick stop in her bathroom to freshen up and then went downstairs to be social.

* * *

The dinner went well with a tinge of déjà vu for everyone. Jay's parents carried on a lively conversation with Bailey's folks, reminiscing about the escapades of their daughters through the years. Eventually, they asked Bailey about her time away from Philadelphia.

She spoke fondly of her life in Florida. "I couldn't believe I was recruited before I finished my internship! Within a year of leaving school, I was able to put together a down payment on an adorable condominium near the beach. Plus, working for a regional bank instead of one of the national chains, was the right move. Smaller companies seem to focus more on the consumers than strictly upon the numbers."

"The strength of the numbers matters too though. Loans can't be decided just on feel good vibes." Jay interjected.

Bailey didn't take the bait and the conversation turned to recreation as Bailey regaled the gathering with tales of her attempts to try new sports during her first year out of college.

Bailey laughed. "The first time I tried to get up on water skis I almost drowned myself! I just didn't understand the physics involved in getting upright until it happened by mistake. Once I managed it, I was able to repeat it. I decided to stick with snorkeling. Keeping up with coral was more my pace." She chuckled at the memory and the others joined her.

"You haven't mentioned one relationship. Did you leave anyone special behind?" Laura asked.

Bailey shook her head with a wry grin. "No, my last relationship ended a little over a year ago. I think I always knew I would come home, and I never dated anyone I could get serious about." She peeked at Jay. *How could she ever explain why things were so messed up between them?* To her surprise, Jay was looking at her as well, and she blushed a little. Jay looked confused as if she was working on a puzzle and the answer was just out of her reach.

* * *

Later, after their guests had left, Jay quietly helped her mom clear the last of the dishes and load the dishwasher.

Her mother leaned against the counter and spoke softly. "Jay, are you ever going to tell me what happened between you two?"

"I don't know what you mean, Mom."

"Yes, you do. That summer break after your freshman year you two suddenly stopped hanging out and Bailey transferred to Florida. She had never mentioned an out of area school before then." Jay started the dishwasher while thinking about that first year at school.

After winter break was over things seemed to change. One evening as Jay watched Bailey get ready for a frat party, she realized that she was jealous of the guys who would get to dance with Bailey. She was too good for them. With a sudden breath, Jay looked at Bailey again. She was in love with her best friend.

- 11 -

She didn't say or do anything that night. She was too afraid of what she was feeling. She might scare Bailey away forever. Just before spring break, Jay finally decided to approach Bailey with her feelings. Bailey was lying in her bed, and Jay could hear her familiar sounds as she got ready for sleep. Jay decided to tell her how she felt.

"Hey, Bail?"

"Yeah, Jay, what's up?" Bailey asked in a sleepy voice.

"Um, have you ever, I mean what would you think..." Jay couldn't seem to find the words or the courage to put voice to her thoughts.

Bailey sat up in bed, suddenly concerned about her best friend. "Spill it, Jay, you've been acting weird most of this term, what's been eating at you? You know you can tell me anything."

Jay took a deep breath, let it out slowly, and screwed up her courage for another attempt. "Have you ever thought about kissing a girl?" It wasn't exactly what she was planning on saying, but it did open the door at least. Bailey was quiet for a moment and Jay waited nervously.

Finally, Bailey replied. "I can't say I've never thought about it, but it isn't really something I've thought seriously about either. Why are you asking, Jay?"

"Um, never mind," Jay mumbled, feeling her heart start to ache. Jay heard the bedclothes move on Bailey's bed and felt her sit down next to her. Bailey put a light hand on Jay's back and started to massage her gently.

"Jay, sweetie, talk to me. You're the best friend I could ever have, and I hate seeing you in pain."

Jay gave a gasp as she felt Bailey's hand on her back and squeezed her eyes shut, trying to keep the tears from escaping. "Bailey, I think I prefer girls," Jay said in a rush, afraid that if she didn't say it fast she wouldn't say it at all.

Bailey's hand stopped briefly then continued rubbing gently. "Is that what's been bugging you? Did you think I would think less of you for being a lesbian?" Bailey asked.

"Jay, you've been my best friend for so long, how could I stop loving you because of who you prefer to date? If I didn't realize how much you must have struggled with this I would be mad at you for keeping secrets."

Jay gave a small smile as part of her worry faded. "I admit I've been afraid of how you would react. I didn't want it to change things between us. I was afraid you would feel awkward around me in our room." Jay knew she had something else to admit but was now unwilling to go further.

Bailey leaned over and gave her a big hug. "You've always been here for me. It's about time I get to be here for you too!"

Jay was relieved that things were fine between them, better in fact, now that Jay had been at least partially honest with Bailey. Better, that is, until the summer break and everything went out of control.

Just as Jay's mother poured two fresh cups of tea, Jay's father came into the room.

"Hey, how long does it take to load one dishwasher?" he teased.

Laura smiled at Steve and offered to make him a cup of tea as well. "Sorry, I was just asking Jay what happened between her and Bailey that ended their friendship. It was pretty evident tonight that whatever it is, the two of them haven't worked it out after all these years."

Steve accepted the tea from his wife. Jay's face reflected the defeat she felt. "Do you want to tell her or shall I?" he asked noting the look on his daughter's face. Laura looked at them both in astonishment.

"You mean you've known all these years and never told me about it?" She glared at her husband until he came over and put a hand on her shoulder.

"Honey, Jay came home one night that summer a little drunk, and she was pretty talkative. You were out of town and by the time you came home, Jay had asked me to keep this a secret."

Jay sighed as she listened to her parents. *It's time I need to get this talk over with, especially if Bailey and I are going to work together.*

"Mom, Dad, let's go into the living room and talk. Mom, I'm sorry I asked Dad to keep a secret from you, but you and I weren't getting along so well back then."

After choosing seats in the comfortable room Jay squirmed in her seat. "I'm not sure where to start," Jay said.

Her mother gave her hand a squeeze. "Start with freshman year of college which is when you and I started having trouble."

Jay nodded. "Okay, we left for school, and we were roommates as you know. We had always been so close. It was Bailey and me against the world. I could hardly remember a time when we weren't friends. As the year progressed, we got even closer since we lived together and spent most of our free time together." Her mother was looking at her intently, and her father gave a nod of encouragement.

"I think I stopped confiding in you Mom because I was afraid you wouldn't handle my feelings when I didn't even understand them myself. One night I watched Bailey get ready for yet another frat party and realized I was jealous of the guys who would get to dance with her. I suddenly understood that I had fallen in love with Bailey." At that, she choked up and her mother gave her a hug.

"Oh honey, I'm sorry this hurts you. Are you sure you want to finish telling me tonight?"

"Yes, I should have told you long ago. I'm sorry, Mom. I didn't mean to shut you out. This is still painful and embarrassing for me."

"You have no reason to be ashamed of anything. You were realizing your attraction to women, and you were frightened of my reaction. I can understand that entirely."

She took a few sips of her tea and then made eye contact with her mother. With a deep breath, she continued her story.

"Well, I didn't say anything to Bailey about my feelings that night. I was afraid that I would scare her away forever. Then summer break happened."

Jay remembered as if it were just yesterday, walking in to that party that led to the best and worst moments of her life.

They had gone to a party at a friend's house after promising her parents that they would be careful. Bailey was more of a party girl, and Jay always tried to watch out for her. Bailey started to drink and work her way through the throng of people with Jay following along trying to look as if she were having fun. Eventually, Bailey was drunk, and Jay was getting sick of the party and its noise. She motioned to Bailey that she was going outside for a few minutes of air. Bailey waved her off and returned to her conversation with a group of guys. After about fifteen minutes, Jay was bored and wandered back inside to look for Bailey. She was hoping to convince her to leave the crowded house and head somewhere more peaceful. Once inside, she couldn't find Bailey anywhere. As panic set in, she headed upstairs and started looking in bedrooms until she found a closed door. When she heard more than one male voice inside, she slammed the door open and stormed in. Her best friend was passed out on the bed with three guys around her. Jay saw red.

"Get the fuck away from her! You jerks! Can't you see she's drunk? Get out! I don't ever want to see you near her again!"

Jay held her friend close, trying to get her to wake up. Finally, Bailey came around, looking confused.

"What happened, Jay? How did we get up here?"

"You don't remember?" Jay tenderly stroked the hair away from Bailey's face.

"I don't remember anything after you left the kitchen. Oh my God, Jay, what did I do?" She sobbed uncontrollably on Jay's shoulder as fear and shame warred with each other on her face.

"I've got you, Bail, you're safe now, sweetie. I won't let them hurt you, I promise." Jay kept murmuring to her as she hugged her. When Bailey finally cried herself out, Jay suggested that they get out of the party and head home.

"You can't tell our parents Jay. I don't want them knowing what an idiot I was tonight. They'll never trust me again." Bailey, suddenly terrified of her parents finding out, begged Jay.

Jay agreed reluctantly. She didn't want to cause trouble when the outcome had been okay, and Bailey seemed to have learned her lesson. She helped straighten her clothes, and they left with Jay supporting Bailey to the car. Bailey leaned into Jay's warmth, snuggling next to her on the drive back to Jay's house. Jay's heart beat faster the whole way home as the reality of how close her friend had come to being raped sank in. Bailey gave a little sigh and wrapped her arm around Jay's waist as she snuggled close, sound asleep. Jay would swear her heart skipped a beat and struggled to focus on the road.

Jay woke Bailey when they arrived and helped her into the house and upstairs to her room. Jay helped Bailey get out of her clothes and into one of her sleep shirts before she stripped, showered, and joined Bailey, more than ready for sleep. Jay was shocked when Bailey reached over in her sleep and snuggled in tightly. In all the years of sleepovers, of sharing beds, this had never happened before. Jay's heart hammered in her chest. The woman she loved more than anyone else was sleeping in her arms! Jay took a long time to settle into sleep but finally closed her eyes to rest.

A couple of hours later, Jay awoke to find that Bailey was half on top of her with both of their sleep shirts pushed up. Their legs were intertwined, and Jay had her arms wrapped around Bailey. She realized that Bailey's head was resting on one breast with her hand cupping Jay's other breast. Jay groaned and couldn't help but arch her back to let her breast come into more contact with Bailey's hand.

Without speaking they kissed, both groaning with the heat of it. Suddenly, Jay's shirt was pushed out of the way, and the woman of her dreams was straddling her.

"Bail, are you sure, I mean..."

"Don't you want me, Jay? We've shared everything else, why not this too?" Bailey started kissing her neck and Jay lost all ability to think clearly. They spent the rest of the night exploring each other and learning how to please one another. In the morning, Jay awoke to find Bailey gone, and only a pleasant soreness as a reminder of last night. She smiled softly as she realized that her fondest dream had come true. *Bailey must be in love with me too!*

After a quick shower, Jay rushed over to Bailey's house. *We should talk,* she thought with a smile. *Yeah, talk among other things.* When she got there, no one was home. She shrugged, feeling a little disappointed, but knowing that Bailey had probably gotten home to find that her mother had plans. Wandering home, she replayed the scenes from the previous night over and over in her head. She smiled, thinking that life was just about perfect.

Of course life is full of surprises as Jay discovered. She couldn't seem to get in touch with Bailey. That was strange since they rarely went more than a day without seeing each other. A day turned into a week before Jay finally heard from her. She received a phone call as she was getting ready for bed one night. When she heard the strain in Bailey's voice, panic gripped Jay's insides.

"Bail, what's wrong? Where have you been all week? Why haven't you called me back?" Jay heard a sigh on the other end of the phone before Bailey spoke in a stilted, slightly frozen manner.

"Jay, I've decided to transfer schools. There is a great program in Florida that I've decided to go into. I'll be near

the beaches and can finally shake Pennsylvania winters."
Bailey tried to sound lighthearted but her laugh was brittle.

Jay gasped. "Florida? When did you decide this? I
thought..."

Bailey sighed again. "I know what you thought, but I
was drunk, and it shouldn't have happened. In fact, I can't
believe you took advantage of the situation like that, Jay."
Jay felt a coldness pierce her heart as if an icicle had just
been driven into her chest. Bailey continued. "I've been
thinking of Florida for a while, and I made my decision this
week. I think it's for the best if we don't see each other for a
while. I think I need time to get over this and I would
appreciate it if you didn't contact me." With that, Bailey
hung up the phone and shattered Jay's heart into a million
pieces.

Jay recounted an abbreviated version of her experience
with Bailey, and the heartbreak that followed. She also filled
Laura in on the surprise interview candidate she'd found outside
of Sharon's office earlier that week.

"Looking back, I know that I didn't force her or take
advantage of her, but at the time I was devastated that perhaps I
might have gotten carried away and misread things. I think she
was simply too afraid to examine what had happened and ran
from it and me."

Jay's mother had tears running down her face as she hugged
her daughter again.

"I'm so sorry you went through all of that on your own.
Thank you for telling me what happened. I'm so proud of what
you've done, and who you've become."

"I was too embarrassed to tell you. Dad only found out
because I was dumb and got drunk shortly after that trying to
forget about what had happened. I made him promise not to tell
you in exchange for my promise to come out to you."

"Jay, you've come a long way. You know I love you for
who you are, don't you?"

"Of course, Mom, we're fine. But, you can understand now why dinner was awkward for me."

Laura paused and then shared a look with her husband. He nodded and gave her a small smile. "Jay, you should know something that Helen told me a couple of years ago." Helen, Bailey's mother was a close friend of Laura's, and it wasn't unusual for the women to share confidences. "Apparently, Bailey came out to them a few years ago. It seems she finally accepted the truth about herself after denying it for a long time." Jay just shook her head and remained silent. "I just thought you should know since you will be working together," her mother continued.

Jay sighed and shook her head. "Such a waste. Maybe it was just me or maybe she wasn't ready to deal with the reality of coming out back then. I think part of me always suspected I wouldn't be her last woman. If she had just been honest back then..."

"From what her mother told me, Bailey didn't figure it out until after college. Helen only told me because she wanted to know how you and I were doing after you told me about your orientation."

"It'll be fine Mom. The past is the past, and I've moved on. She'll be working for me, and as long as she does her job and doesn't cross any lines, everything will work out somehow." With that, Jay stood, kissed both her parents goodnight, and went up to her old room.

* * *

Jay lay in her childhood bed thinking back over the evening. She was a little sad but also physically exhausted by her week and the talk with her parents. All of her memories of Bailey came crashing back to her as she flashed back to when Bailey's family first moved into the neighborhood. The first time the girls met they knew they would be friends. Over the years Jay never saw reason to doubt that initial reaction until that one night.

Jay turned over and pounded her pillow into submission as she tried to forget the feel of Bailey against her. She drifted off to sleep with past and present thoughts of Bailey mixing in her dreams.

* * *

A few houses over, Bailey lay in her old room, struggling with images of her past. She wished she could just run over like they used to. There was so much to say – to apologize for – and she didn't have a clue how to approach her. She had told everyone, including her parents that she had moved home because she missed the change of seasons. She knew deep down the main reason she had come home was to tell Jay the truth... the truth about everything. She wanted to give Jay the chance to make her live through the same pain and rejection that Jay had suffered at her hands.

If they were going to work together, she had better speak with Jay as soon as possible and clear the air. If this wasn't going to work out, she wanted to know before she accepted a job that would torture both of them. Tomorrow morning would be perfect before Jay left her parents' home. With a sigh of relief, Bailey finally drifted off to sleep.

CHAPTER 2

*F*RIDAY MORNING JAY'S supervisor, Sharon, sat in her office, after the morning meeting, thinking about Jay. She had seen the younger woman coming into work. Jay, dressed in a dark tailored suit, white dress shirt with stylish black boots and her honey colored hair pulled into a French braid, looked every inch the successful young banker that she was. Jay was one of the youngest senior lenders in the company and one of the most successful.

This morning had begun as she began every morning, a department meeting to go over new and complex applications, changes in policy and anything else pertinent to the department. Sharon had watched as Jay drifted, noting the smudges under her eyes. She was probably thinking ahead to the meeting that would follow – a conference with her own team, then closings followed by a lunch meeting with managers of the bottom three branches. Sharon had overheard Jay's secretary, Scott, giving her the morning rundown and watched him cock his head asking if Jay felt all right.

"You look a little tired," he had said.

Jay had chuckled. "A little? I'm fine, thanks. Nothing some sleep won't cure."

Sharon had tucked that away for future examination as she moved past them into the conference room. The company was one of a new breed of banks; open seven days a week for the convenience of its customers with full services available during the extended operating hours. That meant a senior member of the lending department, such as Jay, had to be available at all times – at least by telephone to answer the questions from the branch employees and to make lending decisions. As the senior underwriter in her department, Jay was often consulted by newer lenders for advice when dealing with applications that were somewhat murky.

"Did you close those two start-up business loans yesterday?" Sharon asked Jay, looking at her senior lender across the table.

"Yes, both closed with no problems, and I sold a separate line of credit to one of them," Jay answered with a smile.

"Excellent cross-selling! That's what I'm talking about, people. Make the cross-sell on qualified loans," Sharon had said, as her eyes settled one by one on the others in the room. She then moved on to another topic before wrapping up the meeting. As everyone left, Sharon had called Jay back.

"Jay, do you have a minute?'

"Sure," Jay had replied but Sharon saw her jaw clench, knowing full well that she was already thinking of the next meeting.

"Are you feeling all right? You look rundown."

"I'm fine, just a bit tired. It's been a busy month." They walked together into Jay's office, and Sharon shut the door behind them.

"Have you seen a doctor lately?" Sharon asked.

"Yes, within the year. What's this about?" Jay had set her notebook on her desk and looked at Sharon, smiling politely but it didn't touch her eyes.

"You just look worn out, and I was concerned. Anyone special keeping you up at night? If so, you need to be careful and not let it affect you at work," Sharon said cautiously.

"Sharon," Jay had laughed. "I'm married to this job. Who has time for social fun?"

"All right, if you say so, but if you need to talk outside of work, let me know," Sharon had said before she opened the door and left.

Back in her office, Sharon turned in her chair, thinking about her conversation with Jay. She wished things could be different, but it just wasn't possible. Her worry for Jay was more than simply her tired eyes. It was extremely difficult to be a lesbian in this conservative company, and she knew that from firsthand experience. Long ago she had decided to play by the rules and stay in her closet. Her last relationship had ended about five years earlier when her lover couldn't take the secrecy as well as always coming in second to Sharon's job.

She and Jay had run into each other at the Mann Music Center during an Indigo Girls concert shortly after Jay had begun working at the company. Sharon had gone with Sandy in an effort to piece things back together and try to enjoy each other's company once again. It was a warm Philadelphia night, clear and comfortable. They were sitting on a blanket, sharing a picnic dinner before the show when Jay had come up to them.

Sharon had stood and greeted Jay in a quiet voice. "Jay, what a surprise to see you here."

"I thought that was you," Jay said, grinning and happy to see her. "I didn't know you liked the Indigo Girls." She had tilted her head looking at Sandy.

Sharon had ignored Sandy. "Uh, yes, I do. Jay, I don't bring my personal life into work, and I don't want it brought there by anyone else."

Jay looked shocked by the sudden stiffness of her new supervisor. "Sure. I understand – keep things professional at work. Of course, Sharon."

Sharon glanced at Sandy's thin-lipped expression and sighed. "Jay, it's more than that, actually. No one at work knows about me. That's how I've managed to get ahead there. It's a conservative company in a conservative field, and they don't promote people who are different. You might want to keep that in mind for yourself as well."

Jay had blushed furiously. "I see your point. Sorry to have bothered you. Don't worry; I won't bring it up at work. Enjoy your evening." She left and hurried back to her friends.

Sharon sighed, turning back to Sandy on the blanket but caught "the look". She knew what was coming, another "living out and proud" lecture. She tried to stop it before it started. "Sandy, I know how you feel about this issue, but it's best if she learns now what kind of environment we work in and how to deal with it."

Sandy shook her head. "You were rude and didn't even bother to introduce me. Now she's afraid of you and thinks she's going to have to stay closeted for the rest of her life just to do well in your eyes! How is that environment ever going to change if you don't work for change?"

"Can we just agree to disagree on this one, Sandy? You work in a liberal field and don't have to deal with the conservative jerks I have to deal with everyday." She tried to change the subject. "Could we just relax and enjoy the concert tonight. Is that too much to ask?"

Sandy had dropped it, and they had enjoyed the show but their final breakup happened two weeks later.

She swiveled in her chair and stared out of the window. *What's done is done and I'm leaving it in the past.* Over the years that had followed, she'd spent way too much energy keeping Jay at a distance, always afraid that someone might connect them especially since Jay had not taken her advice about staying closeted. Lately, however, she'd begun to reconsider her own life as well as her professional relationship with Jay.

By reaching out to Jay now, she felt as if she was taking a small step in the right direction. Sharon knew she wanted her life to be different but was terrified of upsetting the delicate balance she felt she had achieved. She knew Jay was viewed as highly talented and professional even though she hadn't taken Sharon's advice. Still, she had no idea what Jay's life was like away from the job. After the concert she had completely stopped attending any GLBT community events for fear of running into anyone else.

Her intercom buzzed and reminded Sharon that her next meeting was coming upstairs. She asked her secretary to just send him in when he arrived. There was an opening in Jay's section, and she quickly glanced at the resume of this applicant. Bailey McIntyre, age thirty-four, graduate of the University of Miami, experience in another financial institution with a good reputation as a loan generator and closer. Excellent references, but no reason given for the sudden relocation. Nothing else from HR either. Sharon closed the file raising her eyebrows in a question just as there was a knock on the door.

"Come in," Sharon called and pushed the file to the side.

One of the most stunning women she'd ever seen walked through the doorway. She was the picture of a successful woman in business with stylishly short dark hair, green eyes like emeralds, short, standing around five-three and tastefully dressed in a black skirt suit with small heels. Sharon blinked rapidly before standing and motioning her inside.

"I'm sorry," Sharon said. "You're Bailey McIntyre?"

"Yes. I take it you were expecting a man?" She smiled, showing her dimples. "It happens all the time. My parents met at the Baileys Irish Cream booth at a Taste of Philadelphia event, and they decided to commemorate it."

Pulled into the smile, Sharon shook her head. She'd made the assumption of gender and apologized. "I'm sorry. I haven't even spoken with HR yet and was just going off the resume. Come in, please, and have a seat. Would you like anything to drink?"

Bailey smoothed her skirt and took one of the leather chairs in front of Sharon's desk. "No thanks. I'm fine."

Sharon quickly sat down. "I noticed you are relocating from Florida. May I ask what brought about this sudden wish for cold and icy winters?" She gave the younger woman a genuine smile, still intrigued with the face sitting across from her.

"One too many hurricanes happened," Bailey chuckled. "Seriously, my family lives in this area, and I've decided to move to be closer to them."

They continued the interview until Sharon decided to bring Jay in on the meeting since this would be a new member of her section. She asked Bailey if she would mind waiting in the outer office for a moment while she talked to the section supervisor. As far as she was concerned, the job was Bailey's if Jay had no objections.

During Jay's portion of the interview, Sharon remained quiet. She had not been prepared for Jay's information or reaction, and she watched them carefully. Whatever their history was, she wanted to make sure it didn't taint her department. However, both women were thoroughly professional, and she relaxed. It must not have been any more than just a friendship. Pleased, she again decided to make an offer to Bailey McIntyre.

When Bailey had left, Jay settled into a chair in front of Sharon's desk.

"What did you think?" Sharon asked.

"On paper, she's a great choice. I'm just not sure she's a good fit for this division."

"Jay, she's a go-getter with a lot of loan experience and knowledge. What exactly are your concerns?" Sharon tilted her head as she listened, trying to hear the explanation behind the words. She suspected issues from their past must be at the root of Jay's hesitancy, but she wasn't about to coddle anyone, especially Jay. "Do you have any concrete reasons why we shouldn't give her a chance? I have to tell you that I think she's perfect for the position, and she should have the opportunity to prove herself."

For a moment, Jay looked distressed but instead cleared her throat. "I'm concerned about her ability to blend into our existing setup. She's not used to such an integrated group sharing the workload." She shook her head. "If you feel that strongly, I'll give it a shot. I'm just not sure it will work out."

Sharon smiled. "Jay, I'm not worried. I know you can train and work with anyone. Consider it another management-building session. Working with people we know can be a challenge, but it may be easier since you haven't maintained a friendship over the years. You won't have the issues of trying to manage a friend."

Jay nodded and agreed to give it a try. Sharon said she'd file the paperwork with HR and have them contact Bailey with the offer letter.

* * *

Bailey left the building, got into the car, and sat with her head resting on the steering wheel for a moment, her heart still pounding. It had suddenly hit her that her mother had known Jay worked here. Why hadn't she at least warned her? She swore quietly and finally started the car, heading home to her parents'. She calmed down a bit as she drove, realizing that her mother only knew they hadn't been friends in years and probably assumed the two girls had just lost touch as they built their careers. In fact, neither of her parents had any idea of the real truth behind the split between she and Jay.

With a sigh, Bailey turned into the driveway and parked her blue Toyota Rav-4. She went into the house looking for her mother.

"Mom, where are you?"

"In here, honey. How'd the interview go?" Her mother was in the solarium tending to her plants, her favorite pastime. Bailey perched on a stool watching her mother work with the soil.

How did the interview go? Bailey thought about Jay's frozen expression and the stiff set of her shoulders as she had walked into Sharon's office. She had taken a seat in front of the desk, but Jay had sat on the desk, not beside her. Her heart had been jumping against her ribs as she tried to appear calm and poised. She had been positive Sharon had liked her, but Jay had only looked at her professionally and without a trace of the old warmth. *Could they work together? Could she ever repair their friendship?*

"Why didn't you tell me that Jay works there?"

"Oh, honey, I didn't even think about it. Did you run into her?"

Bailey gave a little short laugh. "Not only did I see her but, if I get this job, I think I'll be working under her." As soon as the words left her mouth, she felt her face warm, immediately thinking of the last time they'd seen each other.

Bailey stirred, slowly awakening and realizing the position they were in. She couldn't remember ever feeling so safe or so aroused in her life. She lifted her head and looked at Jay's half-lidded eyes as she reached to caress the soft skin. She'd had a crush on her for so long, and now she couldn't hold back. Ever since Jay had come out to her at school, Bailey had wanted this but didn't know how to deal with her feelings. Now it didn't matter. She wanted her, and Jay was responding.

The next morning the panic had set in, and she had taken off before Jay awoke. She was terrified of the consequences of the night before. She knew her parents would never understand and feared they might cause trouble for Jay. All she could think of was the high expectations her conservative, church-going family had for her. She was not going to let them down. Instead she ran. Ran from Jay, her family and from herself, all the way to Florida.

Her mother had her back to her but glanced over her shoulder. "That's great, dear. You'll have a chance to renew your friendship! You two were thick as thieves until the first summer after college. Whatever happened to make you lose touch?"

Bailey just shook her head. "I don't know, Mom. I transferred to Florida for school, and we just drifted apart." Even though her parents had finally accepted her sexual identity, she had no intention of sharing the night of her first experience with them.

"Well, you're home now. Perhaps you two can pick things up again. It'd be nice to have a friend to do things with here."

"Uh, sure Mom." Bailey stood and moved to the door. "I'm tired so I think I'll rest for a while. I didn't sleep well last night. Nerves, I guess."

"We're going to the club for dinner so be ready by six."

"Okay," Bailey said, heading to her room as the phone rang. She heard her mother answer and laugh. She had to figure out a way to have her life make sense again. The problem was that she didn't know if it was possible anymore. She may have simply waited too long.

CHAPTER 3

SATURDAY MORNING dawned clear and temperate with the forecast calling for nothing higher than seventy-four degrees. Jay met her father downstairs for a quick breakfast. They grabbed their gym bags and headed for the club. There was a wonderful feeling of homecoming for Jay. It was at this club that she had learned to play golf while still a child. She didn't take the time to play much anymore, but she kept promising herself to make more time. After agreeing on a place to meet, they headed off to the locker rooms. Jay tossed her gear in her locker and changed into the soft spike golf shoes favored by most courses these days.

I must be getting nostalgic. I really miss the clickity clack of those metal spikes, thought Jay with a wry grin. She understood the need for saving the greens and fairways but thought that there was something to be said for tradition as well.

Her father signed them in, got a cart, and they headed out to the range to warm up while waiting for their tee time. Steve watched his powerfully built daughter as she placed a ball on the tee and lined up her shot. He noticed one of the golf pros watching her as well and smiled to himself. He might never get used to people hitting on his daughter but realized that most of the time she was oblivious to the advances of both men and women.

"Nice shot, honey!" he called to her. She smiled and waved before rolling another ball onto the green mat and switching to her seven iron. After the shot, the golf pro walked up to Jay.

"Nice form, try keeping your head down a bit longer," she said. Jay looked up, startled, having been so focused that she hadn't noticed the attractive golf pro.

"Um, thanks. Perhaps you would like to show me what you mean?" Jay suggested. The pro took the club from Jay and set a ball down on the mat. As she settled herself into the shot, Jay smirked. *The pro has a pretty nice form herself.* The pro hit the shot, keeping her head down a bit longer and getting a much cleaner shot than Jay had managed. Jay smiled and took the proffered club. "I see what you mean. Nice shot. I don't suppose you would have time later for a lesson?"

The woman grinned and extended her hand. "I'd be happy to make room for you in my schedule. I'm Riley." Jay took the hand, enjoying the nice firm grip.

"Nice to meet you. I'm Jay. I have a tee time coming up with my father, but perhaps a little later? In fact, maybe you could join me for a late lunch to discuss the details?" Jay didn't usually ask women out but seeing Bailey had rattled her, and she enjoyed the reassurance that she was still attractive to other women. Riley's smile grew, and she agreed to meet Jay at the club's dining room around two. With a final wave, Riley walked off and Steve approached his daughter.

"So, does this mean you're going to ditch your old man after the round?" He grinned as he said it, letting her know that he was fine with her plans.

"I hope you don't mind, Dad. We're going to talk about golf lessons at lunch," Jay said as a blush stained her cheeks.

"Uh-huh. Sure, kiddo. I seriously doubt either of you thinks that you need lessons in golf, but I do think it's about time you had a social life. You join Riley, and I'll have lunch with a few of my friends here. We can meet after lunch and ride home together unless you decide to make other arrangements."

"Dad! It's not as if I'm going back to her place after lunch! I'll gladly meet you to get a ride. Then I'll have to get back to my place and do some work that's been piling up." Father and daughter gathered their clubs and headed to the tee together, laughing as they walked away.

* * *

Jay was nervous about her lunch date. *What has gotten in to me?* she wondered. This worried feeling was so unlike her, especially at her parents' club. *Maybe I've been around Sharon too much at work —her and that giant closet she lives in.* She ran a brush quickly through her hair and pulled it up into a ponytail, not taking the time for her usual French braid. She took a deep breath as she headed for the dining room. Spotting Riley on the verandah, Jay walked over to her and smiled. "Is this seat taken?"

Grinning Riley motioned for her to sit down. "Nice shot on the eighteenth."

"You saw that, huh? Dad liked it too," Jay laughed.

"Yes, it's not everyday someone lands a perfect shot. I guess you might not need lessons after all."

"Lessons?" queried Jay. "Oh right, lessons. I might not since I don't plan on joining the LPGA anytime soon."

They both chuckled and Riley started to speak as the waiter approached their table.

"I may be presuming, but I didn't accept your invitation to lunch because I thought you needed lessons," admitted Riley with a grin.

Jay chuckled. "Good, that isn't why I asked you to lunch. I think we're on the same page."

Riley smiled and Jay noticed her dimples for the first time. She figured Riley was about five-ten, and she hadn't failed to notice the reddish gold hair caught back into a ponytail, the grey eyes, or the athletic build of her lunch companion. After giving the waiter their orders, they lapsed into silence for a moment then they both started to speak at once. Laughing, Jay motioned for Riley to go first.

"I was just going to ask why I haven't seen you here before. You obviously love golf."

"My parents are the regulars although we're all members. I just don't have a lot of time to come out and play. I'm hoping that things change so that I can enjoy more time out here with my folks. I understand from my father that you were a touring pro. What made you give that up to teach amateurs who just use this as another place to do business?" Jay asked as she took a sip from her water.

"Truth?"

Jay nodded at her.

"I hate being mediocre! I was a middle of the pack finisher most of the time. Good enough to make a decent living, but not good enough to place and get the big endorsements or paychecks. Pretty soon, I was worn down by all that travel and I was starting to miss out on things that were important to me."

"I can understand the first part, but what were you missing out on?"

"I have a sister with a son who lives near here, and I didn't want to miss him growing up," said Riley. "I wasn't good enough to make it to the top of the tour, but I am very good at watching people and breaking down their swings. I can help others understand how they can improve their game and their enjoyment of golf. I really enjoy my work here. And," she said with a note of pride in her voice, "I'm one of the most requested instructors in the area. I guess I'm just better as an instructor than a tour player."

Before long they were discussing their families, growing up, and exchanging their coming out stories. Jay usually didn't mention Bailey to anyone, but for some reason she felt comfortable talking with Riley.

"I guess the real reason I came out to my parents was that I was in love with my best friend, and she left me."

Riley looked at her with an understanding expression. "You were lovers then?"

"Not exactly, let's just say that she left the state to get away from me, and I was drunk when I came out to my Dad."

"Ouch! I guess it all worked out though. You and your father are obviously close now."

"Yeah, I'm lucky. Both of my parents are very supportive. I'm not exactly a spokesperson for GLBT rights at work, and they don't understand it since they have no problems with my lesbianism."

Riley looked at her with a steady gaze. "What do you do for a living that you would need a spokesperson?"

"I'm in a conservative financial institution, and they aren't all that fond of anything they don't understand. My boss is a woman, hiding deep in her closet. It makes it hard to be around her sometimes since I know about her, but no one else does." Jay explained what her boss had done at that concert long ago, and how she had dealt with it since.

"Doesn't that make having any friends at work difficult?" asked Riley.

"Well, I don't really have a lot of time right now anyway, with our department being shorthanded. I have some friends there and I'm open about who I am just not obvious about it. I'm busy trying to expand our portfolio at the same time, so you can imagine the hours I put in. So, I'm not exactly hiding my life. I just don't have much of one." Jay gave a rueful smile. "I'm hoping things change soon, but for now, I do what I have to do."

As they ate their lunch, they continued to talk and discovered they had similar interests in theater and music. However, Riley was shocked at Jay's lack of knowledge of current lesbian fiction.

"It isn't like I have a lot of personal reading time," protested Jay. "I read but mostly current affairs and business related studies. I can't even recall the last time I made a trip to the gayborhood."

"That's it young lady, no more of this nonsense," Riley said in a mock stern voice. "Next week I'm personally going to guide you back into the world of lesbians!" She looked startled by her words. "Uh, I mean if you're free. I was thinking we could have a casual dinner and hit the bookstore." Riley blushed as she talked. Jay just sat there until she was done, and answered by writing down her cell phone number and giving it to Riley.

"Call me, and we can set up a time and place to meet. Tuesday or Wednesday would work best for me, but we can decide when you have a chance to look over your schedule." Jay noticed Riley's continued flirting and while she was flattered she just wasn't feeling any sparks. Jay hesitated but decided it was only fair to be honest. "I've really enjoyed this time getting to know you. I would like to see you again, but I'm not sure if I'm interested in, or available enough, for a romantic involvement. Can we try being friends and see what happens?"

Riley grinned at her, showing off her dimples again. "That's cool, I appreciate the honesty, and I agree. I'd enjoy getting to know you better. Besides, I'm the new girl in town. I need all the friends I can get!"

They parted with a hug and a promise to get together that week. Jay joined her father as they watched Riley walk back to the clubhouse.

"Have a good time, honey?"

"Yeah, Dad, she's really nice and easy to talk to, not something I find a lot." They gathered their belongings and headed for the parking lot.

"Well, I think you two looked good together," he stated emphatically.

Jay groaned, playfully shoving her father's shoulder. "Don't go sending out invitations just yet, Dad. We've agreed to be friends and see if anything else develops. I'm not looking for anything serious, and she's cool with my choice. It'll be nice to have a friend with no connection to work though."

* * *

After a quick goodbye to her parents, Jay headed back to Philadelphia. She loved living in a renovated warehouse condominium in Old City, known for its artist enclaves and historical architecture. She pulled into the underground parking area and bounded up the stairs to her second floor unit. Letting herself in and dropping her briefcase on the couch, she headed in to her bedroom to change clothes. Her bedroom was decorated in calming blues and greys with a queen sized oak sleigh bed and an antique wardrobe.

Standing in the doorway to her walk-in closet, she sorted clothes from the overnight bag for dry cleaning and laundry. After changing into sweatpants and a T-shirt, she tossed a load of whites into the washer. She was startled by the telephone ringing and listened as her mother's voice came over the machine.

"Honey, we had a visitor this afternoon and – "

She grabbed the phone. "Hi Mom, I'm here. I was just starting some laundry. What's going on, you can't miss me already, can you?" joked Jay.

"Sorry, honey, I didn't mean to interrupt, but Bailey dropped by just after you headed out. Apparently, she wanted to talk to you before you left and asked if we could pass along her number for you to call her. I didn't give her your number. Was that okay?" Her mother was sounding protective again, not necessarily a bad thing, but she didn't want her folks placed in the middle of any issues she and Bailey had.

"That's fine, Mom. Let me have the number, and I'll call her."

Jay took down the number and ended the call. She went to the kitchen to get a drink and opted for a beer, pulling a Yuengling lager out and pouring it into one of the frosted mugs she kept in her freezer. Sitting down in her living room, she pulled out her files, laptop, and cell phone, setting up her usual weekend workspace. After tuning in her music station of choice, the Retro station, she leaned back, took a few sips of beer, and decided she'd call Bailey, but only after getting through her e-mails.

An hour later, her beer long finished, her inbox was empty and Jay reluctantly picked up her phone. She really didn't want to call, but she also didn't want Bailey to go back to her parents' house looking for her. She glanced at the number, noting that Bailey had been here long enough to get a local cell number. As the phone rang, Jay's palms started to sweat. She berated herself for letting this woman from her past get to her this way. Of course, this wasn't just any woman. This was Bailey, "the one." Even after all that had happened, there was no denying that the pull was as strong as ever.

"This is Bailey."

"Hi, it's Jay. You were looking for me."

"Jay! I'm so glad you called me back. I was wondering how else to reach you since you aren't listed, and I didn't want to wait to call you at work." Bailey gave a little laugh. "The thing is, I know I don't deserve this, but I was hoping we could talk, you know, outside of work or family gatherings. I don't expect you to agree, but I really would like the chance to talk, even if it's just for an hour somewhere over coffee. I'm sorry, I'm babbling." Bailey trailed off.

"Actually, that might be a good idea. You wouldn't have gotten it yet, but you will be receiving an offer letter from the company shortly. Before you decide, I think we should talk about the reality of working in the same department." Jay kept her tone cool and business like though she could hear Bailey's nervousness.

"Um, great, I'm totally wide open, when and where would you like to meet?" asked Bailey.

Jay thought for a minute, *I certainly don't want Bailey in my home. However, there aren't too many places I'll feel secure talking with her.* She quickly decided on Fairmount Park. They could walk along Kelly Drive and be fairly anonymous. She suggested it, and they set a time for the next day at ten in the morning. After hanging up, Jay leaned back and thought of dark hair and emerald bright eyes. Sighing, she sat up and tried to put the next day out of her head and deal with work. She buried herself in a new training program she was developing for use in the branches. When she finally made it to bed in the early morning hours, she barely remembered to set her alarm and quickly fell asleep.

CHAPTER 4

BAILEY HELD HER phone and stared at it in shock. Her heart still raced, and she had to force her fingers to loosen their grip on the phone. Not only had Jay called her back, but she had actually agreed to meet tomorrow. It had been too easy to get Jay to agree, and her tone had been cold and distant. Bailey knew that this would not be an easy meeting. It would be her only chance to explain, and she groaned. She closed her eyes and saw again the honey colored hair, the toffee brown eyes, and the arms that had held and comforted her. She knew that she had to get this right, or there would not be another chance.

Now that she knew that she was being offered the job she wanted, there had to be a way for them to make peace. Bailey had given up hoping for anything more with Jay. She simply didn't feel as if Jay would be able to forgive her.

While in Florida, Bailey had tried to date the guys she met at college but couldn't find anyone she was interested in enough to see more than once or twice. Life didn't make sense without Jay, but it couldn't make sense with Jay. Could it? She immersed herself in things other than relationships. She took guitar lessons, pottery classes, read voraciously, and even started to search for a spiritual path that finally made sense to her. Eventually, she found some peace in her life, but it still didn't feel quite complete.

On the day before her twenty-sixth birthday, Bailey went out to a popular lesbian bar with some friends from work. She found that watching women dancing with women made sense somehow. When a woman asked her to dance she nervously agreed, thankful it was a fast song. Suddenly, the song changed. The new song was slower and the lights dimmed. She was being held by a woman, feeling another woman's breasts against her own, and she found the feeling intoxicating. She flashed back to that one night with Jay, and she felt sick thinking about what she had given up. She was far from home, working for a liberal company with several gays and lesbians in positions of power. In fact, she was at the club with one of her managers. She didn't fight it when the woman she was dancing with pulled her in tighter, or when she leaned in for a kiss. Bailey gave in to the kiss, moaning in the back of her throat. Suddenly, Jay's face flashed in her mind.

She pulled back, apologized to the woman, and stumbled back to the table hoping no one had seen her on the dance floor. She felt a hand on her shoulder and saw that it was her manager, Kelly, looking at her with a little concern.

"Are you okay?" she asked. *Was she?* Bailey had no idea, so she just shook her head before bursting into tears. Kelly pulled her from the chair and took her outside.

"What's the matter, Bail? Did she do something to you? I'm sorry, this place was my idea." Kelly handed Bailey some napkins she had grabbed on her way out the door. Bailey sniffed and wiped her eyes, trying to calm down. She tried to assure her boss that the woman on the floor wasn't at fault for her tears, and Kelly relaxed a little.

"Come on, Bail, talk to me. What bothered you in there?" Suddenly Kelly stopped. "Were you getting into things out there? Perhaps feelings came up you weren't prepared for?"

Bailey nodded her head, afraid she'd be unable to speak without sobbing.

Kelly leaned over and gave her a hug of support. "Is this the first time you have felt an attraction for a woman?"

Bailey shook her head. "No, it's just the first time in a long time that I've had to face it," she said softly. "And I ran from it, just like I always do." She started crying again, and all Kelly could do was hold her gently and whisper words of comfort. She gently rubbed Bailey's back and suggested they head home when the crying eased. Kelly went inside and grabbed their things. She told everyone that Bailey wasn't feeling well, and she would make sure she got home safely.

At her house, Bailey thanked her and asked Kelly in for a drink.

Kelly hesitated, but nodded her head, and followed Bailey into her townhouse.

"What would you like to drink?"

"Just some water would be great. The club gets too hot, and water is always the best thing after that for me."

Bailey got two bottles of water and came back to find Kelly sitting uncomfortably on the edge of the couch. Bailey handed Kelly her water and sat down on the armchair adjacent to the couch. She noticed Kelly start to relax.

"Bailey, I know that tonight was a shock to you. I'm sorry about that, I sure didn't mean for it to happen."

Bailey gave a sad smile. "The only thing you did was help save me after I made a complete fool of myself. I can't believe I reacted that way to a dance."

"You know, I think I reacted in a similar way when I started questioning my sexuality. It's normal to be surprised, shocked, or even want to deny your feelings," Kelly reassured her.

"That's not quite the problem. I mean, yes, I'm a bit shocked. But what really gave me a jolt is that I realized I made a huge mistake and hurt someone very badly back in college. I don't know what to do with all of this now."

Bailey started to cry again as she thought back to Jay's voice when she called to tell her about her move to Florida. Kelly moved over to her and held her, trying to calm her down and give some comfort. Bailey glanced up and found herself entranced by Kelly's gaze. There was such acceptance, sympathy, and tenderness in her eyes. She wondered why she hadn't noticed it sooner. *This woman is someone who could be a real friend. My first real friend since Jay.*

Kelly quickly moved back. "Um, I don't know how to say this without sounding egotistical, but you know we can't be more than friends, right?" asked Kelly. "I mean, I care about you, and I consider you a friend, but I can't have a relationship with a subordinate. It wouldn't be professional." Bailey looked a little shocked and then remembered staring into Kelly's eyes a moment ago.

"Oh! I'm sorry, I didn't mean anything... I was just, I mean... Oh Goddess, how do I get myself into these situations?" Bailey leaned forward. "I'm not about to try to start a relationship now, no worries. I respect you as my boss and my friend. I'm sorry if you thought anything else. I'm just having a really bad night. I think I just figured out that I haven't had a real friend since I left home. I never let anyone else get close enough to me."

Kelly gave her a grateful smile. "I'm happy to be your friend, and if you need to talk more of this out, now or in the future, you can call me. I'd be honored to help you as you find your way. I have to ask though, this woman you mentioned, is she from around here?"

"No, someone I knew back home. That is part of why I never moved back after college. Well, that and I got recruited by a great company out here!"

Bailey got a bit of her normal spark back in her eye as she teased Kelly and Kelly began to smile. They called it a night shortly after that, but they continued to grow closer over time. Bailey came to think of her a bit like the older sister she never had.

* * *

Sunday morning Bailey woke up early and changed outfits four times. Finally, she settled on tan cargo shorts and a blue polo shirt that fit well but not too snugly. She styled her dark hair to look casual and a little tousled. She was ready to go a full hour before she needed to leave. Deciding she would use the time to be early and scope out the area, she jumped in her car and headed out. Nervously, she scanned the area for Jay and was surprised to see her arrive quite early as well. Bailey wondered if Jay was as unsettled as she was.

Walking over to Jay, she handed her a small bottle of fresh squeezed orange juice that she had picked up on her way to the meeting. She knew Jay loved fresh orange juice in the morning.

Jay stood still for a minute. "You remembered, thank you," she finally said softly.

They walked in silence for a few minutes, both trying to settle their thoughts. Finally, Bailey nervously cleared her throat. "Jay, thanks for meeting me like this. I know we both have some concerns about working together. I won't take the job if we can't resolve some of that today. I actually have a lot to apologize for and to share with you. If you'll let me."

Jay could see that the other woman was biting her lip and looking a bit pale. "Bailey, I respect that you thought about this before taking the job. As an employee, I think you will fit into the work group fine. We can keep our relationship strictly professional. I won't treat you any differently than anyone else on my staff."

"Jay, that's just it, I didn't come back here just to change jobs. I came back because I owed you a major apology. I – " Her shoulders slumped a bit as she shook her head in frustration.

"Wait Bailey, you don't owe me anything! What happened between us, happened a long time ago, and we've both moved on." Jay's brown eyes were flashing with anger that she was trying very hard to keep it in check. "I don't want to make this personal."

"Jay, please, just let me say what I have to say. Then take all the time you need to think it over and make up your mind. I will not accept the job without you agreeing to this one request."

Jay finally nodded her agreement. She guided them towards a bench under some trees and away from the main path.

"Okay, go ahead, I won't interrupt again."

Bailey took a deep breath, exhaling slowly and studied those brown eyes she used to know so well. "My apology comes in two parts. I am so sorry that I ran away from you after what we shared that night."

Jay stiffened and the muscles in her jaw jumped as she clenched her teeth.

"I was young, stupid, and scared to death that my parents wouldn't understand. I was fine with you being a lesbian, but I was terrified when that term could be applied to me. It went against everything from church, and it was too much too fast for me. I ran because I couldn't figure out what else to do. I should have talked to you, but I was so afraid, and it was easy to blame the alcohol and you. You didn't do anything wrong, Jay, I initiated everything that night, and I enjoyed it all." Bailey stopped to regroup and assess Jay's reaction.

"The second part of the apology is because not only did I hurt my best friend, I lied to you. I lied about my feelings, and I continued to lie by not getting in touch with you since then. I did finally come out to myself and eventually my folks. We worked through things, and we're fine. Yet, I was still too afraid to contact you. I'm so very sorry for all the pain I may have caused you, Jay. You were the person I would have wanted to protect the most, and instead I hurt you so much."

* * *

Jay sat there, unable to believe what she was hearing. The conversation she had dreamed of for years was actually happening, but she found that she no longer wanted to walk away or toss Bailey's words back in her face.

"I'm not sure what to say, Bailey. You were my best friend for so long, and then I fell in love with you. I resigned myself to you never feeling the same way. But, then we made love, and I thought that you must love me too. I woke up to find you gone and couldn't reach you. The next thing I knew you were leaving for another state, and I never heard from you again. You broke my heart, Bailey!" Jay paused to take a deep breath. "I appreciate the struggle you went through, but... you broke my heart." Tears glistened in both their eyes as they looked at each other.

Bailey's voice came out shaky when she attempted to form the words that would allow them to become friends once more. "Jay, I know you may never trust me again. I know that I have no right to ask for this, but I want to try to rebuild our friendship. You were the most important relationship I've ever had, and I miss you every day. Can we at least try?"

Jay took a deep, shuddering breath, blowing out slowly as she counted to ten.

"Part of me wants to tell you to fuck off, but part of me wants to talk more," admitted Jay. "You just threw a lot at me, and I need time to think about it. The way things happened between us affected a lot of my life. I don't trust easily anymore. I don't let people in."

Bailey nodded and looked is if she might cry.

"I've been thinking about the past a lot and about making some changes in my life. Why don't we try this," Jay offered. "We agree that you will take the job for now, and we'll try to build a professional relationship. In the meantime, give me a little time to absorb this, and I'll call you so we can talk more. I have to admit, I've really missed you and our friendship. I don't know where this will head, if anywhere, but I'm willing to consider it."

Bailey gave a small smile, and tears started to trickle down her face. "Thank you, Jay. I'm willing to spend the rest of my life making things right between us. I've regretted this for so long, but I was too afraid to deal with it."

Jay remained silent as she considered what to say next. "What changed? I mean, why did you finally come back?"

"The truth sounds a little trite, but I promise you nothing but honesty from now on. I lost a close friend of mine recently, my former manager, Kelly. She taught me many things. She helped me come out and come to grips with the mess I made of my personal life. She told me that the one thing I shouldn't do was postpone conversations like this one, because the regret of what might have been is too great."

Jay nodded. "I'm sorry for your loss. Were you lovers?"

Bailey gave a short laugh. "No, never lovers, but good friends. We would have made horrible lovers. She was my only real friend since you, and she died way too young."

Jay remembered her juice suddenly, and gave it a quick shake before opening it. She took a swallow and offered it to Bailey, who took it gratefully, and drank some down before handing it back.

"Do you mind me asking how she died? You don't have to talk about it if you don't want to though."

"It's all right, Jay, I'll answer any question you want. She died of a brain hemorrhage, an aneurism. She actually had two. They got to one in time but couldn't reach the second. It started leaking, and she passed away two days later. Before she lost consciousness, she made me promise to come home to resolve my life. She was right. It was past time for me to take responsibility for myself."

Jay patted her hand and offered her the rest of the juice. Bailey finished it, and then stood up and walked to a trash container before coming back and resuming the conversation.

"I guess things happen for a reason, but sometimes it's hard to see it. I'm sorry, Bailey. I can tell you were close to her."

"Thanks, but enough sadness and tears. Shall we finish our walk back to our cars? I don't want to push my luck today and wear out my welcome."

Jay smiled at her, and they headed back towards the path. "I'm glad you came back, Bailey. No matter what else happens, it was good to hear you admit you missed me too. I always thought you simply forgot about me."

Bailey gasped and looked at her in shock. "Forget about you? Jay, there is no way I could ever forget about you! We grew up together, we went to college together, and, well, you were my first sexual experience. Trust me, you are unforgettable! I've never stopped loving you, Jay. I simply didn't know how to deal with it."

"I'm feeling kind of overwhelmed right now, Bailey. Can I just have some time to absorb everything?"

"I won't push you, Jay. I'm just glad I could apologize and explain things to you today. Thank you for the chance."

Jay smiled warmly at her friend from so long ago. "You're welcome. Thank you for making the effort." Jay was surprised to find they were back in the parking area. She gestured towards her car. "This is me. I'll talk to you soon, I promise."

CHAPTER 5

$\mathcal{B}$Y THE TIME Wednesday rolled around, Jay was ready for the evening out with Riley. She had decided that she certainly wasn't in a place to start any kind of new relationship, but the appeal of a friend outside of the financial world was welcome. She started packing up her things at five-thirty in the afternoon after one last check of her e-mail and messages. Scott looked at her in amazement as she walked past his desk and wished him a good night.

"Is something wrong? You never leave this early!"

"Ha, ha, very funny, I'm allowed to have a life every now and then. The truth was, she rarely did leave the office before seven these days, and she was feeling it. *Guess I'm not as young as I used to be*, she thought with rueful smile.

On her way home to change for her dinner, her cell phone rang.

"Jay? It's Riley."

"Hey, Riley, you aren't calling to cancel on me are you?" Jay asked with bit of concern. She really was looking forward to this evening out.

"Oh no, nothing like that, I just thought that I could swing by and pick you up so we only have one car. Parking can get tricky and expensive in that area."

"Oh! That's really considerate of you. Sure, let me give you my address." Once they hung up, Jay started thinking about what to wear. It had been so long since she went into the "gayborhood"... but this was not a date, and she wasn't looking for one either.

Jay rushed through her condo and looked in her closet for something to throw on. She was just about to get into the shower when her phone rang. Listening to the machine pick up, she heard her mother's voice and decided it didn't sound urgent. She would call her later if there was time. As she showered, Jay mused that machines had voicemail beaten in one major arena, screening calls. A quick soap and rinse, a brisk towel off, and she threw on her favorite pair of jeans, her hiking boots, and a short sleeve polo shirt. Jay ran a brush through her hair and decided to pull it back with a clip. Just then, the doorbell rang. She took a quick peek through the peephole and saw Riley standing there waiting. "Right on time I see. I like that in a chauffeur," teased Jay. "C'mon in while I finish up and grab a jacket."

"Thanks, nice place. Been here long?" Riley was looking out the floor to ceiling windows that overlooked the river.

"A couple of years now. I just wish I saw more of it than I do. Sometimes I feel like I should sell it all and get a foldout couch for my office." Jay grabbed her favorite jean jacket and motioned towards the door. "Shall we? I'm ready for my re-education."

"Your chariot awaits, as does your chauffeur," Riley replied laughing.

* * *

Riley guided her car towards the lot on 13th and Locust that she usually used. "What kind of food are you in the mood for tonight? Anything special?" Riley asked.

"Some kind of comfort food I think. It's been a really stressful few months. What do you suggest?"

"I know just the place," Riley replied in a confident tone. "A bit of an upscale take on comfort food, plus they have great desserts... and not just ice cream!"

"Sounds great, should we go to the bookstore first though? I wouldn't want to miss out on my education tonight," joked Jay.

"No problem, there is a whole world of tasty fiction out there for you to experience," Riley answered. "Let's head there first unless you're starving."

"I'm good for a little while yet. As usual, I ate a late lunch. Besides, I'm curious to see what you think I should be reading instead of my financial regulations and reports."

Walking into Giovanni's Room for the first time in over five years, Jay was immediately impressed with the sheer number of volumes housed in the smallish store. Right up front the local GLBT papers and a selection of magazines were on display, and the counter had a selection of gay pride items and jewelry. Just past the register and up a step was the lesbian fiction section. In another section, there were movies and music for sale as well as a help desk.

Jay gazed at all the books that she hadn't realized existed. She spent several minutes getting oriented to the layout before starting to look over titles in earnest. Riley watched in amusement before asking at the counter about a few books she had ordered the week before. Jay continued to pour over titles and read covers with a look of extreme concentration on her face. Riley laughed to herself and motioned to the clerk. She quickly pointed out something in the jewelry case and had it wrapped, paid for, and in her pocket before Jay even looked up.

Riley strolled over to Jay with a smile firmly in place. "Finding everything okay? If you need any suggestions, I'm familiar with a good portion of the inventory."

"I think I might need some help choosing. There are so many more selections than five years ago! I've never heard of most of these authors."

Riley reached past Jay to grab a book from the shelf. "Well, this is a great one. Do you like action, drama, and romance?"

Jay chuckled. "Of course, especially if it is half as good as that cover!"

Riley handed it to Jay then grabbed a couple of other books from the same author. "Here, you might as well get these too. Once you read the first, you'll want to read more. They're all about a mobster in New Orleans. Oh, and here's a great detective series. Well, she was a private eye, but she became a photographer and the private eye thing just seems to follow her.

You mentioned liking science fiction when you were a kid too. There is a series over here about a woman who is in charge of a kid who is heir to two planets' heads of government. They left their home planet in a hurry and got chased to a space station where they could be safe if they aren't shipped back. Good stuff!"

Riley grabbed the books from that series as well and handed them to Jay.

Jay shook her head in wonder. "I can't believe how much has changed in just five or six years. There was nowhere nearly this selection back then, and most of it was either really deep, angst ridden, or trite. This stuff is a far cry from those days. I think I've hit the jackpot!"

"I don't think you have to buy the store out in one trip. You can always come back and buy more," Riley pointed out with a chuckle. "If we check out now, we can get a table without too much effort. The early dinner rush should be finishing by now."

"Great, all this shopping has made me hungry," Jay laughed, feeling more relaxed all of a sudden. She carried her selections to the counter and paid.

They discussed the books they had purchased while walking the few blocks to the eatery, and continued as they were seated. After looking over the menu, Jay announced that she had found the perfect comfort food with a twist.

Riley raised an eyebrow in question. "Grilled cheese with cheddar and apples in it! How perfect! And I can get mashed potatoes or sweet potato fries, I just can't decide," Jay said.

Riley suggested that they each get one and share. With that major dilemma solved, and the orders placed, they went back to their talk of books.

"When did all of these books appear? I can't believe the changes in the selection." Jay continued to gaze at her new books as she asked her question.

"Well, I think the independent publishers finally started getting things to a more professional level as technology made things more accessible. It helps that they are using well-trained editors in several of the houses now too."

When their food arrived, Jay took a bite of her sandwich and moaned in delight. "This is just what I needed. Thanks for bringing me here today."

Riley finally decided to ask the one question she had avoided. "So, Jay, do you want to tell me what prompted this need for comfort food? Did something happen this week?"

Jay munched on a few sweet potato fries thoughtfully and decided to confide a little.

"I guess my world shifted on its axis last weekend. Someone from my past came back into my life on a professional basis, and we had a talk on Sunday." Jay paused to eat a bit more of her food before continuing. "She was my best friend growing up, the one I mentioned at our lunch? "

"And you were in love with her, right?" Riley remembered from their talk last Saturday. "Hey, it happens to a lot of us."

Jay smiled, deciding she liked the way it felt, having a friend to talk to without having to feel guarded. She was always so tense from work, and she hadn't socialized outside of networking functions for years.

"Actually, yes, I was. We had one night together, and she freaked so badly that she changed schools and moved to Florida the summer after our freshman year of college. I've heard nothing from her since a cold telephone call right before she left informing me that she wasn't the 'same way' I was. Bailey blamed it on too much to drink and confusing her feelings of friendship for me in her head."

"Ouch! So she just took off and never looked back? But, now she is here again and somehow involved in your life. What happened Sunday when you spoke?" Riley pushed her food aside, totally focused on the woman in front of her. When Jay finished explaining what had transpired, she reached across the table and took Jay's hand.

"Thank you for trusting me enough to tell me that." She let go of Jay's hand and leaned back in her chair. Her eyes sparkled a bit in the light as she considered her next words very carefully. "When I left for the LPGA tour, I did so in a hurry. I was afraid of my feelings for one of my friends on my college team. I was too young and scared to know what to do with it. Of course I basically ran away to the lesbian circus, so I gained confidence in myself pretty quickly." They both chuckled at the thought.

"When I came home from the tour on my first break, I told the other girl how I felt. She turned on me in disgust and shut me out of her life. Coming home to talk to you shows that Bailey has a lot of courage. She must really want to work things out with you. She had to be worried that you would simply slam the door in her face, so to speak."

Jay thought that over for a few minutes as they both finished eating. "I know you're right. I think that's what has me confused the most. She's out now, but she's going to work for a very conservative company. My company. She wants us to become friends again, and I don't know how I feel about having her back in my life. Hardly a day has gone by that I haven't missed her and been hurt about how things turned out. I just don't know if I can trust her now."

"Does she realize how reserved you've had to become? I mean, when is the last time you got to hang out with women, friends or otherwise, that didn't have to do with your job? They seem to run you ragged. If it's as conservative as you say, don't they have issues with you being gay? Or are you closeted at work?"

Jay let her frustration show with the situation. "I'm out, but I'm not OUT, if you get my meaning. My boss is a lesbian who is convinced that is makes a difference and has done the closet thing for her whole career. I don't think too many people really care, but I haven't exactly brought a date to any company functions either. I haven't had more than five dates in five years, and it's getting pretty hard to stay there and live this way. I love what I do, but I don't see why it has to rule my life. All I do is work, and I never seem to have the time to just be me anymore.

I feel as if I've lost a part of myself, and I've only recently recognized how empty I've been feeling."

Riley straightened up in her chair, reached into her pocket, and pulled out a small package. "I think I may have a helpful reminder for you," she said. "This is a reminder of today, and the world you are a part of outside of your work."

Jay felt a blush come over her face and started to protest. "I can't, I mean you shouldn't have. We haven't known each other that long and..."

"Relax, Jay, I think we both know we are destined for friendship, not a partnership. This is a gift from one supportive friend to another, nothing more. Just open it." Jay took the gift, thanking her, and opened it. Inside was a long, thin box.

"Um, please tell me this isn't a rainbow pride thing," Jay joked, instinctively knowing that Riley wouldn't give her something that would complicate her work situation.

"Just open it!" Riley grinned, not giving anything away.

Jay opened it and found a sterling silver rope necklace with a three dimensional triangle pendant hanging from it. "Oh, Riley, it's lovely!"

"And the best part," said Riley as she stood and moved to help Jay fasten the clasp, "is that no one will realize that the triangle represents your place in the GLBT community. People see rainbows and think of us. They still haven't caught on to the triangle, especially in a form like this. You can wear this to work and have a reminder that there is a world outside of your job, and it stands ready to embrace you."

Jay brushed away a tear as she stood and gave Riley a big hug. "I can't thank you enough for today, Riley; it's been like a homecoming of sorts for me. I had given up on having friends who could really relate to me on a personal level."

Riley returned her hug and smiled. "Hey, I'm not exactly overrun with friends either, I just moved back here." She did her best Bogart imitation, "Kid, I think this is the start of a beautiful friendship."

Jay groaned and grabbed the check before Riley had a chance to look at it. When Riley protested, Jay pointed out that Riley drove, paid for parking, and bought her a gift. The least Jay could do was buy dinner. Riley conceded, and they gathered their things and walked together to the parking lot. They chatted casually on the way back to Jay's and when Riley pulled up, Jay asked if she wanted to come in and hang out. Riley pointed out the lateness of the hour on a work night and her drive home before thanking her and promising to call soon to do something.

Jay tossed her keys on the table just inside the door, kicked off her boots, and fingered her necklace thoughtfully as she wandered into her bedroom to get ready for bed. She stacked her new books on the bedside table and laughed as the stack wobbled.

"Hmm, maybe I ought to move some of those," she chuckled as she rescued the swaying stack. Jay quickly got ready for bed and crawled in between the covers to settle in with her first book. It was actually early for her to go to bed, but she decided she was taking the night off from work.

* * *

Friday morning Jay headed in to work as usual. She didn't get many early morning calls, so she jumped when her cell phone rang. Hitting the button on her headset she answered and was surprised to hear Bailey on the other end.

"Um, hi, I hope this isn't too early," started Bailey.

"No, it's okay, I'm on my way to the office."

"That's kind of what I wanted to talk to you about. I'm starting on Monday, and I wanted to know if there was anything I should prep for over the weekend."

Jay gave her a few things to go over, mostly just some Pennsylvania lending regulations and laws that differed from the ones in Florida, and then asked, "Was that everything? This really could have waited, Bailey; just enjoy your last free weekend before I get you in my clutches."

Bailey could have sworn the room got a bit warmer at the thought of being in Jay's clutches, but she managed a shaky laugh. "I guess I was wondering about getting together. I thought that maybe we could play a round of golf at the club if you were coming up to your folks' place. I know I shouldn't push, but I just wanted to ask you." Bailey listened intently, not hearing a response. "Jay, are you still there?"

"Um, sorry, I was reviewing my schedule in my head. I can fit in nine holes tomorrow, but I don't think I could make a whole round." She and Riley had plans to go to a movie and try a new Irish pub up in Bucks County. Jay planned on crashing at her parents' house that night.

"That's great, I'll be available all day. Just give me a call, and I can meet you at your parents' house."

"Why don't we just meet at the club for a two o'clock tee time. I'll call it in and let you know if it changes. I have plans after that and can leave from the club if we take separate cars." Jay smiled. It felt good to have plans and even better to be able to say that to Bailey. Granted, it was a little high schoolish of her, but she indulged in it just the same.

"That's great! I'll see you at the club tomorrow." Bailey paused before adding, "I don't want to mess up your plans. Thank you, it means a lot that you are willing to do this."

Hanging up, Jay thought about the conversation and wondered why her heart had sped up when she heard Bailey's voice on the phone. Pushing it from her mind, she focused on the day's schedule and was ready to go when she reached the parking garage at work.

* * *

"Sharon wants to meet with you in her office ASAP," said Scott, standing in Jay's doorway that afternoon.

"Great," grumbled Jay, "I have all the time in the world for more meetings." Eyes flashing in irritation, she gathered her piles of folders into some semblance of order and stood. "Fine, Scott, let her know I'm on my way. When I get back I'm going to need your help on some paper gathering and documentation for two of these loans."

"No problema, boss of mine," he said in an irritatingly chipper tone. Jay took a deep breath, counted to ten before releasing it, and then picked up her day planner on her way out of her office.

* * *

Sharon waited behind her desk for Jay to arrive. She remembered her dream of the night before and again, felt as if her world was about to change. She remembered very little other than it seemed like a regular day at work until Bailey arrived for her first day and chaos ensued. Now Sharon was tense about adding a new person without running it past Jay. She couldn't put her finger on it, but as with many things in her life, Sharon decided the best defense was a good offense.

"Shut that behind you, won't you, Jay?" Sharon sat at her desk, looking the manicured, coiffed picture of perfection for an upper level executive. No one knew how she managed to get through every day without a hair out of place, but yet again, here was the proof. On the other hand, Jay tucked a stray lock of her hair behind her ear, as she sat in one of the visitor chairs in front of Sharon's giant mahogany desk. "I wanted to talk to you about your team, your new employee, and how she'll fit in," Sharon stated.

She saw Jay's hackles rise immediately, though even she had to admit that Jay did an admirable job of hiding her anger. She knew that she hadn't called such a meeting the last time a new member joined Jay's team, and she had expected to get a rise out of Jay with her statement.

"Sure, Sharon, what seems to be the concern?" Jay asked evenly.

"Oh, no concern per se, I just realize that your team has been together for a while now and bringing someone new to the company into the mix can cause difficulties. I just wanted to make sure you have all the tools you'll need at your disposal to ease the transition." Sharon looked over at Jay, wondering if she sounded the least bit convincing.

The truth was Sharon was curious about whatever past there was between Jay and this new hire, Bailey. Sharon saw Jay as her protégé, and she didn't want anything to halt the progress that had been made in advancing Jay's career. Sharon had big plans, and she wanted to continue to use Jay as a cornerstone of her team. *Something about that dream last night... this department, heck, I, don't need any trouble right now.* Sharon just had to make sure that it remained an anxious dream and nothing more.

Jay shrugged, obviously confused about the real purpose of this meeting. "Everything should be great. In fact, I spoke with her today. She's all set for her new employee orientation on Monday morning, and she'll spend the afternoon meeting the team and getting set up with her computer access."

"Oh, all right, I guess you have a handle on things. If you need anything from me, just let me know. As usual with new hires, let's meet every week for a few minutes to discuss her progress."

Jay rose to her feet. "Sounds good, Sharon. Don't worry; I think I was just shocked when I first saw her back in town. I'm sure things will work out just fine. Besides I need the help in the department," Jay grinned. Everyone knew that her team was the most productive in the state and near the top for the company.

Sharon took a moment and then continued in a softer voice. "Jay, are you sure you're okay? You seem to be a bit run down, and I don't think it's all from working too hard. Is there anything I can do to help out?"

Jay was a little surprised by this personal interest. Usually, Sharon made sure to keep things strictly professional with her. "I am feeling a little worn out," Jay admitted grudgingly. "I think I need to start taking vitamins or something. I know I need to get more workout time in my schedule. That usually makes me feel better."

Sharon nodded her head. "I understand and that's why I have the treadmill at home. I can fit in a workout no matter what time it is when I get home. Just don't over do it, kiddo, we need you at full strength around here. Take some time off this weekend and get some R & R in."

Jay laughed. "Okay, boss, no problem."

"Seriously, leave the laptop and files here for the weekend, Jay. They can wait until Monday. Now get out of here and get finished up. I expect you out of here no later than five tonight!"

Jay gave up, raising her arms in a gesture of surrender and laughing lightly as she left her boss's office.

* * *

Sharon can be so unpredictable sometimes, thought Jay. *She can go from slave driver one minute to caring and supportive the next. Might as well take advantage of her generosity today and get going; it was almost five already.*

"Scott, let's get everything put away. It will keep until Monday, and I think we both deserve a fun weekend off."

Scott looked on in amazement as Jay actually started putting her files away in drawers, not in her briefcase. Jay stopped what she was doing and turned an amused eye on her assistant.

"What? Is it impossible for me to try to get us out at a decent hour now and then?" Scott, realizing that he was about to get a reprieve from late hours, just shook his head and started putting away files with Jay. He saw her power down the laptop, but she didn't undock it.

"Coming in over the weekend?" he asked.

"Nope, I'm leaving it here for the whole weekend. Sharon's orders too." Jay was almost gleeful as she said this, watching the expression on Scott's face.

"Wow, I wonder what happened?"

"Who cares, let's get out before anyone changes her mind!" He started clearing his own desk and shut down his workstation. They grabbed their jackets and headed for the stairs, not wanting to risk running into anyone during their escape. With a conspiratorial wink and wave, Jay wished Scott a great weekend and headed for the garage and her CR-V.

* * *

"No, Mom, I won't be home for dinner tomorrow, but I can have Sunday brunch with you guys." Jay was on the telephone with her mother, having forgotten to call her back the other day. "I have a few plans for Saturday, and I figured I could crash at the house and visit with you two. Is that all right, or did you have plans?"

"Jay, you are always welcome here, and you know it," chided her mother gently. "In fact, we were wondering about a round of golf on Saturday before your plans."

"Sorry, Mom, I already have plans for a two o'clock round with Bailey before I go out for the evening. We're going to talk about her new position and play the back nine."

"Sounds fine, dear, whatever you have planned is good. You have your keys, and we'll see you at the club tomorrow. We can catch up over brunch on Sunday, and you can fill me in on this sudden social life you have acquired."

Jay rolled her eyes but smiled, grateful that her parents wanted to know about her life instead of shutting her out. "No problem, Mom, I'll see you both tomorrow, I'm going to go do some laundry and workout now. Have a good night!"

Jay tossed in a load of laundry and climbed on her exercise bike after putting on some good pedaling tunes. She was spinning away when suddenly, she felt light-headed. Jay grabbed at the handlebars and stopped pedaling, reaching for her bottle of water. She took a few sips as she started to regain her breath. Her head seemed to settle down, but she felt the vestiges of dizziness. She rechecked her settings and saw that it was set to her usual workout, nothing too strenuous. Jay decided that the combination of not enough food, and not working out regularly, was the cause of the problem. She went to her fridge and checked around for food she could prepare quickly. Pulling out some eggs and a few other ingredients she whipped up an omelet.

She grabbed a couple of slices of bread, tossed them in the toaster oven, and cleaned up the debris from her preparation. Jay poured a glass of apple juice and took the pumpkin butter from the fridge before she set the table as her omelet finished cooking. Getting everything on a plate, she sat down to her meal and devoured everything. With her obvious hunger as proof that the earlier episode was nothing to worry about, she continued doing laundry and reading from her new book collection. Finally sleepy, Jay tossed a few clothes in an overnight bag for the trip to her folks' and got ready for bed. As she lay down, her mind was a jumble of characters from her life and her book, and with a puzzled look on her face, she slept.

CHAPTER 6

$\mathcal{J}$AY FELT LIKE life was potentially on track. She was cautiously optimistic, and that was a damned good feeling after a few years of pessimistic cynicism. She had someone who was becoming a close friend, work was going well, other than her growing disgust at remaining so carefully closeted, and there was a chance that she could have Bailey back in her life at least as a friend.

Jay had worn her new pendant to work all week, receiving several compliments about it, but no one seemed to suspect it had a meaning, including Sharon. Jay had to chuckle at the thought of Sharon's face if she ever realized what it was Jay had been wearing. Today was sunny and comfortable, and she had plans for the weekend that didn't include any work! Life was feeling good for a change.

Pulling into her parents' driveway, she cut the engine and pulled her overnight bag out of the back seat. As Jay let herself into the house, she saw that her parents had left a note for her telling her they were at the club and had decided to have dinner there as well. Smiling, Jay went up to her room and tossed her bag on the floor. She let herself fall backwards onto her bed and took a minute to review her plans for the rest of the day.

Jay knew she would need to leave soon for her golf date with Bailey. *Golf date? Interesting choice of phrase,* she mused. *Why does this feel like a date? I haven't spoken with her in years, she shows up on my doorstep, and I'm suddenly thinking that we're going on a date? I'm going to be her boss next week! This can't be a date. I don't know if I can trust her that much again. Or, that I want to risk that much pain again.* Jay put her thoughts aside as she gathered the clothes she would need for her plans with Riley that evening and repacked her bag before she left for the club.

Why couldn't Riley and I be a couple? Might make my life simpler if it had happened. Then I could have simply told Bailey she was too late. Or, could I? Jay recognized the pointlessness of her thoughts and closed her bedroom door firmly behind her as she headed to the club.

* * *

Bailey watched from the pro shop as Jay walked towards the locker rooms with a small bag in hand. As she watched, she saw the pro who had helped her earlier coming down the steps from the main door of the club. The two women met at the landing and hugged. Even from a distance Bailey could see the affection between the women. Bailey turned away. *She has plans, and I just saw who those plans involve.* Bailey tried to remind herself that she had no claim on Jay. Just because the sight of Jay made her knees go weak, didn't mean Jay felt the same, especially considering their past. Determined to make the most of her time with Jay, she got the scorecards and loaded their golf bags on the cart just as Jay appeared.

"Hey, thanks for doing that for us," Jay said as she approached. "You know, the subservience doesn't actually start until Monday morning," joked Jay.

"Very funny! I just figured since you had plans this evening, I'd get us all set to go out, and we could take a cart to save some time." Bailey was trying not to let her jealousy of the golf pro show. "I ran into the new pro, and she got your clubs out for me."

"Yeah, she's a great addition to the staff here! She's given me a few pointers I want to try out today," Jay said with enthusiasm.

I just bet she has! Bailey thought. "Why don't we head for the tee?" Bailey said as she tried not to let Jay know she was fuming within.

"I'll drive," they both said at once. Breaking into laughter at the once common occurrence. They decided to take turns, with Bailey driving first since she set the cart up for them. Bailey soaked up the feeling of Jay next to her and relaxed as they headed for the tee.

Jay settled into her seat before she pulled her glove out of her back pocket and pulled it on. As she started to check her first ball for nicks, she finally spoke.

"I'm glad you asked me to play today."

Bailey felt her ears grow warmer and knew they were bright red. She stammered a bit as she tried to reply. "I... I'm glad you agreed to meet with me. I just didn't want things to be too awkward on Monday. I meant what I said about wanting to win back your friendship and trust, Jay."

Jay just nodded and remained silent, her eyes following a pair of ducks swimming in one of the water hazards that ran through the course.

Bailey was relieved when they found the tee empty. They flipped for the first shot after agreeing that they would follow the rules of leader takes first position after the hole. Jay won the flip, casually teed up the ball, and settled in for her first drive. Taking a deep breath, she slowly released it as she swung through the ball, keeping her head down and watching the club sweep through the path she wanted. Bailey's eyes followed the twist of Jay's body as it coiled and uncoiled. She had always liked to watch Jay, but there was something more alluring about this adult version.

"Nice shot, Jay, guess those lessons must be paying off," Bailey said as she got out of the cart and teed up her own ball.

As Bailey lined up her shot, she cleared her mind of everything but the ball and where she wanted it to land. With a strong motion, she swung through and raised her head in time to see her ball land just behind Jay's, both dead center of the fairway.

"Great shot, Bailey! It looks like we're pretty evenly matched these days," Jay complimented. Bailey was reminded that Jay had always out-powered her driver shots. Bailey had to admit that it felt good to be back on a course and able to keep up with Jay.

They walked to the cart and headed towards their balls. "So, um, have you given any thought to our friendship, Jay?" Bailey asked with a hesitant quality to her voice.

Jay blew out a breath and made herself take a second to think. "I have, of course I have. I know it will be ridiculously hard to work together every day and pretend we didn't grow up together. The truth is, I do understand why you ran away. Yes, it hurt, and I think you should have come back sooner to settle things, but you came when you were ready, right?" She sneaked a look at Bailey to see how she was being received.

Bailey nodded. "I did come back as soon as I realized I had to take the chance to make things right. I thought I could ignore it and it would go away, but it ate at me, Jay, I had to come back to you... I mean here."

Jay's breath caught a little at that, but she let it pass. "Okay then, here's what I've decided. We take things one day at a time. It feels comfortable to be with you here and now, but I still find myself on guard. We're both different people than we were all those years ago, and who knows if we'll even have much in common now." Bailey raised an eyebrow, but kept silent, pulling the cart over as they reached their balls.

They hit their second shots and returned to the cart. "I admit I've really missed you and our friendship over the years. I want to say that I would take back that night if I could, but the truth is, it was an amazing night for me." Jay stopped suddenly, seemingly unable to continue for a moment.

"It was for me too, Jay, that's why I ran. It was impossibly good. We were two kids with no clue about the world, and I felt like I had found the other half of my soul. I just didn't know what to do with that, considering the ramifications."

They waved another group through, as they realized that they weren't doing much golfing. They finished the hole, both deep in thought, and when Jay got behind the wheel, she headed for a section of the course closed for renovations.

"Where are we going? Jay, what's going on?" Bailey sounded a little concerned since Jay took off without announcing a change of plans.

Jay saw the confusion on her face. "Relax, I just figured we could keep talking without the whole club coming through the conversation. This section is closed so we can sit and talk for a while."

Bailey nodded and smiled softly. "I'm so glad you want to talk, Jay. I can't tell you how much I've missed talking with you." Jay pulled over behind some trees with a nice view of the lake.

"Let's settle some things without interruptions." Jay said firmly.

Green eyes looked up at Jay, and she almost lost her resolve. Bailey nodded, afraid to speak for fear of saying the wrong thing just when it seemed Jay might actually be open to working on things. She wondered about the golf pro, but pushed her from her mind and continued to look into Jay's deep brown eyes.

Jay settled more firmly into her seat and cleared her throat. "I guess the real question, Bailey, is how much do you want from me, and how much can I give this time?"

Startled, Bailey started to protest, but Jay waved her hand to ask for silence.

"Now Bailey, I don't mean that quite the way it sounded, but the truth is, as much as I understand how things happened, a lot has changed for me. I'm not the trusting soul I was in our younger days." Bailey sat very still, almost afraid to breathe waiting for Jay to continue.

"I don't know how to explain it, but working at this company has changed me, Bail. I've had to work for someone who is so deep in her closet she can't see daylight, and she wanted me to do the same. I've managed to compromise. I don't lie about myself nor do I go out of my way to tell people anything much about my life outside of work. I changed companies about five years ago to get into this lending division, and now I sometimes wonder why."

Bailey kept quiet, but she nodded while instinctively reaching for Jay's hand with hers. She smiled when she felt the warm fingers wrap around her smaller hand.

"The thing is, all this time, I've just been working so hard, and now I'm not even sure I know why anymore. I've started learning more about the upper management of the company, and I'm not sure I want to stay. I need to know, Bailey, what is it you really want from me, from us? Friendship or... " Jay stopped talking; she couldn't even ask what was in her heart. Ever since she first saw Bailey again, she knew that her heart still belonged to the green-eyed woman. Now she was babbling, and it was time to learn the truth behind Bailey's homecoming.

Bailey knew this was the moment. This one moment in time was why she had picked up and moved back from Florida, without a job or a place to live of her own. *Please Goddess,* she begged, *please let me get this right.*

"Jay, I realized something just before Kelly died. I've never gotten serious with anyone because no one could ever capture my heart. My heart has been here with you all these years. It's still yours with no room for another love." Jay stayed silent, but she tightened her grip on Bailey's hand. Bailey gave a tremulous smile. "I found a spiritual path for myself while I was in Florida. There were people just like me searching for a place that accepted our beliefs and lives without threats or damnation. In Wicca I've learned to believe in the duality in nature. Where there is good there is bad, where there is light there is dark. There are both God and Goddess."

"So you left home and became a witch?" Jay asked.

"In a manner of speaking. Not like the movie version of course but I do believe in the magic of the world we live in." Bailey responded. "Does it freak you out Jay?"

Jay shook her head. "Not really. There is a good-sized Wiccan population around here. I've heard enough about it to know that it seems to be a pretty positive approach to life. So, back to what you were saying? God and Goddess I think?"

"Right. Two halves of a whole. Jay, I believe you are my duality, my other half. I want to see if we can build a relationship, a full partnership. I know it's a lot to take in, and even more to ask, after all that has gone before. I know you're seeing the golf pro and – "

"Wait a second!" Jay interrupted. "There is no one in my life right now. I'm not dating Riley or anyone else. Where did you get such an idea?"

"But, I saw you when you got here, you hugged her, and don't you have plans later? It's okay, I don't have any claim on you, I understand."

"Damn it, Bailey. You aren't hearing me. Riley and I are friends, becoming very good friends in fact, and we do have plans later. However, we do not now, nor will we ever have, anything romantic. We've hung out and talked a lot, in fact we've talked a lot about you." Jay ducked her head as she said this, realizing she was admitting to thinking about Bailey a lot since their last meeting.

Bailey gave a big sigh of relief and hugged Jay before she realized what she was doing. "Oh, Jay, I'm sorry, I didn't mean to presume... I'm happy to hear you aren't dating anyone. You've thought of me?" Bailey had just processed that part of the statement through her excitement to find Jay still free of entanglements.

"Of course, you goofball, you came barreling back into my life without warning. Of course you've managed to cross my mind a few times." Jay couldn't help but feel as if she was walking on thin ice with her heart, knowing she still hadn't answered Bailey's statement about their relationship. "I guess you deserve an answer, huh?" Jay trembled a bit, and it dawned on her that they were still holding hands. *Maybe that's a good sign.*

"I don't know how good I'm going to be at this, but I would like to try with you. I miss our friendship, but I lost my heart to you years ago, and it never came back to me." Jay saw tears in those emerald eyes she used to know so well. She felt her own eyes welling up. "I can't make any promises, but I will do my best to put my faith and trust in you, Bail. I've missed you so much."

The tears flowed down both their faces, and they hugged fiercely. After several minutes, they both started to breathe more easily and pulled apart to look at one another. Brown eyes searched green, looking for anything to hold on to, anything to make this moment suspect. They found only honesty and caring with a little wariness.

Jay wiped away her tears. "I need us to take it kind of slow, Bail. This will take me some time to get used to and to trust."

"Absolutely! I'm not toting a U-Haul behind the Rav-4," joked Bailey. "Besides, I'm starting this new job, and I hear the supervisor I have is a stickler for all the work getting done quickly and efficiently. It might cut into my social life a bit."

"Oh crap!" Jay slapped her forehead in frustration and looked earnestly at Bailey. "I have to warn you, Sharon knows I'm a lesbian. She's deep in the closet, but she isn't dumb. She'll catch on to us if we aren't careful. We have to totally keep this under wraps at work, especially with me as your supervisor!"

Bailey nodded her understanding. "Should I look around for a different job? I don't want anything to ruin this chance to make things right with you. I can call up tomorrow and withdraw."

Jay smiled for a moment, her face lighting up at the thought that Bailey would do that for her, for them. "No, it's fine, stay with this for now, and you can form your own opinions. If it becomes a problem, we can discuss it. One of us can always transfer to a different team or something. That part I know we can work out." They both smiled shyly until Bailey noticed the placement of the sun.

"Oops, we better get you back, you have plans tonight! Hot date with the pro wasn't it?" she teased, smiling so Jay knew it was just a joke. They started the cart back towards the clubhouse, holding hands as they drove.

"Do you want me to cancel tonight so we can keep talking? Or, do you want to join us? We're just going to dinner and maybe a movie."

Jay was so cute in her attempt to include Bailey that she took pity on her. "It's fine that you two are going out. I have plans also." Jay raised an eyebrow as if to inquire.

Bailey burst out laughing. "I remember you practicing that look in the mirror for hours! It doesn't fool me, woman! But, to answer your eyebrow, I'm having dinner with our parents here at the club. Mother has a nice young woman she wants me to meet after dinner."

Jay growled at that statement.

Bailey patted her hand reassuringly. "They have no idea it's you I want. Don't worry, I'll take care of that later tonight. That is if you don't mind. You know anything I tell my mother will be back to yours within twenty-four hours."

"Why don't you wait, and we can tell them together? Bring them by my folks around ten in the morning? I'll let my mom know that I've invited your family for brunch. Then we can tell them together that we are exploring a relationship, but taking it slowly. Deal?"

"Deal! You are brilliant, you know. If I told my mother on my own it would be a matter of minutes before she was picking out baby names." Laughing they pulled in at the clubhouse. "I make no promises that they won't do that still, but at least we will be a united front!" They got out of the cart and put their unused golf bags on the racks to be put back into the storage room before heading to the locker room.

Their lockers were in different rows, but they talked quietly as they changed since they had the place to themselves. After finalizing plans, they went in search of their parents before Jay had to meet up with Riley. Jay hugged her parents and greeted the McIntyres before asking her mother for a private word. Laura went willingly and asked Jay what was wrong.

"Nothing, Mom, I just wanted to let you know, I asked Bailey to bring her folks to brunch tomorrow. Is that all right?"

Laura looked at her daughter as if she had grown a second head. "Are you feeling well, dear? I thought you just mentioned brunch with the woman that broke your heart so many years ago."

Jay hugged her mom. "I did, Mom, just trust me and remember Bailey and I are working together now. Things have to get better, right?"

Laura shook her head, looking Jay over, but finding no sign of impending insanity. She resigned herself to waiting to find out what was really going on. She knew her daughter well enough to know that she had something up her sleeve, but she couldn't guess what was going to come out at brunch tomorrow. They walked back to the group just as Riley came through the door looking for her.

"Oh, there's Riley, we're headed out to dinner. I'll see you tomorrow!" She took off with a quick wave to everyone.

* * *

"Why do I feel as if I missed something crucial today?" asked Riley as they headed out to dinner. They had taken the CR-V back to Jay's parents' house before heading out in Riley's Jeep for the night. Jay collapsed against the seat in laughter. She laughed until she had tears forming in her eyes.

"That is the understatement of the week!" said Jay when she could speak again. "Do you mind if we go some place quiet for dinner and talk? Maybe skip the movie?" Jay asked once she had control of herself. Riley looked at her but didn't read anything from her expression.

"Sure, we can still go to the pub I told you about. We can get seated in the downstairs dining room if we can't get a corner booth. Either one will give us a chance to talk."

"Perfect," Jay said. "I just need to get a handle on some stuff and talking with you seems to help. I think I should buy dinner since you're playing therapist again." Jay had been teasing Riley for the past week that she should go back to school to become a social worker or therapist since she was so easy to talk to and gave such great advice.

They got a corner booth that opened up just as they walked in. They waited for the server to deposit menus and take their drink orders. The two friends talked over the menu, finally picking a couple of dishes to share. The server dropped off their drinks, took their orders and Riley made a toast.

"To friends, new and old." They clinked their mugs of ale and each took a sip.

"So, I take it you have me figured out already," Jay said with a slight smirk.

Riley gave her a much bigger smirk. "I had you figured out a week ago! You were the slow one, girly! But please, tell me what exactly happened as even my wise and wonderful powers have failed to tell me how you came to the obvious conclusion."

Jay groaned, but grinned as she did it. Leaning her elbows on the table Jay started out by filling Riley in on the telephone call Friday morning and continuing up to the part about brunch.

"Whoa, dude, you mean to tell me you are having brunch tomorrow and announcing your fledgling relationship to all four parental units? You got a big pair of ovaries there." Riley took a big sip of her ale, sighing with pleasure as she drank it. "I almost wish I could be a fly on the wall for that one. How do you think it will go over?"

Jay grimaced as she had second thoughts, however brief they were. "I'm sure it will be fine. In fact, doesn't every parent want his or her kid to date the girl next door?"

Riley broke out in a huge belly laugh, turning heads in their direction. "I don't think this is the 'typical' situation, Jay, my friend. Besides your folks know what happened before, right?"

Jay nodded slowly, her eyes never straying from her ale.

"What makes you think they will be so willing to let you risk your heart with the same girl again? Don't you think they'll be a bit upset?"

Jay shook her head firmly. "I'm sure they will have some reservations but they've always wanted me to live my life the way I thought best. I can't not give this a try. I've always wondered what could have been if we had waited or things had gone differently. Now, I'll know for sure if it is meant to be, or if I've been holding on to a fantasy all this time."

"Okay, girly, I expect to be kept in the loop. You aren't going to dump me because of this are you?" Jay was surprised to find Riley looking nervous as she asked that question.

"Oh, Rye, of course not! You've come to mean so much to me, there is no way I'm letting go of such a good friend. You're gonna have to work pretty hard to shake me loose. Besides, I need all the free golf tips I can get." Jay laughed as she said it, trying to bring a lighter tone to the table. It worked, and as their food arrived, talk turned to the happenings at the club, Rye's family, and the books they were reading.

They finally left the pub sometime after midnight when Riley noticed Jay yawning into her beer.

"You've got to learn to hold a couple of beers better than that, Conway! You're letting down the Irish side," she kidded as they walked to the Jeep.

Jay gave her a sleepy smile. "It's weird. I've been really tired lately. I can gear up and get going during the day, but I'm going to bed earlier and earlier, and sleeping later on weekends. I guess I'm getting older." Jay shrugged it off and Rye teased her about her age since Jay was a few months older. They arrived in short order at Jay's parents', and Riley shut the Jeep off for a minute.

"Good luck tomorrow. If you need anything, I'll have my cell on me all day. I want a report tomorrow night no matter what!" Riley ordered.

"Yes, dear," laughed Jay in her best hen-pecked voice. "Now go home and let me get some sleep, youngin'. No respect for your elders these days." Jay joked as she gave Riley a quick hug and got out of the Jeep. "Seriously Rye, thanks for being here for me. It helps to know there is someone in my corner."

"Anytime my friend, anytime. Go get some sleep, we'll talk tomorrow."

* * *

Morning came faster than Jay realized as she awoke to the smell of coffee wafting up from the kitchen. She hurried through her morning routine, threw on shorts and a T-shirt, and then changed again into a polo shirt. After quickly drying her hair and running a brush through it, Jay decided to leave it down for now. She made her bed and left her room to help her mom get brunch together.

"Morning, Mom. Morning, Dad," she said dropping a kiss on each one's cheek and heading for the coffee. She poured a half of a cup and added milk and sugar. Her mother watched in amusement.

"I still don't understand why you even bother drinking it like that. It's just coffee flavored milk."

"Exactly! I like it this way!" She stuck her tongue out at her mother with a giggle. Her parents exchanged looks but kept quiet. "So, can I help? I can make my killer French toast if you would like," Jay offered.

"Sure, honey, I think we have everything you need for it."

Jay gathered the necessary ingredients and then sliced up a large loaf of Brioche. She quickly had the food for their brunch well underway. Her dad added sliced fruit while her Mom scrambled eggs with a touch of dill, a family favorite.

"So, honey, how was your night out with your friend Riley?" her dad asked.

"It was great, thanks. We went to that new Irish pub near here and split a couple of entrées and dessert. They had great rice pudding!"

"You still drink beer when you eat your rice pudding?" he teased with a grin.

"Very funny, old man! No, I switched to water for dessert and then went back to beer, thank you very much." She knew he couldn't resist teasing her about the time they went out, just after she turned twenty-one. She insisted on having beer with her entire meal, dessert included. She spent a good portion of the night learning why pudding and beer don't mix well. She made a face at him and then laughed at the memory. "Anything else I can do, Mom?"

"No, we're all done, the table on the patio is set, and the juice is in the fridge waiting for everyone to get here. Are you going to tell me now what brought on this fit of neighborliness?"

"Sorry, Mom, you just have to accept that I'm getting nicer in my old age." She threw a wink over her shoulder as she went to answer the knock on the door.

Jay greeted the McIntyres and led them through the house to the patio. She offered them drinks and took the flowers they brought to put into a vase for the table. She hardly got a second to look at Bailey, never mind a moment alone with her.

Once everyone was seated at the table on the patio, the conversation quickly turned to how much like old times it was. Before long everyone had finished, and Jay got up to clear the table. Laura started to rise to help her, but Bailey motioned for her to remain seated.

"It's okay, Mrs. C., I've got it. If it's going to be like old times, might as well let the kids do the dishes." Bailey grinned at her parents and helped Jay clear the table and load the dishwasher.

Finally, alone in the kitchen and out of sight of the older folks, they exchanged a quick hug.

"Still feel like this is the time to tell them?" asked Bailey.

"Yes, positive, but we have to do it now before I lose my nerve." She grinned as she said it, but the truth was that Jay was nervous about this announcement. There was no going back, they were definitely going to try dating as adults, and they hadn't even kissed yet! Realizing that, Jay leaned in and gave Bailey a quick, soft kiss on her lips leaving the other woman slightly dazed and surprised.

"What brought that on? Not that I mind, but...?" Jay quickly explained her train of thought, and they shared a laugh. Taking a deep breath, they headed back into the other room and their parents.

"Enough shenanigans, kids, tell us the real reason we're having brunch after more than a decade of you two not speaking." Marc, Bailey's father didn't pull any punches, he knew there was an agenda, and he was tired of waiting.

Jay looked in Bailey's green eyes, saw the faith and trust in them, and she was ready. "Well, we've been doing some talking about our past and why we stopped being friends. We've worked it out to our satisfaction and... " at that point Jay stalled out and looked to Bailey for aid.

"What Jay is saying, is that we've decided to explore, very slowly, a romantic relationship. Slowly that is...." She was almost afraid to look at their parents, but when she did, Bailey was almost as shocked as Jay to see all four of them passing money around the table.

"What the hell is going on?" sputtered Jay. "Were you guys betting on us?"

"Well, it wasn't like it was if you would get together or not. We simply had a pool on how long it would take you two to tell us today," said Marc with a grin as he counted his winnings.

They looked at each other and started laughing until tears ran from their eyes. *Go figure,* thought Jay, *we're stressed and they already know what we're going to say.*

"Are you okay with this, Mom?" Jay leaned over to whisper to her mother.

"Honey, I've often thought that the two of you should have ended up together. I'm so proud of you for taking a chance on love after all the pain you've dealt with."

"Thanks, Mom," Jay wrapped her mother up in a hug.

Steve did have one question. "How are you going to handle things at work? It's not the most liberal environment and dating a subordinate won't be looked upon well."

Bailey explained their plans and all the parents nodded approval. After a little more chatting, Jay excused herself to head back to her place in the city or she'd get stuck in traffic returning from the shore. She went upstairs to get her bag and Bailey followed. While Jay looked around to make sure she had packed everything she needed, Bailey collapsed with relief on the bed.

"I can't believe they had a pool going," she said with a laugh.

"Hey, it is better than the alternatives," pointed out Jay. She looked at Bailey on her bed, just like so many other times when they were growing up. Only this time it was different too, and she felt a little awkward about it.

Bailey shot her a questioning glance. "What's going on, Jay? You got really still all of a sudden."

"I was just thinking how many times you've lain on that bed, and how nice it is that you're doing it again." Bailey moved over to Jay and wrapped her arms around the taller woman.

"You are very sweet, Jay Conway. If you keep this up it's going to be very hard to get rid of me." Bailey's voice wavered as she said the last part, but she kept looking into Jay's dark brown eyes.

Jay hugged the smaller woman and brushed a kiss gently across the top of her head. "What makes you think I want to get rid of you, McIntyre? I've put the past to rest. Let's see where the future leads."

Bailey's hold on Jay tightened into a bear hug. She was unable to believe her luck that Jay was willing to give them a chance. "I'll try to focus on that, Jay, I promise."

They walked downstairs together, and Jay dropped her bag off in her car before heading inside to say her goodbyes. After a round of hugs and promises to get together with her parents for golf sometime soon, the two women walked back out to Jay's CR-V holding hands.

Jay chuckled and when Bailey gave her a questioning look, she explained. "I feel like this is a reverse high school date. You're walking me to my car but in my parents' driveway. And I'm the one driving away. It just struck me as odd."

Bailey gave a short laugh and agreed. "Call me later so I know you got in? I'll be around and suffering from first day nerves and all that stuff." Jay gave her one last hug and agreed to call when she got home. Jay saw Bailey standing in the driveway through her rearview mirror as she drove away feeling a little sad and yet filled with the promise of a fresh start.

* * *

Monday morning, Bailey was up and out the door about an hour earlier than she needed, but she was too excited to stay at her parents' house any more. She decided to get downtown early, and spend her time in a café looking over rental ads. She ordered her usual caffeine of choice, a large Chai latte and settled into a comfortable chair in the corner. Taking out a pen, she went over the paper's rental section, circling those she felt good about. Deciding to call about them at lunch, she folded up the ads and stuck them in her messenger bag.

"Mind if I join you?"

Bailey looked up in surprise. Smiling widely. "You can join me anytime! What are you doing here, Jay?"

"It so happens this is my typical morning stop for Chai and a bagel. I'm not too surprised that you found it so quickly."

Bailey laughed. "I should have known since it's in the same building you, I mean we, work in. I was just getting ready to head up."

"Well then, let's head up together, and I'll get you introduced to the team before your morning orientation session with HR."

Greeting people as they went, Jay led the way up to their offices, stopping to drop her things off along the way. Jay introduced Bailey to Scott and explained that he was her right arm.

"If you need anything, the odds are Scott can help. He holds the team together with scotch tape and baling wire."

Scott blushed and held out his hand. "Nice to meet you, Ms. McIntyre. Welcome aboard and feel free to call on me if you need help locating anything."

"Please, call me Bailey, and I might just take you up on that until I get my sea legs." With that Jay took Bailey around the floor, introducing her to the members of the team and ending up in front of the HR suite just before the appointed time.

"See Scott when you get done. He'll show you to your workspace and get you set up with passwords and such. Spend the rest of the day getting your e-mail and other programs set up to your liking, and we'll hit the ground running tomorrow. Later this week, I'll take you around to the branches that will report to you for concurrences and decisions, and introduce you to the branch level lenders you will be responsible for helping along in the program."

"Whew, sounds like a lot, but I'm ready. See you later?"

Jay shook her head. "Not likely, I'm in meetings off site by the time you get out of here." She lowered her voice so it wouldn't carry. "Give me a call when you head out, maybe we can get dinner or at least talk for a while." Smiling, Bailey nodded and let herself into the HR suite.

CHAPTER 7

TIME FLEW BY, the weeks passing, and summer would give way to autumn soon. Bailey had found a small one-bedroom apartment in Old City, easing her commute time considerably. She and Jay were working on things, spending time together outside of work, and regaining the closeness they had in their younger days. Things were going so well that Bailey was actually a little nervous about it. Jay teased her mercilessly; saying that waiting for the other shoe to drop was negative conditioning and a total waste of time. Maybe so, she conceded, but life just seemed so good.

Labor Day weekend was coming up, and they were heading to Bucks County for a backyard shindig at the Conways' house. Bailey was excited to see her folks. Things had been so busy that she hadn't gotten out of the city much at all. There had been the occasional round of golf with her folks or Jay at the club, a dinner here or there, but not a lot of time overall.

Thinking over the past weeks, she marveled at how far she and Jay had come in a relatively short time. They were dating now, taking things slowly, but enjoying the time together as they grew closer. They still hadn't slept together, and Bailey was getting ready to implode. She found herself thinking about tackling Jay and strapping her down so she could have her way with her, but recognized that Jay needed to rebuild her trust before they took that important step.

They were making strides towards that trust at least by talking about the years they had spent apart. The previous weekend had been a huge step down that path for both of them. Bailey had talked about her time in Florida with Jay, sharing information that she had worried about telling her. They had finally covered the topic of religion and how their beliefs had affected their lives.

"What about religion? Do you still go to church?" Bailey asked Jay.

"Not really. I'm sure you remember that Mom gave me the out when I hit my teen-age years. They don't go other than major holidays. I've kind of just stopped going altogether. Too much goes along with it that I just don't believe in or like." Jay shrugged. "I still believe in something, but I'm not sure what anymore. What about you?"

"You remember my friend Kelly?" Jay nodded. "She introduced me to a group of Wiccans that she practiced with, and I ended up studying with them. I think one of the hardest parts of accepting my sexuality was that it went against what I was taught in church. Wicca has given me a way to be spiritual while honoring nature and believing that I am a strong woman."

"You mentioned this once before. I know you said you aren't a witch but what does it all mean? Do you do spell and stuff? Are you going to turn me into a frog if we have a fight?" Jay chuckled to make sure Bailey knew she was teasing but she was curious.

Bailey slapped Jay lightly on the shoulder. "No you big goof! I don't do spells, though some Wiccan's call their rituals spell work. To me, it is just another form of prayer. I worship and pray just like people in other religions do. I just do it in a different format. I will hold the frog thing in reserve though." Bailey shot Jay a playful grin. "Just in case you step out of line."

"I'll remember that." Jay replied. "But seriously, I'm glad you found something that works for you," Jay replied. "I didn't realize that church had been affecting you so much in school."

"I didn't really go to church back then because I knew that their teachings went against things I felt. I think it was a huge factor in my running from you." Bailey stopped walking and looked at Jay with a sad expression. "I didn't know then what I know now. We can be faithful to God and Goddess and still love whomever we love. It is all part of nature. Knowing that homosexuality exists in nature somehow helped me accept myself finally."

Jay tugged her into a hug. "I'm glad you found your way back to me, Bail. Whatever path it took to get you here, I'm just so glad you made it here."

* * *

With a sigh, Bailey tossed her files aside, knowing that she wasn't going to get any more work done today. She thought about stopping in Jay's office before she left, but she tried to maintain distance from her at work. She gathered her things and headed towards the elevator, almost bumping into Sharon as she too headed out for the weekend.

"Bailey, how are you settling in here? I've heard great things about you from your teammates." Sharon smiled, happy that her choice for the opening on Jay's team had fit in so well, especially after Jay's initial reservations.

"Oh, hi, Sharon. Things are great. Everyone is keeping me busy. I sent you and Jay an e-mail recommending one of my branch lenders for an award. He's brought in more business this quarter than any two branches, and he's a new graduate of our lending training."

"I did see that and made a note. It sounds like he's a solid choice for the Lender of the Quarter award. You've done a good job, Bailey. Keep up the good work. Enjoy the long weekend!" They parted ways in the parking garage and Bailey headed home to wait for Jay's call letting her know she was done for the weekend.

Jay sighed, rubbed her eyes, and leaned back in her chair. After a quick glance at the clock, she realized that she needed to get out of her office. She was having trouble focusing, and reading through credit reports wasn't helping matters. All she could think about was her long weekend, the chance to spend time with Bailey, and hopefully, she could get a decent night's sleep. Lately, it seemed like she was having more and more trouble sleeping through the night. She didn't know why, but she was still tired when she woke up most mornings. She knew that she had pushed herself hard all spring and most of the summer, but by now she should be recovering from that extra work.

Jay pushed those thoughts out of her head, thinking instead about the special evening she had planned for her and Bailey the following night. Jay knew Bailey was frustrated with their lack of physical intimacy, and Jay planned to remedy that situation this weekend. She appreciated Bailey's patience and understanding, and she finally felt ready. Her trust in Bailey and in their relationship, had grown with the time they had spent getting reacquainted, and she was going to take things to the next level.

* * *

Bailey awoke to a persistent ringing. She slapped at her alarm clock, frustrated that she had set it out of habit. That didn't stop it, and she realized it was her telephone. Snatching it up she mumbled, "Lo?" She heard the warm chuckle that could only be Jay on the other end. "Stop laughing at me, it's the crack of dawn."

Jay laughed outright at that. "Bail, it's almost nine-thirty, we're supposed to get together in about an hour to go to the Italian Market. Did you forget?"

"Oh crap! I'll be ready, I promise!"

Jay smiled, knowing that she would end up waiting a little while when she got there, but that was fine. They had no real schedule today.

"It's fine, Bail, I'll get to your place around ten-thirty as planned. Just come out when you're ready, it's so gorgeous out that I won't mind waiting. I'll just bring a book and read outside."

Bailey swore as she stumbled around her bed trying to get oriented.

"You can come in you know. I'll get ready as quickly as possible. Shorts are okay for today, right?"

"Yeah, you'll be fine in shorts. It isn't cool enough for jeans today. Take your time and don't hurt yourself getting ready. And I would rather wait outside in case I don't get decent parking. I'll see you soon." Jay hung up and looked around her condo to make sure things were ready for later.

The CD player was loaded up with Loreena McKinnet, and the candles were set up on the mantle and the dining room table. The table was already set for tonight's dinner, and the wine was waiting in the fridge. The bed had fresh sheets, there were candles on her dresser, and the bathroom was even clean, with extra towels and a new toothbrush still in the wrapping. Thinking of tomorrow's plans with her parents, Jay set the alarm clock next to the bed, just in case there was a reason to oversleep. Feeling a familiar tingle run through her at the thoughts she was having, Jay smiled. She never would have believed this was possible, but she was getting ready to have a romantic night with the woman of her dreams after she was sure she had lost her.

Having delayed all she could, Jay grabbed a book and headed for the CR-V in the condo association's garage. Bailey's place was close enough to walk, but they would head to South Philly's famous Italian Market, an outdoor market full of great vendors for fresh fruits and veggies, along with any kind of meat, poultry, fish, and cheese you could think of wanting. There were also a couple of great bakeries where she planned to get a loaf of good semolina bread for tonight. She also needed to pick up a dessert for tomorrow's get together at her folks since she'd been too busy to bake anything.

She waited in her vehicle reading for about twenty minutes before Bailey appeared. Jumping out Jay walked around to open the door for her and got a quick hug and kiss on the cheek for her efforts. Jay grinned as she shut the passenger door and got back in looking over at Bailey with eyes shining brightly.

"Ready for our culinary adventure?"

"You bet! Lead on, oh great chef." Bailey had to admit, one of the things that she loved about Jay was her willingness to be adventurous in food. They both loved to cook and found that they could collaborate nicely in the kitchen.

They found parking on a small street just off Washington, the main thoroughfare near the market area. Grabbing Jay's hand Bailey was off and ready to shop for tonight's dinner adventure. Jay stopped walking, and Bailey looked up at her.

"Is everything okay? Something I should know about?"

"Everything is fine, but I have a specific menu in mind for tonight. Is that all right with you? I know we usually pick everything out together, but I kind of planned it out this time."

Bailey tilted her head to the side, trying to read the hidden message in Jay's eyes, and then she shrugged and grinned. "That's fine. I don't care as long as I'm spending the day with you. I trust you to feed me well."

They wandered among the open-air vendors and ventured into the small family owned shops along the market, tasting, and sampling, picking up things here and there as they went until they were both loaded down with bags. Jay finally decided she had everything she needed and suggested they head back to her place so they could get started on dinner as it would take a bit of time to prepare. Bailey looked a little baffled, having still not guessed the menu for the evening. Jay smiled to herself as they made their way back to her CR-V. She had bought some stuff to use during the week, knowing the weird mixture of purchases would keep Bailey guessing.

They got back to Jay's and carried in the groceries, putting things away together. Jay was swept away by the domesticity of the scene. She asked Bailey to switch on the music so they could have some cooking tunes for inspiration. Bailey raised an eyebrow when she heard the sounds of Loreena Mckinnet fill the room, but she didn't comment. She just washed her hands and asked for her first sous-chef assignment.

"Why don't you pound the chicken breasts out? I need them as thin as you can get them without breaking through."

"I'm on it," replied Bailey as they settled into their dinner prep. Jay was gathering things from the fridge and pantry, and had pulled out her food processor, raising Bailey's curiosity by at least a factor of five.

Jay started by taking fresh spinach, after washing and drying it, she added it to the food processor, then some ricotta, fresh mozzarella, sun dried tomatoes, an egg, various fresh herbs, and some breadcrumbs. With a few quick whirs, her concoction was done and put it in the fridge to chill. The broccoli rabe, garlic, onions, and portabella mushrooms where all cleaned, prepped and ready to go at the last minute.

"All set with the chicken, what's next?" Bailey reported.

"Are you in the mood to slice tomatoes?" Jay asked after a little thought.

Bailey laughed, tomatoes were one of her favorite foods. "That depends, did you get me an extra one to eat while I slice?" With a flourish, Jay presented her with two perfectly ripe New Jersey tomatoes for her munching pleasure, as well as a couple to slice for the tomato and mozzarella salad she had planned.

"Aw, Jay, you spoil me, thank you!" Standing up, Bailey reached up to Jay to give her a quick kiss. To her surprise, Jay put her arms around her and deepened the kiss, their tongues doing battle with one another until they had to break apart for air.

"Wow! I'll play sous-chef for you anytime if that's my payment," Bailey joked, while she tried not to let Jay see how much their kiss had stirred her.

Jay struggled to keep from acting on her feelings right then. She wanted Bailey, wanted her right then and there, but she wanted to do this right. This was, for all intents and purposes, going to be their first time together, and she wanted Bailey to have a romantic, slow seduction. Since Bailey had taken the initiative to come back and rekindle things, the least Jay could do was show her how worth the wait it was for her. Trying to refocus on the food preparation instead of the ache in her groin, she remembered the tomatoes.

"Um, okay, you slice those, and I'll slice the mozzarella and prep the fresh basil." Bailey looked up at Jay with such a sweet smile that Jay just had to lean down and kiss her one more time.

They got the tomato salad together and let it marinate in a little extra virgin olive oil, a splash of balsamic vinegar, some sea salt, and pepper. Jay took the chicken breasts that were pounded paper-thin and scooped some of her cheese and spinach mixture into each one, spreading it out and rolling each one into a cylinder shape. Each roll got dipped in an egg wash and rolled in breadcrumbs, before being put on a parchment-lined pan.

"We're all set," said Jay with a last wipe of the counter. "I'll set those to bake for a while, and then I just have to sauté the broccoli rabe while they rest, and we'll have a nice little Italian dinner." They looked at each other and laughed, and Bailey said what they were both thinking.

"Yeah, the two Irish chicks made a nice Italian dinner."

By the time they got the food together and the kitchen cleaned up, it was a little before five in the evening. Jay brought out the tomato salad and poured them each a glass of wine. They carried everything into the living room and settled in together on the floor in front of the couch.

"This is great. In fact, this whole day has been wonderful, Jay, thank you," Bailey spoke softly as she leaned into Jay a little. Jay wrapped her arm around Bailey's shoulder and gave her a light squeeze.

"My pleasure. It's so easy being with you like this, spending the day running errands and cooking. It feels so right, like this is how life is supposed to be."

"Mm, I know how right this part feels," said Bailey as she snuggled into the warmth of Jay's embrace. "I know what you mean though, just doing ordinary things seems so much better when you're with me. I can't thank you enough for taking another chance on me."

"Shh, enough of that," soothed Jay "We're long past the need to apologize. This is about our present and our future." With that, Jay leaned down and claimed her mouth in a soulful kiss that seemed to penetrate right to Bailey's heart. Bailey turned into her and ran her fingers through Jay's hair, smoothing her hands down her back.

Jay moved her mouth to the hollow of Bailey's neck where the pulse beat insistently. Bailey groaned and arched into Jay, encouraging her to continue. Jay let one hand wander down Bailey's side, pausing at her hip, reveling in the soft curve she found there. Bailey started nipping at Jay's ear before placing little kisses down the side of Jay's neck, heading for the opening of her polo shirt. Jay felt the pulse beat between her thighs, she knew she could continue and neither would complain about the outcome. She raised her head to suggest they move to a more comfortable location when the oven timer rang.

"Damn, I forgot about that," said Jay sheepishly. Bailey was looking at her with desire in her eyes. It took all of Jay's willpower to move away and resettle her clothing as she headed for the kitchen to save the chicken. Bailey came up behind her just as she put the covered pan on the stove top to rest. She wrapped her arms around Jay from behind and gave her a good squeeze. She slid her hands down, appreciating the slight roundness to her ass before running her hands back up to Jay's arms.

"I'm fine, you know, I told you we will take things as slow as you need," Bailey spoke softly to Jay. "I'm not going anywhere, there's no rush. I enjoy whatever time I get with you, however we spend it. No worries, Jay."

Jay turned around so she was facing Bailey. "I know, you've been great. I just needed a minute to settle myself down I guess." Jay looked into those emerald eyes that captivated her so long ago, and she saw the desire mixed with concern. "Really,

Bail, I'm fine, nothing happened that I didn't want. In fact, I wanted more," she said with a huskiness to her voice. "Maybe later we can pick up where we left off?"

Bailey gave her another hug. "Sweetie, we can pick up anywhere you want, whenever you want."

Jay paused, that was the first time either of them had used a term of endearment and she decided she liked it, a lot. With silly grins on both of their faces, they went about the kitchen finishing the dinner preparations.

Jay grabbed the veggies from the fridge and sautéed the broccoli rabe with the onions and garlic, adding in the mushrooms last. It all got a healthy dose of lemon juice and kosher salt, and a final few flips in the skillet before Jay declared dinner ready. Jay ran into the dining room to light the candles and lower the lighting. She then ushered Bailey into her chair. Bailey smiled in surprise, having not seen the table before now. Jay carried in the salad, semolina bread, and broccoli, and went back for the chicken. She quickly sliced the chicken into rounds that showed off the pinwheel effect of the stuffing, and arranged it all on the platter bringing that in with the wine.

Bailey looked at her with sparkling eyes. "You did all this for me?"

"For us," answered Jay. "This is for us, to the start of our new relationship. I know I'm a bit corny and old fashioned, but it only seems right that I show you how I feel." Bailey was certain that she would fall in love with Jay at that minute if she weren't already head over heels for the woman. Jay finished pouring the wine and serving them, sitting at the corner adjacent to her rather than across the table.

They talked quietly as they ate. Jay discovered she wasn't all that hungry. She was more nervous about the rest of the evening. When they finished eating, Jay moved back into the kitchen and pulled out a bottle of sparkling wine. She popped the cork and poured as a surprised Bailey looked on.

She handed Bailey her glass and raised her own. She offered a toast.

"My Wild Irish Rose
The sweetest flower that grows
You may search everywhere
But none can compare to my Wild Irish Rose
My Wild Irish Rose
The sweetest flower that grows
Someday for my sake she may let me take
A bloom from my Wild Irish Rose"

After Jay finished the traditional Celtic toast, she touched her glass to Bailey's and took a sip of her sparkling wine. Bailey, flushed and amazed, took a sip of her own and looked at Jay, speechless. Jay became a little uncomfortable when Bailey said nothing. "Was it too much? Is it too soon? Bail, please tell me what you're thinking!"

Bailey shook her head slightly as if coming out of a dream and looked at Jay almost as if she was seeing her for the first time. "I don't think anyone has ever done anything so sweet and romantic for me, Jay. That was the toast my father made to my mother at their wedding."

"I know," Jay replied. "I heard all those stories growing up too you know. I thought it was the perfect way to tell you how I feel about you."

Bailey stood, holding her hand out to Jay. Jay took it and clasped it tightly.

"Jay, if you don't take me to bed right now, I might explode."

"Can't have you making a mess in my clean house," joked Jay as she scooped her up and carried her into the bedroom, placing her gently on the bed.

She quickly lit the candles there as well and stood looking at Bailey, licking her lips nervously.

"Jay, we can still take this slowly, just tell me if anything I do makes you uncomfortable."

"Bailey, I want you so much it hurts, please, just make love with me."

"Oh yes." Bailey reached for Jay and pulled her down next to her on the bed. She leaned in and started kissing Jay, deepening the kiss and slowly guiding them further up on the bed until they were lying next to each other. Jay's mouth started traveling towards the open neck of Bailey's shirt, finding the swell of her breasts too tantalizing to resist further. Bailey started exploring Jay's strong back, edging her hands underneath Jay's shirt. She worked her way towards Jay's bra strap and then paused.

"Is this okay, honey?" she asked Jay.

"Oh God, yes, please," cried Jay, her body screaming in need at this point. Jay then urged Bailey's shirt up and over her head, tossing it across the room and then eased her bra off. Jay gazed down at her. "You are more beautiful than I remember, and I need to taste you. May I?" Jay asked with a mixture of pleading and admiration. When Bailey moaned and nodded, Jay lowered her head and started by placing light kisses down the line of her collarbone, then circling her breasts while gently cupping them. Slowly she started kissing the valley between Bailey's breasts, reveling in the texture and the scent that meant Bailey to her. With almost agonizing slowness, she worked her way to a hard nipple and enveloped it in her warm mouth.

Jay groaned and sucked more of the breast into her mouth as Bailey's hands urged her closer. Jay switched to the other breast, her hand fondling the one she had just left. Then her hand started making a journey south, followed closely by her mouth. She kissed and licked her way to the top of Bailey's jeans, looking up for permission. Bailey, her hips already rocking, fumbled to help her get the offending garment off as quickly as possible. Jay stood and stripped away the last of Bailey's clothing before quickly removing her own.

Both women sighed with relief as their naked bodies came together for the first time in over thirteen years. Jay quickly started where she had left off, kissing her way down Bailey's abdomen and down each leg, stopping at the knee and moving back up in a teasing manner.

"Oh God, Jay, you're killing me, please... " Bailey begged for Jay's touch. Jay moved up and kissed her with such tenderness and caring that it brought tears to Bailey's eyes.

"Are you sure, Bail? Please be sure." Jay questioned as she looked straight into the eyes of the other woman. A small part of Jay was terrified that she would lose her again to fear.

Bailey recognized it and took the time to ease her fears.

"I'm totally sure and here, Jay, this is you and me as adults. I want you to make love to me. I want to make love to you until we can't move anymore."

Jay nodded slowly and moved her hand down into the softness at the juncture of Bailey's legs. They both moaned as Jay's fingers searched through her heat and wetness, finding the hooded prominence of her clit. Jay slowly moved her hand so that she could enter Bailey as well as give her clit some stimulation. Slowly, she eased in two fingers, feeling the heat and the smooth muscles as they gripped her. She was home, and she knew it. She kissed Bailey repeatedly as she rocked into her, feeling the tension build in them both. Suddenly, Bailey's hand was reaching for her, stroking her softly as they rocked together. Jay moaned at the additional contact, already close to coming.

"Oh God! Bailey, what are you doing to me?"

Bailey kissed her again and spoke into her ear. "I'm making sure you know you are mine," she whispered as her fingers slipped into Jay.

Suddenly, they both stiffened. Jay let out a moan as Bailey shouted Jay's name. Jay could feel the ripples as Bailey's body reached an orgasm. She gave a final shudder before slowly easing down next to Bailey and reclaiming her hand.

"Jay, honey, are you okay? Talk to me please." Bailey was worried that the past would come back to Jay now, and she wanted to reassure her that she wasn't going anywhere.

Jay nodded and smiled. "I'm not afraid, Bail, I believe in us. I love you, Bailey." Jay held her tightly as she spoke, hoping it wasn't too soon but she had to say what she felt.

"Oh Jay, I love you too, I've loved you for so long, but I didn't want to scare you."

Bailey sniffed as tears started rolling down her cheeks. Jay reached to her bedside table for a tissue and handed it to her.

"Sweetie? Why are you crying? Did I do something wrong?" Jay was starting to worry now.

"Jay, you are the absolute sweetest woman I know. I'm not crying because you did anything wrong, but because you did something so very right." Bailey hugged her tightly, then reached up and kissed her lightly on the lips. "I'm going to spend the rest of tonight showing you just how right you are," purred Bailey as she moved over her lover.

* * *

"How much time do we have before we have to leave?" asked Bailey as she came back into the bedroom after her shower. It was her second one, the first turned into a shower for two, which led to them running a bit behind schedule, Jay remembered with a flush.

"Um, well we're stopping by your place so you can change, right? So I guess we should head out soon. I cleaned up the kitchen while you finished in the shower." They had been in such a hurry last night that the remaining food sat out all night. *All the work was worth it,* thought Jay.

"Just let me run a brush through my hair, and I'll be ready to go," replied Bailey as she glanced over at her lover. For a moment, her breath caught as she recalled their passion of the previous night, and several times throughout the night too. Quickly, she realized that she was staring and got her things together. She pulled on her clothes that Jay had recovered from around the room and lain out on the bed for her. "You know, it's too bad you're so damn tall, or I could just borrow some of your clothes," laughed Bailey.

"Hey, I'm not the vertically challenged one here," teased Jay. "Now, get that cute butt in gear so we aren't too late. I'm not going to be the one to tell your parents why we were delayed this morning." Laughing, Bailey finished up and headed out the door following Jay.

They made the short drive to Bailey's place, and then they headed up 95 North to Bucks County and their parents. The Labor Day picnic was something of a tradition, and truth be told, Jay usually enjoyed it. Today, she was a little apprehensive since it was really their first family event as a couple. Just then, as if sensing Jay's case of nerves, Bailey reached over and took her hand. She raised it to her lips and gently kissed the knuckles before holding it with her smaller hand. Jay smiled over at her and counted her blessings.

"So, who's coming today? I mean other than our families," asked Bailey.

Jay thought about it and answered. "I'm not really sure, since the guest list is usually somewhat eclectic. My parents still invite anyone with no place to hang out or people they haven't gotten to spend much time with over the summer. I did mention that Riley is coming, right?"

"Yeah, you did. I already apologized for thinking you two were an item. She is darn cute after all, and you're a total catch!" Bailey chuckled at Jay's sudden blush and let her off the hook. "Honey, it's fine, she's your close friend so we have to learn to socialize at some point, might as well do it now, right?" Jay smiled at Bailey's willingness to accept her friend. Riley had been so busy with wrapping up the regular season stuff at the club that they didn't think she would be able to make it today until her boss suddenly gave her the day off. Jay suspected her father had a hand in that, but she kept her mouth shut and accepted the good fortune.

Jay found a parking space and followed the noise around back, carrying the strawberry pie she had purchased during their Italian Market trip. It was her mother's favorite so she knew it would be well received. Bailey carried in two bottles of wine for the party and stopped to greet her parents before going over to Jay and her parents.

"Thanks, ladies, good timing," said Steve. "The main work is done, and I'm getting ready to throw the chicken on the grill," he teased Jay.

Laura nudged him. "Don't listen to him, you just get a drink and mingle. Go spend some time with Riley. She just got here a few minutes ago."

"Thanks, Mom," replied Jay, giving her a quick hug and kiss on the cheek.

They poured themselves glasses of wine and made their way across the yard to where Riley was engaged in conversation with a few people from the club.

After a quick hug from Jay, Riley extended her hand to Bailey. "It's great to see you again." Bailey gave an exasperated sigh before pulling Riley into a hug too.

"If you are a friend of Jay's, then I like you enough to hug you too," she explained with a twinkle in her eye. Riley chuckled and returned the hug before asking how Jay was feeling. She had been run down the past couple of weeks, and Riley was a little concerned.

"I'm fine. I just need to get caught up on sleep, I think. Now that my latest team member is outshining everyone else, I should get a break." Jay glanced at Bailey and saw her smile at the compliment.

They chatted for a while about the books they were reading and the deplorable state of gay rights at various companies. Bailey introduced Riley officially to her parents. They knew her from the club but hadn't realized that she was a friend of Jay's as well. Everyone was having a good time, and Jay relaxed. She was far away from work and her weekday stress. Without any apparent thought, Jay reached out and took Bailey's hand, holding it gently in her own. Bailey knew that was a big step for Jay. She wasn't a PDA kind of person. Smiling, she gave Jay's hand a quick squeeze while continuing her conversation with her parents.

As the party wound down, just after sunset, Jay and Bailey helped clean up the yard and kitchen. Jay's parents kept protesting, but the women had decided they would help with clean up since they were too late to help prepare for the party. While they finished up, both sets of parents sat out on the screened in patio enjoying the cool evening. Jay and Bailey joined them when they were finished to sit for a few minutes and talk about the day.

"Honey, are you staying with us tonight?" Bailey's mother asked.

Bailey almost choked on her tea.

Before she could answer, her dad, Marc, chimed in. "Of course Jay is welcome as well." At that, no one looked comfortable, and both daughters were blushing furiously.

Jay coughed. "Thanks, but we rode together, and I have plans in the morning so I thought we'd head back shortly."

"I think our young women would rather be alone," Helen contributed causing Laura to laugh out loud.

"MOM!" bellowed Jay. Jay suddenly realized they were all just teasing them, apparently having worked it out while she and Bailey were still cleaning.

"On that note, since we're done being the butt of your jokes, I think we'll head back to the city," Jay said with a shake of her head.

"Aw, come on Jay, we were just teasing our two favorite people," said her father.

"No, Dad, really, it has been a long day and a longer week. I've been really tired lately too. I need to go if I'm going to make the drive back."

"Give an old man a hug, kiddo, and get out of here. I'm just happy that you look so happy," he said quietly. From the looks of things, Bailey was having a similar talk with her mother. They finally got themselves together and out the door.

On the way back to Philadelphia, Bailey started laughing suddenly. Jay turned to look at her as if she had lost her mind.

"I'm sorry, but the look on your face when my dad suggested we both stay there. It was pure panic and embarrassment."

Jay chuckled along with her. "Well, I couldn't possibly do to you what I want to do with your parents just down the hall. It just wouldn't be right."

"Oh yeah? What do you have in mind?" queried Bailey.

"You'll just have to wait and see, I guess," Jay replied. "Did you bring an overnight bag with you?"

"Yup, it's in the back seat. No need to go back to my place until tomorrow evening."

At that, Jay's heart lurched a little. She knew it was somewhat stereotypical, but she didn't want Bailey going anywhere. *At least it took longer than their second date*, she thought with a rueful smile.

Pushing those thoughts from her head, Jay realized that it made sense for them to not spend every night together. Besides, they couldn't really start showing up at work together, could they? Jay thought about it, they could carpool, at least some days, if they were both in the office. She mentioned it to Bailey, who looked thoughtful.

"I don't see why not. With us working in the same department and living so close, it does make sense." They decided to wait a week or two and make sure they weren't obvious around the office before starting the carpooling idea.

When they got back to Jay's, they practically raced each other to the bedroom, pulling clothes off as they went. Jay stopped Bailey from leaping on the bed by suggesting a shower together first. They took a long shower, spending plenty of time soaping, rinsing, and testing with their tongues to make sure all the soap was gone. Finally, they toweled each other off and made it into bed.

Jay hugged Bailey to her. "I'm so glad you're here. That empty part of me isn't empty anymore."

Bailey hugged her back. "You never have to be without me again, sweetie. I'm here for you always," she whispered.

Jay pulled back a bit to get a better look at Bailey. "I wish we could live together. I just don't see how we could though, do you? I mean, it wouldn't look good at work since I am still your supervisor."

"Jay, we'll work it all out, I promise. Don't let this stress you out. If I have to leave the company, I'll gladly do it so we can be together. Let's cross that bridge when we come to it. For now, let's just revel in finding each other again."

Jay resolved to do just that as she closed her eyes and fell into sleep.

CHAPTER 8

$\mathcal{L}$IFE SEEMED TO settle into a good rhythm for Jay as September drew to a close. She was surprised to be called in for a meeting with Sharon. Unable to pick up any vibes on why she was there, she sat and waited for Sharon's attention. Thankfully, Sharon got right down to business.

"Jay, we're getting direction from headquarters on a new structure for the consumer lending division, and I need your input."

Jay wasn't surprised as there had been talk for months that there would be a shifting of responsibilities. Jay just hoped her team didn't lose anyone. Things were finally rolling smoothly.

"Sure, Sharon, what can I do to help?"

"I'll get right to the bottom line, Jay. I know you're busy. Upstairs is talking about, well hell, they are restructuring the regions. When that happens, your area of responsibility will just about double."

Jay let out a shocked gasp and then quickly got a handle on herself. She knew that she couldn't let Sharon see her fear. "It'll be really tight. Is there any chance of gaining a few more people to help out the team?" asked Jay hopefully.

Sharon smiled. "Jay, I haven't gotten to the good part yet. I'm the new President of Lending, and you will be named as a Senior VP of Consumer Lending with another Senior VP of Consumer Lending to co-chair the department for this region. We will be adding a second team to your department and assigning you both ultimate control of your division, under me of course." Sharon let that sink in a minute, "Congratulations, Jay, it's a well earned promotion for you!"

Jay was stunned but managed to thank Sharon and give a wan grin.

"I think I have the perfect person in mind to be your Co-Chair, but she doesn't have as much seniority as you. You will keep your team members, and we'll form a new team under the other Co-Chair. Both teams will gain people as well." Sharon continued with her news.

Jay nodded. She was starting to like what she was hearing. With luck this might actually decrease her overall workload.

"So, after looking at the recent reviews, loan numbers, and talking to some of the branch staff, I know who I want to promote. It might make things a little difficult because the only thing missing is seniority," Sharon continued.

"Of course, I mean Bailey. I realize it would be a loss to your team but we'll fill her slot with anyone you choose. I would need you to work closely with her, teaching her the responsibilities, but it's a huge step for her as well. This puts you both firmly in upper management. This should make your friendship easier with the difference of rank gone, and you no longer acting as her supervisor."

"It isn't easy having to supervise your friends," Jay admitted. "But I think it's gone well."

"Oh, it has," agreed Sharon. "But this way I'll be responsible for her reviews, and you will essentially be peers. It is just a little extra benefit." Sharon waited for Jay's response.

"Wow! I knew there was a restructure coming, but I didn't envision this. I thought I would lose people, not gain them. When does it start?" Jay asked.

* ⁎ ⁎

They called Bailey in to share the news, and then went over some of the details. Sharon told them that since it was Friday they should leave early and do something to celebrate their new promotions. They walked out of Sharon's office together and looked at each other glad that they had car pooled for the first time that day.

"Meet me at my office in fifteen minutes?" Jay asked.

"Make it ten," laughed Bailey, and headed for her office.

Scott looked at Jay and asked her what was going on.

"Stick with me, Scott, I can't tell you just yet, but next week you will know before anyone else, I promise. For now, get out of here, have a great weekend, and I'm going to do the same." To emphasize her point, Jay shut down her computer and left it docked, locked up her files, and was ready to go before Bailey returned. The two of them headed for the parking garage, barely containing their excitement.

"Your place?" Bailey asked since she had driven that morning. Jay nodded, grinning ear to ear. As they pulled away, they both let out shouts of joy, and Jay pumped her fist in the air.

"What do you think the Board would say if they realized that their new consumer lending managers are a couple?" Bailey asked with a chuckle.

Jay snorted and then shook her head. "At least you no longer answer to me for reviews and such, so we're as legit a couple as we'll get there. At least no one can claim favoritism since Sharon selected you for the job, not me."

"Jay! This is a happy day, stop with the negative stuff," chastised Bailey.

"You're right, I'm sorry, sweetie, let's celebrate. What do you want to do?"

Bailey gave her a credible leer. "You!"

Jay laughed, held out her hand, and granted her wish. They got back to Jay's, where Bailey now had some clothes and things for convenience, and headed for the bedroom. Bailey was aggressive, pinning Jay down and lavishing her body with attention.

"If this is what happens when one of us gets promoted, I'm going to work much harder," gasped Jay when they took a break. Bailey laughed and curled up next to Jay and let her hand wander over her lover's neck and chest.

"Honey, what's this? It feels like a bump under your skin. Has it always been there?" Bailey asked with concern.

"What? Where is it?" Jay asked a bit sleepily. Bailey guided Jay's hand to the pea-sized lump. It rested just under her jaw line on the left side.

"I don't know babe, probably a bug bite, or a lymph node. I'm sure it's nothing." Jay yawned.

"I'm going to keep an eye on it, Jay. I don't like it. I don't remember it being there, and it doesn't look like a bug bite."

Bailey spoke with enough conviction that Jay was compelled to make an offer. "Tell you what, if it's still there next week, I'll take a run into my doctor, I promise. I don't want you to worry about me." Jay gave her a kiss on the forehead and snuggled Bailey in tight against her. They both took a nap before celebrating their promotions throughout the night.

* * *

Bailey awoke to the smell of something yummy baking. She smelled cinnamon, but she wasn't awake enough to figure it out yet. Just as she started to sit up, Jay walked in with a breakfast tray completely filled with homemade cinnamon buns, fresh squeezed orange juice, cut up fruit, and a single red rose in a bud vase with a spray of baby's breath keeping it company.

"When did you have time to do all of this, Jay? What time did you get up?"

Jay set the tray down, gave Bailey a kiss on her forehead, and sat next to her on the edge of the bed.

"I got up a little while ago. I remembered how much you loved cinnamon buns so I whipped up a batch. No big deal. I ran down to the corner store for the rose while the dough rose. That left me plenty of time to make the juice and cut up the fruit."

"You are the sweetest woman, Jay, thank you so much. Now, come here and get next to me so we can share."

Bailey couldn't believe her luck. Jay really didn't seem to understand how sweet her romantic gesture was. It was another example of Jay just being Jay.

They finished breakfast and decided to call their parents and let them in on the big news. Before they called, they had to decide if they wanted to celebrate with their folks that night or not because it would certainly be suggested. They didn't really have plans, so they decided their parents should come down to the city, and they would go out somewhere fun. With that agreed upon, they picked up their cell phones and dialed. Everyone agreed to meet at the restaurant that Bailey and Jay chose. It was a fairly new Middle Eastern place in Center City that had gotten some good reviews.

They decided to stay in and be slugs for the rest of the morning. They made the bed, cleaned up from breakfast, and they cuddled up on the couch to listen to music and read. A little after one o'clock Jay's cell rang and she grimaced as she looked at the caller ID.

"Hey, Sharon, to what do I owe the pleasure this afternoon?"

Bailey made a face and Jay turned away so she wouldn't laugh. After a few minutes, Jay hung up and settled back into the couch and her comfortable position.

"Are you really going to make me ask?"

Jay smirked. "I wanted to see how long it would take."

"Well?"

"It's no big deal. She was just calling to ask about having a lunch meeting on Monday. I think it has to do with the announcement of the restructure." Jay gave her a quick kiss and settled back into her book.

* * *

Everyone had a good time at dinner and Jay had to admit it had been fun. She didn't really want to make a big deal of her promotion. She wanted to celebrate Bailey's achievement. They walked their parents back to the parking lot they had used and bid them a safe drive and good night.

"What next M'Lady? Shall we head somewhere else or shall we head home. I think I have a new Netflix that came in. We could watch that if you want." Jay asked as she took Bailey's hand.

Bailey looked into the dark brown eyes that she loved more than anything and gave a contented sigh. "Anything is fine, why don't we go home and watch the movie after we get into snuggly clothes? We've both been pushing pretty hard, and I just want to relax this weekend."

"Your wish is my command, this way to your horseless carriage M'Lady." Jay offered her arm and gave a quick bow.

"You know, one of the first things I can remember about you is that you could always make me laugh. No matter what the situation, no matter how tense or troubled I was, you could always make me laugh. Thank you for that, honey!" She rose to her toes and gave Jay a quick peck on her cheek.

Jay blushed and ducked her head. "It's all part of the service, ma'am. Just doing my part." She grinned cheekily and looked forward to getting them home.

CHAPTER 9

$\mathcal{J}$AY WAS READING through files and sifting through documents at work on Tuesday when Scott interrupted.

"Hey, boss, I'm going to go grab a sandwich, want anything from the deli?"

"No thanks, Scott. I'm not feeling that hungry. Go enjoy your lunch. Just make sure you forward the phones, please."

"Sure thing," he said as he headed out.

Jay was still at her desk, checking e-mail when she leaned against her left hand. That's when she felt it, that small bump Bailey had mentioned. Strange, she thought as she poked at it, it wasn't there last week, and now it felt bigger than a pea. As she thought about it, Jay remembered waking up several times drenched with sweat. She had blamed it on the heat Bailey put out as she slept, but now she wondered if it wasn't something else. Jay decided to see her doctor and made the call right away. As it turned out, they had a cancellation for the next day. After checking her schedule, she agreed to the afternoon appointment and went back to work. She sent Bailey and Sharon a quick e-mail to let them know she would be out of the office the next afternoon.

About five minutes after she sent the e-mail, Sharon was at her door. "What's going on Jay? You're never sick, are you feeling okay? You've looked pretty tired lately." Sharon bombarded her with questions and comments.

Waiting for the eventual break in Sharon's questions Jay was ready with an answer.

"It's just a basic check up, Sharon. I've been feeling run down, and I thought they could suggest some vitamins or something. It's no big deal, this was just when they could fit me in. If taking off is a problem, let me know."

Sharon shook her head. "Jay, you don't really have to ask me anymore. But please, let me know how it goes with the doctor when you get in on Thursday. In fact, go home early today and rest."

"Thanks, Sharon, but I actually rode in with Bailey today. The CR-V is getting an oil change."

"You two really have rebuilt your friendship. See, you were worried needlessly when I wanted to hire her."

"I'm sorry I doubted you. She was a great choice both professionally and personally." Jay bit back a grin but Sharon missed the double entendre.

"Jay, give her a call and tell her I want you out of here for the day. If you want to take the whole day off tomorrow, do it."

"Thanks, Sharon, I should be fine, and it will keep my mind off things to come to work for the morning. Have a good night."

As soon as Sharon left, Jay called over to Bailey's office. "Hey, are you busy?" she asked when Bailey got on the line.

"Nothing too pressing," she said, sounding a little distracted.

"Ready for some boss dictated hooky?" Jay asked.

"What are you talking about, Jay? Does this have something to do with the e-mail you sent me? I haven't had a chance to read it yet." Bailey pursed her lips as she changed screens to get to her e-mail program. Jay was explaining as she opened the e-mail and read it.

"Is something wrong, Jay? I can be ready to leave in a few minutes."

"Take your time and come over when you're ready. I'm fine, but we were ordered to leave early when I explained you had brought me in so my CR-V could get an oil change."

Bailey smiled as she shut down her computer. "I'll be right over, shut down your computer and get ready."

Scott came into Jay's office holding a deli bag. "Here you go, turkey on wheat with thousand island and lettuce. I know you said you weren't hungry, but you have to eat, Jay. If you don't mind me saying, you've been looking pretty ragged."

"Thanks, Scott. You really didn't have to but thanks. I know I've been run down which is why I'm leaving for the day. I'm also leaving at noon tomorrow. Move my calls around as needed. If it is urgent by your standards, not someone who is panicking, get me on my cell. Otherwise route things to the on call lender or Bailey."

Scott looked surprised. Jay rarely left early, especially two days in a row. "Things okay with you, Jay? Anything I can do?"

Jay was touched, and he really did look worried. "No, I'm sure it's nothing. I just thought it might be a good idea to get a check up and see about some vitamins or something." She paused and smiled at him. "Thanks for asking, you're a sweet guy."

He blushed and wished her well and went back to his desk just as Bailey arrived and they left for the day.

* * *

Jay didn't think about her appointment until her e-mail alarm reminded her to go. She arrived at the doctor's office with five minutes to spare and checked in. Musing about the irony that she struggled to get there on time, yet no one else ran on time, she waited a few minutes until her name was called. She followed the nurse to the exam room where they began with the ritual of vital signs and a weigh-in. Next, the questions started about what brought her in. Jay pointed out the small lump and admitted to fatigue for several months, some lightheaded moments, and recently some night sweats.

The nurse left and the doctor came in a few minutes later. They exchanged small talk while he washed his hands and took a seat on the round stool on wheels that lives in every exam room.

"Let's see what's going on with you, Jay. You're usually healthy as the proverbial horse."

Dr. Stewart felt along her jaw and down her neck before examining the inside of her nose and mouth.

"So Doc, did you find the answers to the universe in there?" joked Jay. She knew she was just letting off some nervous tension, but it made her feel better.

"Actually, Jay, I'm a little concerned. Lymph nodes vary in placement depending on an individual's physiology. However, I'm not sure that your swollen area is a lymph node. I'd like to take some blood and send you for a CAT scan. I think I'm also going to refer you to a good Ear, Nose, and Throat specialist."

Jay looked a little startled. "You mean there might really be something wrong?"

Dr. Stewart smiled reassuringly at her. "Jay, I'm not saying it is something, just that I would rather be safe than sorry with your health. The test is painless and harmless, you just lie down and they scan you in a tube. I can draw the blood here today, so you don't have to make a separate trip for that as well."

"What could it be?"

"I don't want to speculate, Jay. It could be absolutely nothing. Since I don't know what it is, I just want to be safe. Let's just do the tests and go from there."

Jay agreed and got the referrals she needed to schedule the other appointments. After they drew the blood, she decided to go home for the rest of the day instead of going back to the office.

After checking in with Scott and letting him know her plans, Jay drove home trying not to think about the lump in her neck. The first thing she did when she got home was call to schedule the appointments, and then she changed into her "hang around the house" sweats. She decided to read until Bailey would be free. Around four Bailey called to check on her, and they decided to order in Chinese food so that they could talk about the appointment and the tests the doctor ordered.

* * *

It was almost seven before Bailey got to Jay's house, and she let herself in with the key Jay had given her a few weeks before. She found Jay curled up on the couch reading a book in the fading light. For some reason she felt a mild panic start to grip her.

"Jay, why is it so dark in here? What's wrong?" Jay looked startled to see her, then got up, stretched, and gave her a hug.

"Sorry, I was so wrapped up in my book that I didn't realize it was getting darker. Sure does explain why my eyes are a little tired though." Jay gave a sheepish grin as she turned on a light. "How was your day? You looked pretty busy when I saw you this morning."

"Nothing that won't keep, I'm starving, let's order, and then I'll change. After that, I want to talk about your day."

Jay nodded and got the menu. "Just order the usual?" she asked.

"Sure, honey, thanks, I'll go change while you do that."

While they waited for the food to arrive, Bailey insisted that Jay go over her entire visit with the doctor. She watched Jay for signs of anxiety, fear, or anything that might indicate that there was something more going on than what she was being told. Bailey found none and started to relax after making a mental note to search the Internet the next day for things that could be the cause of Jay's lump and symptoms.

"Well, whatever it is, we'll deal with it together," Bailey said emphatically. She leaned into Jay, loving the feel of her lover's strength and warmth. She gave a little prayer that everything would check out and then focused on Jay for the rest of the evening.

* * *

Riley called Jay to let her know she was five minutes away. She was picking Jay up for her CAT scan appointment. The three women had gotten together over the weekend, and both Riley and Bailey decided they wanted someone to accompany Jay. The problem was that Bailey couldn't take off without tipping their hand at work about their relationship. Riley offered to take Jay, and then they had decided to hit the bookstore and replenish Jay's supplies. Jay was waiting outside when Riley pulled up so she just hopped in, and they headed to University Hospital. Jay wasn't really feeling nervous, but she was glad to have the company of her friend. It made the waiting easier at least.

"So, any more book suggestions for me? I'm running low with all this waiting around I've been doing," joked Jay.

"Yeah, I'll help you spend your money, that's what friends are for," Riley replied. "Though I don't know how you have much time to read with a new relationship," she teased.

"Actually, the work situation has gotten better. With the work more evenly divided I get more time to myself and more time for Bailey," said Jay with a chuckle. Jay frowned as she admitted to herself that she'd really been too tired the past week or two to do much more than cuddle.

* * *

Two weeks later, Jay packed up her briefcase, grabbed her jacket from her closet, and met Bailey at the elevator. Today was her appointment with the ENT, and lucky for her it was late enough that Bailey could drive her as if they were simply carpooling. Once they were in the car and headed for the specialist, Jay took Bailey's hand, needing to feel her strength and comfort. Bailey gave her hand a squeeze and shot her a comforting look before returning her attention to the rush hour traffic.

"It'll be fine, sweetie. No matter what, I'm here for you," Bailey reassured her frightened partner.

Jay tried not to show how deep her fear ran. Over the past two weeks, the lump had grown and Jay felt obsessed with checking the size and shape throughout the day. It now stretched for a good inch parallel to her jaw line but just under it and was almost an inch wide. It didn't hurt, but it was getting scary, especially with the night sweats growing more frequent, and her fatigue growing by the day. Suddenly everything seemed to be getting worse very quickly. Jay didn't want to voice it but she had to. "What if it is serious, babe? What then?"

"Then we deal with it, Jay, together."

Bailey knew what Jay was really asking, would she stick around or would she run? No matter what else happened, Bailey knew that Jay was her soul mate, the one she was meant to be with, and she wasn't letting go now that they had finally found each other again. They went in to the doctor's office and filled out the usual forms, then sat waiting for Jay's name to be called.

Once they took seats in the exam room, and the usual things were out of the way, a resident came and introduced himself. He took a history, both general and specific to the cause of Jay's visit. Jay handed over the CAT scan results, and after the resident did a quick physical check of the lump, he left them alone again.

"I'm scared, Bail, I'm so scared!" Jay's voice quivered as she grabbed Bailey's hand. Bailey made some soothing sounds and held her lover tightly while she struggled to regain her composure. Just as Jay pulled it together, the doctor walked into the room.

Dr. Brown was highly recommended in the area and was the head of the department in his hospital, but he was also kind and compassionate. It showed in his greeting of the two women, and his empathy as he listened to Jay retell her recent history. He gently examined the area, took some measurements, and verified some details. After checking in her nose and throat, he sat down with her chart and the CAT scan report.

"I'm a big believer in telling people exactly what I'm thinking and why. Does that work for you?"

Jay nodded. "Please make a note in my chart that Bailey is my partner and should be given full disclosure as well."

"Not a problem," he said, making a note. "If you have any supporting paperwork, we'd like copies, but your request is enough for me. Now, down to the business at hand. This is officially a tumor, but we don't yet know what kind. It could be a fatty tumor, it could be a pre-cancerous tumor, or it could be cancer. Are you with me so far?"

The women held hands tightly and nodded their understanding.

"Here's my standard procedure. I treat everything as if it is cancerous until I can prove it's not. That way, I've taken every precaution to prevent the spread to the rest of the body if it turns out to be cancerous. Does that make sense?"

Jay looked a little pale. "So, better safe than sorry? Be aggressive until we're sure it's harmless, right?"

Dr. Brown nodded. "Exactly the idea. What I would like to do next is a needle biopsy to try to determine what we're working with here. I can do it right now in the office if you agree. It should give us a better look at the make up of the tumor."

"Is there much pain involved? And how much can you see with a needle?" Bailey asked the doctor.

"Good questions, the pain will be minimal since I will use a local anesthetic as well as a topical." The doctor paused as if to consider how much they were ready to hear. "The truth is the needle biopsy could give a definite answer, but it is such a small sampling that we could miss the important cells. Either way, the tumor needs to come out, especially since it's growing."

Jay let out a long breath, and her hand became clammy in Bailey's.

"So, we're talking surgery either way? Why not just wait to biopsy it when you take it out?"

"We would like to see what we are dealing with as soon as possible. If it were to come back malignant, it would give us an idea of what to expect when we go in, otherwise there will be the possibility of changing direction midstream as it were. I'll give you two a moment to digest it all and check back in a few minutes."

They nodded, and he left the room.

"I guess I should do that biopsy, it might at least tell us something. I'm going to have to take a leave from work to get the surgery. I have to tell my folks, and what will I tell Sharon?"

Jay was panicking and pacing in the small room. Bailey stood back. She understood that her lover needed to pace, but she kept an eye on her.

"Honey, let's do one thing at a time. First, we'll let him do the biopsy, and I'll be here with you through that procedure. Next, we'll go home and get you into a bubble bath while I make dinner. After dinner, we'll call our folks and let them know what we know."

Jay smiled gratefully at her lover, knowing that she was right.

"You're right, sweetie. I'm sorry, panic mode is off for now. We do need to discuss how much to tell Sharon and when. At least I can telecommute some of the time so I won't miss as much work while I heal."

"That's the spirit, honey. We'll figure it out as we go. I can help with the workload too so don't worry. I'll let the doctor know we're ready," Bailey reassured her.

Jay put her arms out for a hug and held on tightly as Bailey settled in her embrace. "Let's do this thing!"

The doctor and his resident came in with an intern in tow to watch the biopsy. Jay closed her eyes and gave the go ahead to the doctor. She listened to him tell the students what he was doing and why as she felt the pressure and some momentary twinges of pain. Bailey held her hand through it all, and Jay could feel her strength and energy through their bond. Soon the doctor was snapping his gloves off.

"Leave the bandage in place for the next four hours, then it is fine to remove it. You'll hear from the office as soon as we have results."

"What about the surgery? Should we schedule it now or wait?" asked Jay.

"I operate on Wednesdays, and I'm booked this week. Let's schedule you for next week. Does that give you time to arrange your schedule?" he asked.

"Whoa! That's quick. I didn't really think... I'll make it happen. I want this thing out of me, especially now that we know it could be dangerous."

"Good girl! I'll see you that day before the surgery, and I should have some answers by the time you wake up. My nurse will call and give you instructions a couple of days before the surgery but please don't hesitate to call if you have any other questions." He left and the two women stood looking at each other in a bit of shock. It had all happened so quickly.

"Let's get you home and in a bath, everything else will wait." Bailey ushered her lover to the reception desk to schedule everything and then to the car and home.

* * *

That night in bed, they lay in each other's arms trying to decide how to handle things at work. Both sets of parents had been concerned and supportive, and of course Riley offered to help with anything she could since it was the slow season at the club. Now they were trying to determine what to do about work and Sharon.

"I don't care, I want to be there when you have surgery damn it! Sharon can be damned if she doesn't like it."

Bailey was adamant that Jay and her needs came first, but Jay thought she should be at work covering things on that front.

"Honey, I'll be sleeping. It's not like I'm going to be awake, and you could keep me company. Riley can drop me off, or you could before work, and I'll be awake to see you by the time you get out of work."

Jay thought it a logical plan, but she had spent more time sublimating her life in favor of the needs of the company.

"Let me explain this to you, Jay." Bailey pulled away and sat up, her voice started to increase in volume with her frustration. "I wasted too many years not being here for you and with you. That stopped the moment you were willing to talk to me again. Where you go, I go. That means I go as close to that surgical suite as they let me, and I wait there until I can see you awake and healthy. I will stay there until they kick me out, and then I'm back as soon as they let me in the morning."

Jay felt tears well up as she heard the emotion in Bailey's voice. Jay's voice was husky when she tried to speak. "I get it honey, and I love you for it. Having you with me today made all the difference, and I don't want to be without you either. I have no idea how to approach this at work though."

Bailey settled down and gathered Jay in her arms. "Frankly and honestly? Maybe they just never had to deal with a couple that told them the truth. Maybe that's why some people think you can't get ahead as a couple within the company. We aren't the only people in that company dating, Jay, that can't be too big of an issue."

"I'm listening. What do you suggest?"

Bailey let out a breath. "I suggest we go into Sharon's office tomorrow and tell her about the surgery, and that I will need a couple of days off then to take care of you. Assuming she asks why, we tell her the truth that we are a couple, and that is what couples do."

Jay smiled, admiring her lover's spark and persistence. "And what do you suggest when she either tells you no or threatens our jobs?" She paused a moment before continuing. "Bailey you have to know that Sharon won't just roll over and agree to have her two top officers out at one time, especially if word gets out why we're out at the same time."

"Well, there are two options. We tell her we are going to HR and filing discrimination claims, or we tell her that her little secret might not remain such a secret."

Jay pulled back in shock. "You can't threaten to out her, Bail. She'll know that info came from me. I can't just out someone. How she lives is her choice."

"Okay, you're right. I'm just so frustrated. The whole closet thing is just such a Catch-22. People fear coming out because they may face discrimination, but the discrimination continues because people hide and allow it to continue. I will contact HR about it if I have to do so. Either way, I'm coming with you to that surgery. End of story!"

"Yes, dear," Jay joked.

"That's right, you keep practicing those words, woman! Now get over here and show me how much you appreciate me." Jay complied willingly, ending all other conversation for the night.

CHAPTER 10

SHARON SAT IN shock, unsure if she was hearing correctly. "So, you're telling me that you are in a serious relationship with the woman who was your subordinate? Is that what I'm hearing, Jay? And on top of it, you need to take off for potentially serious surgery?"

With a mild look of embarrassment, Jay nodded.

"And you, Bailey, dated your supervisor for months, and now that you are essentially peers, you want to take off time to be with her during this surgery and her recovery? Exactly how am I to explain that to my bosses?"

Bailey nodded and opened her mouth to make a suggestion, but Sharon continued her rant. "The whole point of having the two overlapping positions was to avoid a lack of coverage like this one. People already realize you two are close friends, but car-pooling is one thing, sitting in the hospital all day is another! What a freakin' mess you two have made." Sharon collapsed into her leather chair with a groan.

Jay stood up, her eyes blazing and spoke sharply. "Sharon, that is enough already! I admit it wasn't the best move to date someone in my chain of command, but let's face facts. Our beloved CEO married his secretary that he was screwing on company time while he was still married to the woman that helped fund this company to begin with! Ethics shouldn't be a factor here. We are two consenting adults and are more professional in here than half the staff. This company has been lucky not to get hit with more sexual harassment lawsuits." Pausing, Jay visibly refocused her thoughts and spoke more calmly as she continued. "Now, this is my surgery we're talking about, my life for God's sake! Is it too much to ask that you be a little sensitive about that?"

Bailey sat in silence, cheering Jay on in her head and smiling proudly at her. Jay remained standing waiting for Sharon's reply.

"You've made your point, Jay, but I thought I made mine five years ago. Keep your personal stuff personal and don't bring your life in here. This could kill your advancement in this company if it gets out – for both of you."

Jay snorted. "I've gotten higher already than I expected. I really don't want to go any higher and deal with the crap you deal with every day. If they want to take away my division, they can have it. I have to worry about possibly having cancer, and you want to shove me in a closet? Plenty of people here know I'm gay, Sharon. I honestly thought you might have learned by now that it doesn't matter to anyone but you." Jay seemed to lose some steam and took a seat next to Bailey, shaking her head slowly.

Sharon looked over at Bailey and nodded. "Go ahead, I'm sure you have plenty to say as well."

"I think Jay did a great job, but I will add this, I am going to have the time off I need to be with her. I am willing to keep my Blackberry with me and handle things remotely as much as I can. During her recuperation, I will work from her house until she is well enough to be on her own during the day. As she regains strength, she can back me up from home. I'll come in if I have to for quick meetings or to run out to a branch, but not the first couple of days. That is my offer. If you don't go for it, then I'm leaving here to file a complaint with HR.

It was Jay's turn to look on in admiration and amazement. She gave Bailey a look full of love and pride, not caring that Sharon was standing right there.

Sharon sighed and stood to pace as she thought quickly. She looked at the two women before her and wondered how it happened in her department of all places. Sharon realized that this was her chance to start effecting the changes that she had felt welling up in her for months. She wasn't sure how, but she was going to try to help them, if she could do it without endangering herself.

"Since I'm not insensitive to the situation, and I do appreciate you trusting me with this information, let's try this for now. Jay, obviously your medical leave will be approved with no questions asked, and I do hope it turns out to be nothing but a scare." She paused, wondering how she was going to justify this next part to her superiors.

"Bailey, you will be off for the day of the surgery and the following two days with a third if it is needed. I will need you to work from home, um, I mean Jay's house once she's home and recovering. Your teams should be fine during the day of her surgery. Take that day off entirely, other than to call me and let me know how everything goes. If there is anything I can do, please let me know. All I ask in return is that we keep this as quiet as possible and keep the lines of communication open between us."

Jay looked at Sharon and then at Bailey in disbelief. "That's it? No lectures about closets, glass ceilings, or hate mongers?"

Sharon grimaced. "I admit, five years ago I was more concerned than I am now. You were right before. Fewer people seem to care these days. Maybe I have some more thinking to do about that, but for now let's focus on you. Your situation is a little tougher because of the supervisory relationship the two of you had before this restructure. We'll deal with it as it comes. Now, get out of here. Go make us some money. And Jay?"

Jay looked over at her as she stood from her chair.

"I really do hope this turns out to be a scare and nothing more. Let me know if you need anything, okay?"

Jay nodded. "Thanks, Sharon."

* * *

"See, I told you it would work," crowed Bailey. Jay nodded absently, wondering what had caused Sharon to buckle so easily. She mentally shrugged her shoulders.

"I'm surprised but happy of course. Now we just have to get things ready for us to be out. Prepare your team, and I'll prepare mine. We'll meet with both teams Monday to let them know that I'll be out of the office for at least a week, and let's just tell them what Sharon suggested about you."

The cover story Sharon came up with was that Bailey was already registered for a series of executive workshops offsite, and would only be available during breaks for a few days. Since the surgery was a recent item, it couldn't be helped, and the teams would have to pull together and cover things for a few days. With that, they parted, heading to their respective offices and piles of paperwork and messages to return.

* * *

The day before her surgery, Jay was trying to block everything out but work. She arrived a couple of hours early and started clearing her inbox as quickly as she could. She was so engrossed in her laptop that she didn't even hear the first knock on her door. When she heard the second, louder, knock she raised her head, slightly disoriented when she realized it was already ten in the morning.

"Come in," she called as she straightened up her desk. She was surprised to see Sharon enter and close the door.

"Jay, I just wanted to let you know that I hope everything goes well tomorrow, and you two will be in my thoughts. I know I'm a hard ass at times, but I really care about both of you." Sharon started pacing like a caged animal. "I'm simply not as brave as you two are. I could never have faced off with my boss the way you did with me."

Jay smiled, surprised by Sharon's admissions. "Sharon, part of what made it easier to talk to you was that you have been a decent boss, hard and tough, but fair. Also, knowing your personal situation, well, I suspected that things would go either very well or very badly. Thankfully, they went well. I'm sorry if we put you in a bad spot, but we've loved each other since we were kids. And we were lucky enough to get together now. I'm willing to risk everything to keep her in my life. Do you understand?"

Sharon stopped pacing and nodded, smiling sadly. "I respect you and your choices. I'll back you up as much as I can, but I think we view the powers that be here very differently. Maybe, since I have no one to go home to at night, I just don't think it's worth the fight. Either way, I'm happy that you two are happy together, and I'm grateful you've been so discreet at work."

"Hey, professional is the only way to be here, perhaps one day you can come out to dinner with us. Who knows, maybe you'll get a chance to reconnect with your other self." Jay was feeling bold since she was going into the hospital the next day. "Either way, thanks for helping us, Sharon. I won't forget it." Sharon wished her luck again, reminded her that she wanted updates, and left her to her work.

A few members of the team either stopped in or e-mailed throughout the day to wish her luck and let her know she was in their prayers. By the end of the day, she was sick of good wishes, work, and people in general. Jay slammed her briefcase on to the desk so she could load her laptop into it and grimaced. It wasn't the briefcase's fault that she was so grumpy. She was nervous and needed to relax. She had been warned to stay away from alcohol and most medication for the week prior to the surgery, but Jay decided she knew the perfect cure for her jitters.

Just then, Bailey showed up, to see if Jay was ready to leave for the day. They hefted their briefcases, loaded with laptops, cables, and paperwork and headed for the garage. They stopped by the Thai place near Jay's and got take out, before heading back to the condo. Bailey got dinner on the table while Jay shucked off her business clothes in favor of sweats and a T-shirt. Bailey took a minute to change as well while Jay finished setting the table and turning on some Loreena Mckinnet.

Bailey came back in the room, listened to the music, and smiled. Jay was so predictable. She always played Loreena when she had something important to discuss. They sat down, passed the food back and forth, and made small talk for a while, skirting any major issues until after dinner. They cleaned up in a companionable silence and then went to the living room with some herbal tea.

"So, when are you going to tell me what's on your mind?" asked Bailey. Jay smiled at her lover.

"You think you know me so well, don't you?" Jay stuck her tongue out at Bailey before laughing and admitting something was on her mind.

"I know it's a little fast, but I was wondering, since you spend so much time here, I mean, would you, what would you think of movinginwithme?" she asked, finishing in a big rush of words. *Smooth*, she thought as she waited, holding her breath, for Bailey to respond. Thankfully, Bailey had seen this coming. In fact, she had thought of suggesting it herself, but she understood that Jay needed to suggest it.

"Honey, are you sure? I'm more than happy to move, but I want to make sure you're ready. I'm fine with keeping my place even if I'm not there much."

Jay's heart fell a little. "You want to keep your place?"

"Jay, I didn't mean it like that, honey." Bailey pulled Jay into her arms. "I simply meant if you wanted me to, then I would as a safety net. But if you're sure, I can give my notice to my landlord anytime. It's a month to month lease so it isn't a problem."

Jay jumped up, almost knocking over the tea and the coffee table, and she pulled Bailey up with her.

"I've never been more certain of anything, Bailey! I want you with me for the rest of our lives and I don't want to wait anymore. How about you bring what you need over while we're off from work, and then after I'm better, we'll pack you up and move you in."

Bailey agreed, knowing that her lover needed to have control over something in her life. "Take me to your bed... no, I mean our bed, " Bailey said.

Jay laughed as she swept Bailey into her arms and carried her to their bedroom.

* * *

Jay was startled awake by her alarm, and she realized that she had actually gotten some sleep. Of course it helped that there had been plenty of activity when they first went to bed, and that Bailey held her tightly all night. She gently kissed Bailey awake.

"Honey, it's time to get up if we're going to take showers before we head out."

Bailey groaned. It was only three forty-five in the morning, and her body needed more sleep. She rolled out of bed and padded after Jay, deciding that she would at least take a shower with her lover before they had to leave.

They arrived at the hospital just before five o'clock and checked in before they were directed to the surgical section where a nurse greeted them. She took Jay back to a pre-operative room to change into the standard hospital gown and footies. Jay answered all the usual questions from the nurse and waited anxiously for her to finish so Bailey could join her.

Just minutes after the nurse finished her work, Bailey stuck her head in the door and saw Jay reclined in the bed with her eyes closed and her headphones in place. She started to move into the room as Jay opened her eyes.

"I'm sorry, sweetie, get some rest. I didn't mean to wake you." Bailey took a seat next to Jay's bed and smiled tremulously.

"I was awake, just waiting for you. The nurse said that Dr. Brown has it in my chart that you are my partner and to give you access. He's pretty cool, huh?"

Bailey leaned over and gave Jay's hand a light squeeze. "Yeah, but the real test of how cool he is will be the scar. I wonder if he's going to give you a nice sexy pirate type of scar."

Jay smiled, noting the twinkle in Bailey's eyes. "I'll make sure to request something sexy when I see him, just for you."

"Thanks. Now, why don't you put on your headphones while we wait. Get some rest, and I'll be here for you."

"You don't want to talk?"

"Is there something you wanted to talk about, honey? If so, then sure. Otherwise, you don't have to entertain me. I'm fine, this is about you, okay?"

Jay gently kissed her partner's knuckles before she put her headphones back on. "You're right. I'm just being silly. I should do those breathing exercises and stuff I guess." Before hitting the play button she looked up once more. "You know I love you, right, Bail? I mean, if anything does happen – "

"Nothing is going to happen, and I need you to know that. But yeah, I know you love me, and I love you. We're going to be fine. I'm here no matter what. Get some rest, baby."

Jay tried to relax, using breathing methods that she had learned in Yoga, and she listened to her music. Thankfully, they were both still tired and managed naps while holding hands. The next thing Jay knew, orderlies were waking her and having her hand over all valuables to Bailey. She removed the necklace that Riley had given her and had Bailey put it on to wear for safekeeping. After passing over her iPod and headset, she gave Bailey a hug and kiss as they reassured each other that everything would be fine.

Jay was wheeled into the recovery area that also doubled as the holding area for patients about to go in. Dr. Brown came by with one of his residents to check on her before they went in to scrub.

"All set, Jay?"

"Sure thing, Doc. You know what you're doing, right?"

He laughed. "Yes, but I still have trouble getting the ear back on correctly. I'll try to make sure yours is on straight for you."

Jay chuckled, amazed that she could find humor right before surgery. "You do that, Doc. I just got a great pair of sunglasses, and I would hate for them to look unbalanced!"

"Anything for you, Jay. Now you get comfortable while we go scrub. Any questions?"

"Well, Bailey did want me to ask if you could make my scar a sexy pirate-type scar... but other than that? Nope, just do a good job and get it all out, Doc. Thanks again."

"My pleasure, Jay. I'll see you in there. I'll be the handsome guy behind the mask."

Jay grinned at him as he walked away, hoping that he was as talented with a scalpel as he was with his bedside manner.

* * *

Bailey was sitting between her mother and Laura. They were flanked in turn by their husbands. Everyone was trying to remain positive and upbeat, but the surgery seemed to be taking longer than they expected. The atmosphere was tense, everyone wondering what was in store for the young woman in the operating room.

The door to the waiting room swung open and a man wearing scrubs came in and zeroed in on Bailey. Bailey stood as he approached.

"Dr. Brown? What happened? Why did it take so long?"

"Let's sit down a moment. She's in recovery and doing fine. I promise. But I think we should talk about what happens next. I assume these are your parents and Jay's parents?"

Bailey nodded and made the introductions as they all sat down. The doctor pulled a chair over to join them.

"The surgery itself went very well. The tumor was encapsulated so we were able to get the whole thing out, but due to the placement we did take her parotid gland." He motioned to the area under the left jaw as he continued. "That means she has only one salivary gland on the left side, but that isn't a big deal. I also took one lymph node that looked suspect. The frozen section of the tumor came back malignant." He paused and looked carefully at Bailey.

Bailey was surprised. She knew it was likely cancer after all the research she had done online, but it was still hard to hear that her partner had cancer. She looked over at her parents for strength before she lifted her eyes to meet the doctor's gaze.

"Cancer. What do we do now? I won't lose her, Doctor, tell me what we do next."

He spent some time going over the process to ensure that Bailey understood things. After answering everyone's immediate questions, he excused himself and promised to drop in on Jay later in her room.

Bailey buried her face in her mother's neck. She sobbed for what felt like hours but was probably only a few minutes. After she pulled herself together, the five people who loved Jay most in the world began to plan how they could best help Jay through her battle.

* * *

"Jay, wake up, can you hear me?" Jay struggled to open her eyes, hearing the voice and not knowing where it came from. "C'mon Jay, wake up, the surgery is over and it went very well. You're in the recovery room." Slowly the face of a male nurse floated into view. Jay felt a mask being removed from her face. "How are you feeling?"

"Sleepy," Jay croaked. The nurse gave her a couple of ice chips to ease the dryness in her mouth and took her vitals. Once Jay was back in her hospital room, Bailey joined her and waited for her lover to come out of the anesthesia.

Dozing on and off, Jay finally awoke in her hospital room to find Bailey waiting for her.

"How do you feel?" asked Bailey.

"I'm fine, just tired, and sore," Jay managed in more of a mumble.

"How bad do I look?" Jay asked.

Bailey took a moment and looked her over. "You look tired, and there is a bandage. There is also a rubber tube attached to a ball like thing. I guess it's a drain of some kind."

"Did you see the doc?" asked Jay.

"He came out to see me after the surgery," Bailey admitted.

"Tell me," Jay said.

"He said that the frozen section they looked at was cancerous." Bailey held on to her lover's hand as she shared the news and leaned closer to give Jay strength from her presence. "It looks like some form of lymphoma, but they'll know more after the lab has more time to examine it. He said he'd be by in a while to talk to you about everything." She watched Jay carefully as her thumb smoothed back and forth over Jay's hand.

Jay slowly turned her head a little to the right to look more closely at Bailey.

"I really have cancer?" she asked in small voice.

Bailey tried to look reassuring, even though she was terrified.

"It's going to be all right, honey. Lymphoma is very treatable, especially if we got it early. I looked it up on the Internet while you were in recovery. That Blackberry came in handy after all. We'll beat it, and I'll be with you every step of the way," Bailey struggled to put on a confident and reassuring face. She didn't want Jay to know just how devastated she had been by it all.

Jay looked shell shocked. "Cancer? I have cancer?" she whispered.

A lone tear escaped Jay's right eye. Bailey leaned over and gently kissed it away while doing her best to keep from letting her own tears slip out.

Jay closed her eyes. Bailey wasn't sure if she had nodded off or not, so she pulled a chair over and sat next to the bed, holding Jay's hand in her own.

* * *

Jay wasn't sleeping. She was trying to figure things out in her head. *How can I have cancer? I'm usually pretty healthy. Why now? I finally have my life on track; I finally have love and success at work.* She knew going in that it was a possibility, but she hadn't really considered it. *I just asked Bailey to move in with me. Will this change things?* Jay's mind was spinning, and her eyes opened to find Bailey looking back at her with love blazing in her sparkling emerald eyes. There was very little sign of fear, just strength and love.

"We'll get through this, right? Jay asked.

"Of course, honey, it's just a set back. All that this means is that you're going to have to work from home a little more in the future depending on what the treatments will be. I'm still moving in, and we will still be together." Suddenly, a thought occurred to Bailey, "You still want that, don't you, Jay?"

Jay was worn out but she nodded. "I don't think it's fair to you, but I'm going to be selfish. I need you with me more than ever."

Bailey smiled and laced her fingers through Jay's. "I'm moving in, and it will take dynamite to get me out!"

They sat in silence. Their fingers entwined. Drawing comfort and strength from each other. Bailey broke the silence when she remembered their parents.

"Our folks are outside waiting to see you. They wanted to let us have a few minutes alone first. Do you want me to get them?" Bailey asked.

"They must be freaking out. Why don't you go get them?" Jay replied.

A couple of hours later, long after their parents had gone for the day, Dr. Brown came in the room with his resident. He looked over his handiwork, and then he was ready to talk with Jay.

"I'm sorry, but the lab did send back a result of possible lymphoma from the frozen section they did while you were in surgery." He looked her straight in the eyes as he spoke.

As he related the details of the surgery, Jay steeled herself for what would come next.

"Do you have any questions, Jay?" Dr. Brown asked.

Jay took a breath trying to gather her thoughts and questions. "What is the next step? What do I do about it?"

"The first thing is heal and rest from the surgery. We'll wait for the lab to bring back a full report on all the sections removed and when I get those results, I'll have you come in to go over them with me. We're most likely looking at Hodgkin's or something similar, and the success rate of treatment in early detection Hodgkin's is about ninety-five percent."

"Right, so I rest, then you call me, and we meet with you. Should I find an oncologist in the meantime?"

"Not yet, though if you want to get referrals, you can of course. All an oncologist will do for now is wait for the lab results, just as we are." He paused and put his hand on her right shoulder. "Jay, you are a trooper and you came through this splendidly. I have no reason to doubt that you will continue to do so. Get some rest, and I'll be back tomorrow to remove your drain and send you home if all looks good."

Jay nodded and thanked him, closing her eyes as he left the room.

* * *

Jay had been home for a couple of hours when she got a delivery of flowers from Sharon. Bailey had filled Sharon in after they got Jay home from the hospital. The flowers were a nice gesture, and Sharon had been supportive when they talked by phone that evening.

Riley was pitching in by helping Bailey move her things over to the condo the next afternoon. Jay was grateful for Riley's help since she was still too tired. She was also under strict orders to not lift more than five pounds for another week.

Jay tried to focus on her work. She used her laptop, sorting through e-mails and answering those she needed to as succinctly as possible. Her neck was still swollen, and the stitches weren't due to come out for a couple more days. She wasn't going back to work until after the stitches were removed. Jay decided she needed something to lose herself in not to bury herself in, so she gave up on the laptop and picked up a book and started reading.

CHAPTER 11

$\mathcal{B}$AILEY COLLAPSED on the sofa next to Riley, relieved that her personal stuff was moved in. She had arranged to sell what furniture she had to the next tenant. She hadn't unpacked some of her boxes from her last move so this move wasn't as bad as it could have been. She struggled to her feet and offered Riley a drink.

"I'd kill for an ice cold beer right now," Riley said.

"Coming right up, I'll fix a plate of munchies too."

While Bailey was in the kitchen, Jay wandered out of the bedroom where she had been napping and sat in her leather chair.

"Hey, what's up, Rye? How did the moving go?"

Riley grinned and flexed her muscles. "Not a problem for a strong woman like me. Seriously, it was fine. Your woman is pretty organized."

Jay chuckled. "You don't know the half of it! She has her socks arranged like a color palette, going from white to black with the colors in the middle."

Riley started laughing as Bailey came into the room with their beers and a platter of cheese, crackers, and pepperoni. She set it all down and gave Jay a quick kiss.

"Want anything to drink, honey?" asked Bailey.

"I'll get it myself, but thanks. Have a sip of that beer for me though, will you?" Jay wandered into the kitchen in search of a beverage, and the two women got started on their snacks.

"So, how's she really doing?" Riley asked.

Bailey took a swallow from her beer before replying. "Good and bad days. There hasn't been a lot of time for it to sink in yet, but we're talking and trying to deal with the feelings."

Jay returned to the room and perched on the arm of the chair Bailey had chosen.

"You guys about done talking about me?"

Bailey stuck her tongue out at her. "Is that a promise, honey? I can kick Rye out right now if it is." Jay tried for a convincing leer.

Everyone laughed, glad to see some of Jay's humor returning. "In answer to your questions about me, I'm really fine right now. I'm waiting until we hear exactly what we're dealing with before I freak out anymore. Mostly I'm just tired and a little sore." Jay explained to her friend.

Riley nodded, helping herself to more of the snacks. "You know if you need anything, I'm only a phone call away, right? Either of you!" she looked pointedly at each of them.

"Yes, Mom," they chorused before laughing.

Jay grew serious and looked at Bailey before turning to Riley. "Thanks, Rye, that really means a lot. I don't want it all to fall on Bailey, and I'm honest enough to admit that we'll need some help with things."

* * *

On Thursday the week after her surgery, Jay went in to have her stitches removed. Bailey left work early so she could drive her. They would also hear the results of the study since the lab had finished their report the previous day. After being shown into the exam room, the resident came in, removed the stitches, and cleaned up her neck. Then she applied more of the salve and made sure that Jay still had enough at home. The resident went out to fetch Dr. Brown, leaving them alone in the room.

"Well, well, looks like I got your ear on straight after all, Jay. You are healing very nicely. Any pain or problems with the surgical site?"

"Nope, some twinges of pain now and then, but mostly it feels fine now. So, how long are you going to make us wait for the results, Doc? Just spit it out, the wait is driving me nuts."

"Jay, Bailey, the lab report came back yesterday, and to be honest I was totally surprised by the results." He leaned back against the counter and opened a file he held. "The lab found that the tumor actually consisted of a different cancer than we thought. It's called Merkel Cell Carcinoma."

Jay looked at him, holding tightly to Bailey's hand for comfort.

"What is it? I've never heard of it before." Bailey said.

"Honestly, I've only heard of it recently myself. I'm sorry, this was a total surprise to the lab and to me. It's a very rare cancer, also very aggressive. It's not considered a true skin cancer but it is related. Typically, it affects Caucasian men sixty-five to seventy-five years of age, and there are less than a thousand cases in the entire U.S each year."

Bailey gripped Jay's hand tightly and tried to remember to breathe. Jay was looking very pale, but her eyes showed her strength.

"How do we beat it? What do I do next?" Jay asked.

Dr. Brown looked on approvingly. "That's the right attitude! Have you gotten the names of any oncologists yet?"

"Not yet, I was waiting to see what we were facing."

"I can give you some names but also check with your primary doctor for a referral. I also printed out the data I have on it. I'm sorry to say, it isn't much, but it was everything I could find quickly in layman's terms."

"Thanks, Doc."

"Take care and keep in touch, I'll be sure to follow your case."

* * *

Jay sat on the couch searching the Internet for information on Merkel Cell Carcinoma. She figured out quickly that it would be hard to find studies or definite information. The cancer was known as MCC, and there were only a few places on the East Coast with much experience treating it. The two top doctors were in Boston and Seattle and were available for consultation.

She decided to find someone local first and was waiting on a return call from her primary doctor's office. Bailey was at work, and Riley was on her way over with take out and some information about a cancer center in North East Philadelphia, Fox Chase Cancer Center.

She sat for a moment contemplating the major changes in her life over the past year. *A promotion, reuniting with Bailey, deciding to live together, and now the cancer. No wonder my head is spinning.*

Jay decided to take a break from research and answer some work e-mails until Riley got there. The first e-mail she saw was from Sharon letting her know that Bailey had filled her in and that whatever she needed to do time wise was fine. She also offered to help if she could, even if it was just coming over to relieve boredom or help her run errands. Jay sighed. She knew people meant well, but she wasn't an invalid yet, and she didn't want everyone acting like she was half-dead. She replied politely to Sharon, thanking her and letting her know things were fine for now. Just as she hit send, the doorbell rang, and there was Riley with food, information, and laughter. *Just what I need*, thought Jay gratefully.

They set up in the living room, and Riley grabbed paper plates and utensils from the kitchen. They dished up the food and settled in before they started talking things out.

"So girlie, what's your thinking about things? How are you handling?" Riley asked.

Jay rolled her eyes and explained about the conflicting information out there. Some doctors suggested only radiation or only chemo, and some still relied on both treatments. There was nothing definitive and less information than she wanted, especially since the mortality rate was skewed in her mind. It was based on old men who were more likely to die anyway.

"I'm up and down. I do the why me thing for a while. I curse fate then I think of all the good in my life and figure at least I have a good strong support team. I guess I'm bouncing through all the stages of grief at once. I don't know what normal is for this, but I think I'm close to it."

Riley looked her friend over. "Hey, at least you approached normal on something," she teased.

Jay laughed and tossed her napkin at Riley. "I knew I could count on you for some laughs. I think Court Jester might become your job through this mess."

"Anything you need, my friend. I'll lend you my library. I'll get you more books, more music for your iPod, whatever I can to distract you. I have a decent DVD collection too if you get interested in it."

Jay marveled at her fortune for having such a friend as Riley.

* * *

Bailey was working at her desk when her phone rang. It was Sharon.

"Bailey, when you have a few minutes, will you please come to my office?"

"Sure, any files I should bring?"

"No, just you will be fine, thanks." Sharon hung up, and Bailey was a bit confused but grabbed her Blackberry just in case and walked over to Sharon's office. Giving a quick knock, she went in and sat down in one of the chairs in front of Sharon's desk.

"What's up? Do you need me to do something?" asked Bailey.

"No, actually, I want to be able to do something for you, well, you and Jay," Sharon replied. "It's hard for me since I'm not supposed to know about you two, but I do know, and I realize that her illness affects you both. I'd like to help in some way. I've known Jay for a while now, I consider her something of a protégé and a braver version of myself. I know she's stubborn and has her pride, but if there is ever anything I can do, please don't hesitate to ask."

Bailey, not being privy to the e-mail Sharon had sent Jay, was flabbergasted. She had expected Sharon to put as much distance between herself and them as possible. It was almost inevitable that during the course of Jay's illness, their relationship would become common knowledge. Bailey figured Sharon would want to disavow any knowledge if she should be called in front of her superiors.

"Sharon, thank you, that's very kind of you. Right now, we're still finding an oncologist and doing research. I promise to keep you in the loop and get you involved if I can."

"Thanks, Bailey, I'd really like to help. How's Jay really handling things? This happened so fast, but I've been wondering if I should have made her go to a doctor sooner. She looked worn out so often over the past several months." Bailey nodded, having wondered the same thing at times.

"I don't think they would have found it any sooner, not really. It wasn't visible until that small lump formed, and she went in quickly after we found it. We think it was caught early enough for her to have the upper hand." Bailey refused to think of it any other way. She refused to lose Jay after having just found her again.

"Well, please tell her I'm thinking of her often, and you're both in my prayers. I'll let you get back to work, but if you need help with your caseload, just let me know. I know Jay's helping from home, but if you need field coverage, I can help out."

"Thanks, Sharon, for everything. I'll pass it along to Jay tonight." With that, she stood and left to head back to her own office for another futile attempt to drown her worries in work.

* * *

The choice was made. Fox Chase was the only cancer center with a good amount of experience treating MCC within a two-hour drive, and Jay wanted to stay local if possible. She had a meeting scheduled with what would become her team of doctors. There would be a surgeon, a radiology oncologist, and an oncologist for chemotherapy. In addition, they were sending her for more testing to determine if the cancer had spread. She had learned that the only definite thing in cancer treatment was that nothing was an exact science. Jay was growing frustrated. In her world, both your credit score and debt to income ratio were good, or they weren't good. It was all based on the strength of the numbers. All of this gray area was making her nervous.

The day for Jay's first visit arrived. Sharon was covering a branch event for Bailey in the afternoon which freed her schedule up enough to take a half-day. Jay was nervous but felt prepared. She had spent time on the LiveStrong website printing out lists of questions that other cancer patients had learned it was important to ask. Survivor, that was the word the website used, and both she and Bailey were trying to remember to use it as well. She was a cancer survivor. Hell, she was willing to call herself anything if she could beat this thing. Jay chose to drive them to the appointment. It was her first time driving since her surgery. Even though her neck was still stiff, it was better, and she wanted to get used to driving with the feeling.

Bailey was nervous also, but she was trying to hide it and be strong for Jay. She knew that Jay was scared out of her mind. She tossed and turned at night, grinding her teeth, until Bailey could soothe her back into more peaceful slumber. Bailey had spent hours doing research on the Internet.

Bailey was already gathering support from her family, Jay's family, Riley, and a few people from work. She knew Jay wouldn't want the people from work to see her when she was really sick and weak, but Bailey figured that they could at least help for the early portion if needed. Besides, people felt better if they could do something other than offer sympathy. Bailey understood that, she wanted to beat the hell out of the disease if she could only grab hold of it.

Bailey reached out for Jay's hand as they drove down interstate 95N. "How you holding up, sweetie? Do you want to go over anything or talk about anything before we get there?"

Jay let out a sigh of frustration. "No, I have the list of questions so I guess I'm okay for now. I just wish... Fuck it, it doesn't matter what I wish, does it?" she finished, her voice full of bitterness.

"Oh, baby, I'm so sorry. I know this sucks, I hate that it happened, but we will get through it."

"*We* will? I think I'm going to be the one losing my hair, puking my guts out, getting radiation burns, and feeling like shit. Oh, and the best part? There's absolutely no guarantee that any of it will work! Sounds like a barrel of laughs to me!" Jay spat out.

Bailey took a deep breath. She had been waiting for this, but it still hurt to hear Jay assume this was all her problem. She fought to remain calm and steady as she addressed her lover.

"Jay, I understand that the physical part is happening to you. I get that, I really do. But first, we don't even know what your treatment will be so we can't assume what the side effects will be. Plus, I'm the one who will be holding your head while you puke, cleaning up, buying you hats, scarves or whatever. I will be here, hurting for you and wanting to help you get through this, as painlessly as possible. Don't tell me this disease is only affecting you because isn't. We, as a couple, have cancer and we will beat it together. Got it?"

Jay looked a little stunned and a little hurt. Then her face changed and a look of understanding and embarrassment came over her features.

"I guess I'm being an ass about it, aren't I? Logically I know it's affecting us both, but I've been having a bit of a pity party for myself. You're right though, we both have to fight it as a team. I'm sorry. Forgive me?"

"There's nothing to forgive, this is all part of dealing with it, just remember I'm here to lean on." Bailey gave her hand a squeeze, and Jay squeezed back, letting Bailey know the point was made.

* * *

They signed in at the main desk feeling a little overwhelmed by the number of people walking around them.

After filling out some forms and signing some paperwork, the two women were directed to another registration desk. Jay looked at Bailey, took a deep breath, and squeezed her hand.

"We can do this, right?" she asked with a slight quiver in her voice.

"You bet, baby!" Bailey answered.

Jay sat on the exam table nervously swinging her legs while Bailey sat in one of the chairs nearby. Jay focused on her breathing, afraid that she would hyperventilate from her nerves. All she could think was, *Why me? Why now? Please let me live now that I finally seem to be on track.*

Finally, there was a knock at the door and it opened. In walked a man with an entourage and he introduced himself as Dr. Zacharias.

"Everyone calls me Dr. Zach," he smiled. He introduced his staff of interns and residents and his primary nurse, Pat. He examined the area of Jay's neck where the surgery was done. "Beautiful job, it is healing nicely." He explained the possible course of radiation he was contemplating.

"When would I be starting this treatment and what are the side effects," Jay asked. She was starting to sound a little more in control, handling this as if she were interviewing a loan applicant.

"When we start depends upon whether or not the team thinks you need additional surgery. Once you meet with the other doctors, we'll have a team meeting and discuss your combined treatment plan. Jay nodded and Bailey was taking notes. "As to side effects, we actually have a handout for you about that and I want to review it with you." His nurse handed each woman a copy of the handout and then handed Dr. Zach the final copy.

Jay seemed to stare at it, reading it and thinking.

"I might lose my teeth?" she asked. "That doesn't seem fair after spending so much time in braces." She chuckled, "My folks will have a fit!"

Bailey gave her a look, wondering if her partner was breaking under the strain already.

"Got it," Jay said, as she sobered again. "See a dentist, get fluoride, and lotion my neck and face. I'm ready when you are."

"Excellent!" the doctor said. "That is exactly the attitude we need for you to have. Maintaining a sense of humor and a positive attitude has been shown to help patients recover faster and stronger." He shook hands with both of them, wished them well, and let them know that his nurse would be in touch shortly about scheduling. With that, he swept from the room, entourage in tow.

Bailey and Jay looked at each other laughed.

"Wow! What a ball of energy he is, huh?" Bailey asked. She moved closer to Jay and gave her a quick hug and kiss on the cheek. "How are you holding up? Did you like him?"

Jay leaned against Bailey, their foreheads touching. "He seems great. I guess I'm doing fine, it's just nerve-wracking, I hadn't thought about more surgery until he mentioned it. That kind of bothers me I think."

Bailey rubbed her back slowly in small soothing circles. "I hear ya, babe, but we'll do whatever we have to do to get you healthy again."

Jay nodded slowly and just let herself lean into Bailey's warmth.

There was a quick knock and the door opened again, letting in a tall, thin woman with long dark hair, and a smaller woman with a large clipboard. Bailey remained standing next to Jay with one arm around her waist while Jay sat on the edge of the exam table. The taller woman introduced herself as Dr. Langston, the surgeon assigned to Jay's team.

"I've looked over your CAT and PET Scans, read your surgeon's notes, and read the most recent research on Merkel Cell. Based on all of that, I'm suggesting that we do a left neck dissection."

Jay looked a little pale, and Bailey had pulled out her notebook and started taking notes.

"It sounds bad, but it's not really. I would follow the same track your previous surgeon took, but extend it down to here," she motioned on her own neck, following a line that ran from the top of her left ear, down around part of her neck, and ending at the area of her neck directly under her chin. "I'll do my best to minimize scarring of course. The purpose of the surgery is to remove as many lymph nodes as possible to prevent any spread of the cancer through the lymphatic system. With me so far?" They both nodded mutely, trying to absorb everything.

"The PET scan lit up only in the area of the original tumor. We can't tell if that means there is more cancer, or if it was reacting to the recent trauma in the area. Just to be safe, I would prefer to be cautious."

Jay was really starting to feel shell-shocked, but she hung in. "When would we do this? I don't want to wait since this is such an aggressive cancer," Jay said.

"No problem, I've already looked at my schedule, and we can schedule you for a week from tomorrow."

Jay blew out a breath and looked at Bailey who nodded in encouragement.

"If you were me, would you have the surgery? I mean we don't know that there is anything left, right?"

"Honestly, considering the type of cancer, I'd have it done in a heartbeat. If it has made it into the lymph system, we need to cut it out before it can spread through your body."

"Let's do it then." Jay made the decision and prayed it was the right one.

* * *

"Baby, I'm so sorry you have to go through more surgery, but I think it's the right thing to do." Bailey leaned into Jay again, wrapping her in a tight embrace.

Jay sat silently; confused and scared, feeling like her whole world was spinning out of control. Bailey was worried about her but just held her, waiting silently for the hemo oncologist, the chemotherapy doctor, to come in. She started making lists in her notebook of all the things they needed to handle before Jay's surgery. Dr. Goldman explained his part in Jay's treatment but kept things brief as he would not plan her chemo treatment until after the results of the surgery came in.

Finally, they were free to go. Jay walked slowly, almost trudging across the floor to the lobby and into the parking garage. Bailey walked beside her. She ran a hand through her thick dark hair and sighed inwardly. She hated seeing her lover so defeated, but she didn't know what she could do to help. When they got to the truck, Jay asked Bailey to drive back to their condo, so she could think and close her eyes.

"Sure, honey, I'll take care of it. Did you want to stop any place on the way?"

"No thanks, I'm just too tired." Jay answered. She closed her eyes and turned her head towards the window, not even bothering to turn her cell phone on.

Bailey flipped on a calm radio station with the volume low, just for background noise, and they drove home in relative silence. She thought about everything that had been discussed with the doctors and found her head swimming. She was thankful she had taken notes. Her heart hurt for all that Jay would have to go through in the months to come. If she could find a way to ease Jay's pain and discomfort, then she would. Bailey resolved to search the Internet for things to help out, thinking she could get nicer bed sheets, nutritional information, things to distract her from her environment and help her that way.

CHAPTER 12

$\mathcal{T}$HE DAY AFTER their visit to Fox Chase, Jay went back to her office for the first time since her surgery. She met with Sharon to fill her in on the upcoming events after deciding that she would play her time off by ear. She also met with her team to praise and thank them for handling things as well as they had in her absence. After attending a scheduled meeting for the various vice presidents of all the lending sections, she returned to her office and sat behind her desk with a sigh of relief.

Scott was in her office in a flash. "Can I get you anything, Jay? A drink or something?"

Jay looked up, bemused. "Since when do you offer to fetch and carry? I thought it wasn't part of the job?" she teased.

Scott blushed. "I admit it, I was worried about you. You're one of the good bosses, and I'm just glad to see you back."

She thanked him and declined the offer of a beverage. She did fill him in on her future absences, glossing over the details but giving rough time estimates. He then left her to her work, which she tackled gratefully, working until after one in the afternoon before thinking about lunch.

"Scott, can you get Sharon on the phone for me please?" she called. He buzzed her a minute later to let her know Sharon was on line two.

"Hi, Sharon, I was wondering if you had gotten lunch yet?" Jay knew Sharon didn't usually eat until close to two most days.

"No, not yet."

"Would you like to get together for lunch, maybe step out for a bit?" Jay really wanted to talk to her outside of the office about some concerns and thought this was the most casual way to handle it.

"Uh, sure, Jay, did you have a place in mind? We could go to that new Italian place around the corner."

"Sounds great, I'll meet you in your office in fifteen?"

"Sure, see you then."

Jay hung up and thought through how she wanted to approach Sharon, and then got ready to head out.

* * *

They had their Pellegrino and were waiting on their entrees before Jay got down to the reason for her lunch request.

"Sharon, I'm going to need some help during the upcoming months. The way I figured it, from the estimates given to me by the doctors, we're talking about six months total which includes surgery, recovery, and treatments. It could go a little longer. It could, hopefully, be less time."

"Jay, you take whatever time you need, you have a ton of vacation and sick time saved up, a great team in place, and Bailey has been doing a great job. I don't want you to worry. Your job is safe, your department is safe, and I just want you to focus on beating this and coming back healthy."

Jay was a bit surprised by Sharon's comment, but it opened the door for what she was really concerned about.

"That's great Sharon, and I appreciate the support, but I'm actually more concerned about Bailey. She won't qualify for FMLA since the company doesn't recognize domestic partners, but there will be times when she's going to want to be with me, or that I'll need her at home. I don't want this to become a problem, you know the work will get done, but this is a problem we're both facing, not just me."

Sharon took a drink of her mineral water to stall while she thought of how to respond.

"Jay, you know I'm sympathetic to your situation. I really am. I'm not sure how I'll justify Bailey's absences from the office. I can't just tell people that you're her partner, and she needs to be with you, can I?"

Surprised that it could be this easy, Jay went ahead. "Yes, you can. By acknowledging our status and showing the humanity to allow her the time off we need, you can set the bar in this company. We can use this to bring more awareness to the company of same sex couples, and maybe we can make things better."

"You want me to out you both? I don't know if I can do that, Jay."

"Of course you can if it helps us. Besides, people know we're gay so it isn't an outing per se. We're proud to be a couple, and though I know it is unorthodox, I really think that times have changed enough that this won't be a major issue. If something good can come out of this mess, then let this be it. Partnership rights are something we should be giving our staff, no matter what. The fact remains that Bailey will need some time occasionally, and she's taking it either way. Money isn't a huge issue. I've invested well and lived frugally. We'll be fine financially for quite a while even if we both quit. We like what we do, and we work where we do because it is overall a good company. But, another company would take us both, gladly, in a heartbeat, and we both know it. Our company is going to have to change eventually, and this is a tool to make it happen."

Taken aback, Sharon slowly nodded her head. "What about all the gays and lesbians hiding in the company now? Have you thought about how this affects them? Some people just aren't comfortable being out at work."

Jay waited for the waiter to deposit their food and leave before responding. "Of course I have. They have the option of staying closeted or coming out and helping us fight for equal rights and recognition. I'm sorry, Sharon, I know that group includes you, but I've said all along that we should be able to offer equal benefits no matter what the gender of our employees' partners. I have to go with my heart on this one. This isn't going to start a hunt for those staying in the closet, and I suspect more people than you expect would speak out for this idea."

Sharon looked at her with a little fear but a lot of respect. "Sounds like you thought this through, Jay. Let's say I go along with this, how and who did you want me to approach on this first?" Jay outlined her plan as they ate, and by the time they left the restaurant and headed back to work, Sharon was fully on board with the plan. She understood what she needed to do to try to help Jay.

* * *

Saturday evening, Bailey and Jay headed to Bucks County for dinner with their parents. They had decided in advance that they would spend the night at Jay's parents' house because she would be most comfortable there. They would share their plans with everyone tonight and ask for help with transportation. Jay understood that she wouldn't be able to drive herself once the chemo started so they were looking into other options. Bailey had already talked to Riley, without Jay, and knew that Riley was willing to stay with them part-time to be available for Jay's treatments. She only had one day a week that she had to be at the club so she could cover four days if needed, but she knew Jay wouldn't want to have Riley that tied up in her illness.

As they pulled into the driveway, Steve came out to meet them and grabbed Jay's overnight bag from her hand.

"Dad, I'm not crippled, and I'm not in treatments yet, I can carry it," Jay complained. "But thanks, Dad, I appreciate you caring that much," she added more quietly. Jay reached out, gave him a hug, and took her bag back from him.

He greeted Bailey with a hug as well and walked into the house with them. They left their bags at the bottom of the stairs and headed out to the enclosed patio to see everyone. It was getting cooler so Jay's dad had put in the storm windows and fired up the heater. With the heater on, it was a useable room almost all year round so most gatherings still happened there.

After greeting everyone and getting drinks, the questions started flying. Jay and Bailey took turns filling them in on the meetings with the doctors and the upcoming surgery. There were some questions, but mostly everyone just listened until they were done.

"What can we do to help you two?" Jay's mom asked. "It will be hard enough trying to get everything done that you normally do, but Jay won't be able to drive, and Bailey, you can't miss all that work. Can I help out? I'm a woman of leisure these days." She had retired two years before, and though she kept busy with charitable works, gardening, and other things, her daughter was her number one priority.

Jay decided it was time to fill them in on her talk with Sharon as well. With a glance at Bailey, she started talking about the lunch they had shared a couple of days before. There were a few chuckles, and an "atta girl" from Bailey's dad, but they listened until she was done. Bailey chuckled, wishing again that she could have seen the look on Sharon's face but also knowing that things went smoother because of the length of time Sharon had known Jay. It might have backfired if Bailey had been present as well.

"That's a big step, isn't it? Essentially you are taking on the Board, aren't you?" Steve questioned.

"Yeah, but I don't think the Board is really the problem. I think no one has ever taken a stand on the subject before. The highest person in the chain of command who would care is Sharon, and she's still a closet case. A lot of the employees just go about their lives never thinking that they could effect change on topics like this one. I'm in a position to take a stand, and I don't have anything to lose by doing it. A lot of people may stand to gain by me taking this chance."

"What about the income?" Laura asked. "What if they decide to let you or Bailey go over the issue of you two dating?"

"Mom, I know it's going to spread through a lot of the company, and they may use us to make an example, but I don't care. The reality is, we don't need the income. Although the health insurance is nice, I can use Cobra if I have to until I find insurance elsewhere. I know that staying there is the best possible thing insurance wise, but other than that screw them all if they can't understand that I need my partner, and she needs me through this thing."

Bailey almost glowed with pride hearing Jay speak with such passion about their relationship. She walked over to Jay and stood behind her with her hands on Jay's shoulders. "Honestly, I'm not as well off as Jay, she's been in a higher paying position longer than me, but I've done pretty well on my investments. It really won't be a burden if I have to leave to take care of her, and I can always find something else after she's done with treatment."

Helen and Marc gazed proudly at their daughter, happy that they had raised such a caring woman. Laura and Steve echoed the thought and were thrilled that these two had finally gotten together.

"I think you have made a wise choice in both a partner and an issue to fight for within your company," Steve said with a smile. "I think I speak for all four of us when I say that if you need any help, financial or otherwise, just ask. We stand behind both of you one hundred percent."

Jay looked around and saw everyone looking misty eyed. "Hey, Mom, didn't you cook anything? I'm starving!"

With a laugh everyone mobilized, getting the table set and the food served in record time. Helen and Marc left around ten thirty and the two women headed up to bed shortly after.

"So, you think it went well"? Bailey asked as they got ready for bed. "They seemed fine with everything."

"Fine? Are you kidding, they looked immensely proud of us, honey."

Bailey chuckled, but when she thought of how her parents had looked at her, she choked up a bit. She wished that things could be different, but at least their parents knew what was going on and were prepared to help out if needed.

Jay's breath caught as she studied her partner. Struck yet again by just how beautiful she was. Jay lay down in bed and held her arms out to Bailey, "Come to bed, babe, I need to hold you."

Bailey gladly turned off the lights and snuggled in with Jay, wishing that the moment could last forever.

* * *

The day before Jay's surgery they went out to dinner with Riley to keep their minds off things. Riley was bemoaning her lack of a social life when Bailey teased her. "Hey, your lack of a life means we get to have you around to help out at least."

"Glad to be of service to someone."

Jay actually felt bad for Riley. She knew she was much happier with Bailey in her life, and she wanted that happiness for Riley too. She was such a good friend to them both that she'd become a part of the family. Jay's parents even had Riley over for dinner during the week occasionally as almost a substitute daughter. They were laughing and kidding around, Jay's spirits were good, and everyone was having fun.

Riley checked her watch and saw that it was getting late. "Hey, do you guys need to get home and get to bed? You have to be up early tomorrow."

"Why? I'm just going to sleep all day anyway," joked Jay.

"I don't mind. I just want Jay to have some fun tonight." stated Bailey a bit more sedately.

"Do you want to go to that pub near your place? They have live music tonight, and it might be fun."

"Sure, might as well check it out." Bailey agreed, and they headed off to the pub.

* * *

Bailey and Jay got in around midnight. The pub had been fun, and they were glad of the extra time out with Riley. Jay gave Bailey a hug and suggested that they shower since they would have to leave early.

"Good idea. Together?" Bailey asked with a hopeful lilt in her voice.

Jay looked at her rakishly. "Of course, baby, I won't get to for a while after the surgery, might as well take advantage now."

They raced each other for the door to the bathroom, shedding clothes as they went. Bailey got the shower going, and while it warmed up, Jay took her in her arms.

Jay relished the feel of her naked lover in her arms. "I don't know how I got so lucky, but I'm so thankful you came back to me."

"Honey, I'm the lucky one here, I was welcomed back into your life when you could have shut me out. You amazed me with your generosity."

Jay leaned down and kissed her gently. "I didn't have a choice, you always had my heart."

They got in the shower together, and Jay started shampooing Bailey's hair, savoring the feel of it in her hands. Bailey returned the favor, having Jay bend over a little so she could reach. As Bailey ran her hands through Jay's hair, she felt a brief sadness, knowing that Jay could lose all that hair soon to chemotherapy. She shook off the sadness and focused on the woman in front of her. Jay sensed something was wrong and turned to face her.

"Sweetie, what's wrong?"

"Nothing, just being silly."

"C'mon, if it's making you sad, then it's not nothing. We're best friends, not just lovers. Tell me so we can work it out."

Bailey related what she had been thinking, and Jay looked into her eyes. "It will grow back. I might not lose it at all, and if I do, it will return," Jay promised. "The important thing is getting the treatment so I can stay with you for a lot longer."

"I know. Like I said, it's silly. I just don't want you to have to go through this mess. I'm fine though, it was just a bad moment," Bailey assured her.

The water temperature started to fluctuate so they quickly finished their shower and dried off.

"Do you think it's worth trying to sleep?" Jay asked as she noted the time on the bedside clock. "We have to get up in two hours anyway."

"What did you have in mind?" asked Bailey, noticing a twinkle in Jay's eyes.

Jay pulled Bailey down on the bed and settled on top of her gently. "I think I can think of something I'd rather do than sleep the rest of tonight."

Jay leaned down and started kissing her, gently at first, and then she deepened the kiss. Bailey moaned into her mouth, and Jay could feel her wetness against her abdomen. She worked her way down Bailey's body, cupping her breasts, and taking turns lavishing attention on each nipple with her tongue and teeth. Bailey pressed up into her mouth, and her fingers were pulling at the sheets. Jay moved lower, kissing and licking her way down Bailey's body until she reached the junction between her thighs. She lowered her head and inhaled the wonderful scent that was Bailey. She dipped her head and caressed the swollen folds with her tongue, gently at first, dipping into her, then taking turns sucking and licking her clit until she could feel how ready Bailey was for her.

Jay slipped two fingers inside and curled them up to reach Bailey's G-spot and kept the pressure there, rubbing in time with her tongue. She felt Bailey tighten and increased her pressure and tempo, pulling her over the edge. Bailey let out a cry as she came, tensing, and then relaxing back onto the bed. Gently, Jay pulled out and eased up the bed to lie next to Bailey and hold her as the last of the tremors rolled over her.

"Oh my Goddess, you are amazing," breathed Bailey. She started kissing Jay's ear before moving to her jaw line. She leaned over, kissing Jay, and tasting herself on her lips. She kissed down Jay's neck and shoulders, marveling at the smooth, strong feel of Jay's body beneath her own. She moved down between Jay's breasts, then leaned over and enclosed a nipple in her mouth while teasing the other one with her hand. She switched sides and then let her hand wander down and slide between Jay's labia. She groaned feeling how wet Jay was, just for her.

"Please," choked out Jay. Not able to hold back anymore, Bailey started trailing her lips down, following her hand when Jay reached out and stopped her.

"Come up here, babe, I want you again, please?"

Bailey groaned at the thought and shifted so that her hips settled over Jay's mouth, and her mouth was right where she wanted it, teasing Jay's clit. Bailey worked her faster; sliding her fingers into Jay and feeling the smooth, hot muscle surround her. She felt Jay start bucking and knew she was close. Suddenly, Jay let out a muffled moan, and her orgasm pushed Bailey over the edge again as well.

When she could move, Bailey slid around and settled in next to Jay, her head on her shoulder. They sighed in contentment, and Jay pulled her a little closer.

"I love you so much, baby," Jay whispered

"Hmm, me too. Do we have to get up yet?"

Jay checked the clock and realized they did, as they both needed showers again. "Yeah, I think another shower is in order, and then we should head out."

Once they had showered, they got the rest of Jay's things together for the hospital. All Jay could have was a few sips of water so Bailey decided to wait until Jay was in surgery before grabbing something to eat.

Jay drove, after announcing it was her last chance for a little while, and she would enjoy it. They held hands the whole trip and mostly stayed quiet, listening to the radio, and soaking up the simple pleasure of being together.

CHAPTER 13

*S*INGING, SOMEONE IS singing, thought Jay. *What? Did
something go wrong? Why am I hearing singing?* She felt a
hand holding hers but she couldn't open her eyes. She was
drifting rather pleasantly, and her body didn't seem to want to
stop yet. The singing moved closer to her, and she could hear
other voices talking. She thought she heard her name being
called from a distance. She knew she was supposed to respond.
Slowly, like rising from the bottom of a pool, she swam up to
consciousness. There was a man singing in her room as he
checked her vitals. He was the one trying to wake her up. She
tried to turn her head and a sudden pain shot through her neck
before she remembered where she was and why. Bailey leaned
over and gave her a kiss on her forehead.

"Welcome back, Jay, everything went just fine. I'm here
honey, and your parents are downstairs getting coffee."

Jay groaned, and the man introduced himself as her medical
tech for the evening shift. He offered to get the nurse to give her
pain medication, and she gratefully accepted. As he went off in
search of the nurse to dispense the medication, Jay looked
around her room and realized she had a roommate. She could
turn her head to the right a little, but it was easier to turn towards
the left where the surgery had been done.

A youngish woman came in wearing scrubs and said she
was the evening nurse with medication for the pain. "I'll be
giving you morphine, Jay, let me know if it makes you feel
uncomfortable or sick."

Jay grunted, still not quite awake enough to speak. Bailey
leaned over holding a spoon with ice.

"Open up, sweetie, I have some ice chips so you can wet
your mouth a little."

Jay took the ice, and then felt the morphine hit her, hard. She could feel it wash across her body from the IV until it had reached every part of her body. "Did you see the doc yet?" croaked Jay. Her throat was sorer than after the last surgery.

"Yeah, she stopped in the waiting room after the surgery. She just said everything went well, and she'd see you when you woke up. I guess the nurse went to call her."

Jay leaned back. The head of her bed was raised slightly making it easier for her to rest. Jay was curious about the results of the surgery, but she would wait. She felt two rubber bulbs pinned to the front of her hospital gown and realized those were the drains. She felt as if she were slowly orienting at least. The fuzzy feeling in her head was kind of pleasant, but she preferred to know what was going on around her.

A little while later, the surgeon showed up with a resident who had assisted with the surgery.

"Hey, Doc, how did you do?" asked Jay, trying to joke but nervous about the answer.

"Everything went very well, Jay. I took out a total of fifty lymph nodes from just above your original site and down your shoulder. Only one showed immediate signs of cancer, and they will study the rest in the lab. The one that did show signs was right next to the original tumor site so it hopefully hasn't spread."

Jay sagged back, and Bailey looked relieved. "Thanks, Doc. Did you get my ear on straight?"

"I think I put it back on pretty well," joked the surgeon. She took a quick look at the surgical area, which was undressed, just covered in some kind of greasy stuff. "Everything looks great. If you have pain, let the nurses know. We don't believe in pain. We believe in pain management. Don't be a hero, okay?"

Jay nodded at her, too weary to answer.

"I'll check back tomorrow and see how you're doing. I'll probably want you to spend some time out of bed tomorrow. For tonight, you can go to the bathroom as long as you have help, but otherwise I want you in bed until I see you in the morning, understood?"

"No worries, Doc. I don't really feel like going for a walk just yet."

"Any questions, Bailey? You've been quiet."

"I'm fine, thanks, just grateful to you and your team for keeping her with me."

The surgeon smiled gently and took her hand. "We have a family and friends support center here too. If you need help, there's no shame in asking for it. I think you're doing great, but as things progress, think about yourself a little too."

The doctors left, and they were on their own. Her roommate's curtain was drawn, and there was a low murmur of voices from the other side.

Jay's parents came in, and Bailey filled them in on the doctor's visit. Jay napped on and off while the three visited and discussed her health. She was too tired to care, and the morphine was keeping her head fuzzy. Her mom sat next to her, holding her hand, and smoothing back her hair from her face.

"Mom?" Jay whispered.

"I'm here, Jay, I'm here, and you are going to be fine."

"I know, Mom, but can you make sure Bailey eats something? She's spent all her time here with me, and I want her to take care of herself too."

Laura smiled, so very proud of this strong and caring woman she had helped raise. "I'll take care of it, honey, don't worry, just get some rest."

Bailey and Jay's parents left to get dinner, and Bailey kissed her goodbye telling her she'd be back first thing in the morning.

"'K, love you."

"I love you too, baby, sleep well."

* * *

On the second day after her surgery, Jay got two additional visitors, one she expected, and one she didn't. Bailey had gone into work for a few hours, promising to come by after work. Riley came by about mid-morning to hang out and play PSP games with Jay. They had just finished a round of racing when a new visitor stuck her head in the door after knocking. Jay looked up assuming it was for her roommate and was surprised to find Sharon standing in the doorway, looking a bit uncertain.

"Hey, Sharon. This is a surprise. Come on in."

Riley stood up and held her hand out. "Hi, I'm Riley, a friend of Jay and Bailey's."

Sharon took the offered hand and was surprised by the small jolt of electricity that shot through her as she stammered, "Um, hi, I'm uh, Sharon, I work with them..."

Jay looked from one to the other, puzzled about Sharon's sudden case of stuttering, but she was on pain medication so she didn't really have the strength to think about it. Riley offered Sharon a seat and pulled up another chair for herself, glancing over at her now and then.

"Sharon is actually our boss, Riley. She's just a little too modest sometimes. So, how are things at the office?"

"Good, busy, we miss you around there, Jay." Sharon glanced over at Riley and caught her looking back. Flustered, she turned to Jay, "So, when are you getting out of this place? Any idea yet?"

"They said maybe tomorrow or the next day. It depends on the drains and some other stuff, I think. They are sending me home with the drains in this time," Jay answered.

They talked about things for a while before Sharon stood and took her leave, saying she had to head back to the office for a meeting late in the afternoon.

Riley stood and offered her hand again. "It has been a pleasure meeting you. Maybe I'll see you again... you know, taking care of Jay and all..."

After Sharon left, Riley looked a little dazed as she sat down.

"Dude! Why have I never met her before?"

"Who, Sharon? She's my boss, we don't hang out usually. I'm shocked she came to see me here. Why?"

Riley looked at Jay as if she had three heads. "She's cool! I'm just wondering why I hadn't met her when we went out to dinner or something."

"Uh huh, whatever, we don't usually hang out like I said."

"Oh," said Riley, sounding excited and dejected all at once.

* * *

"I CAN'T FUCKING DO THIS!" shouted Jay. She had been home for about five hours, and it was time to empty and measure her drains. The angles weren't quite right, so she couldn't see what she needed to see in order to squeeze out and empty the tubes.

"Do you trust me, Jay?" asked Bailey in a calm voice.

"Of course, but this isn't your job."

"Sweetie, it isn't about whose job something is or isn't. It needs to be done, and I can do it. I had the nurse show me how to do it while you napped yesterday. Let me help you by doing this for you."

Jay nodded grudgingly. She hated being unable to take care of things on her own. Bailey was going to work from home for the next few days before going back to the office. She didn't look at the drains as Bailey squeezed and milked them to clean the tubing and emptied the bulb like collection containers. After following the instructions on measuring and recording the output, Bailey cleaned up and tucked the supplies away.

Bailey kissed Jay's forehead and resettled her under a light blanket on the couch. Then she made sure that Jay had plenty to drink before going to Jay's favorite chair to do some work. She worked steadily on the laptop, answering e-mails, concurring with loan decisions, and filing reports. Finally, she was done and looked over at Jay, sleeping on the couch. Bailey's heart broke for her, but she knew that Jay wouldn't welcome anything that felt like pity. She could see the lines of pain etched across her lover's face as she slept, but it wasn't time yet for another pain pill. Sighing, Bailey got up, did a load of laundry, and put away some clothes. Then she went to the kitchen to start dinner; figuring softer foods would be better for Jay right now.

Deciding on something quick and healthy, she looked through the cupboards and made a choice. She would make a light pasta salad with salmon and peas that could hold well.

About an hour later when the food was ready, she woke Jay and helped her to the bathroom to clean up. By the time Jay was back, the pasta she had made was out of the fridge, the table was set, and some soft music was playing.

"Jay, I can bring this to you on the couch if you're more comfortable there." Jay would have to sleep on the couch the next few nights at least because she couldn't fully recline yet.

"Let me try the table, and I'll move if I can't handle it."

Bailey helped Jay get situated before she dished up some of the pasta salad. She poured some sparkling water for them and raised a glass. Jay looked at her curiously but raised her own as well.

"To having you home with me where you belong." They clinked glasses and drank before starting on the dinner.

"Honey, this is great! The hospital sure didn't serve food like this!" Jay was a bit of a food snob and wasn't afraid to admit it. "They used so much canned stuff, it wasn't very good. Thanks for cooking."

Bailey's eyes sparkled at the compliment. "You know I love cooking for you. I just can't wait until you can cook with me again." She paused to take a bite of food and grinned. "Do you remember those messes we made in high school? It's amazing either of us was ever allowed back in a kitchen again."

They laughed and continued reminiscing as they ate. Jay decided that she wanted to watch a movie so Bailey popped in a DVD after cleaning up from dinner and starting the dishwasher. She sat on the end of the couch, pulled Jay's legs onto her lap, and rubbed her feet as they watched. Jay fell asleep about halfway through the movie, and Bailey eased out from under her legs and tucked her in before turning off the TV and the lights.

She left the hall light on just in case and went to the master bedroom to get ready for bed. It wasn't that late, but they were both tired, and she knew she should rest while she could.

* * *

Just over a week after her surgery, Riley took Jay back to the cancer center to have her drains and staples removed. Riley had taken her in for the appointment so that Bailey could stay at work. She had only been back for a few days and so far hadn't reported any problems.

"Did ya need to stop anywhere? Need to go to your office for anything?" Riley asked as they got in the car after the appointment.

"Uh, I hadn't planned on it. I'm pretty sensitive about showing my scar still, and I can't keep it covered yet because fabric irritates it. Plus, my shoulder and neck feel all weird since they cut some nerves. It's like I'm numb but overly sensitive at the same time."

Riley made a sympathetic noise but had a slightly disappointed look on her face.

"Did you want to stop someplace, Rye?"

"Oh, um, no that's fine. I just wondered, you know, if you needed anything from your office or something."

"Thanks, but if I need anything, Bailey will just bring it home with her."

"Oh yeah, right, makes sense. Home it is then!"

Riley put on an Indigo Girls CD and jammed away to it as they drove back through the city. Jay looked out the window wondering if she would ever feel confident in her appearance again. The new scar followed the older one, but that made it larger also. It was very red, raised, and seemed large. The staple marks made her neck look like it was a railroad track, plus there were the two holes from the drains and the nerve damage. She was afraid to go out, that's why she didn't have Riley take her anywhere. Truthfully, she would have loved to stop by the office and at least say hello to people, but she couldn't bear the thought of them seeing her like this. *How will I ever go back to work?*

Riley glanced over at Jay as she drove. Jay's expressions changed from time to time, but she didn't speak. Riley had an idea what was going on in Jay's head, but she didn't know how to reassure her that the scarring wasn't that bad. It was still fresh and had a lot more healing to do. Eventually it would fade away. She wished she could cheer her friend up, but mostly she felt a little helpless which was one reason she was glad to be able to help with transportation. At least she knew there was something she could do to help her friends.

CHAPTER 14

"*H*ONEY I'M HOME," Bailey still loved being able to yell that out when she got home.

"In here," yelled Jay from the kitchen.

"What are you doing? Something smells great in here!"

"I felt pretty good this afternoon, so I decided I would cook dinner. I finished going through all my work e-mails. I thought lasagna sounded really good."

Bailey groaned in appreciation, then quirked an eyebrow at her lover. "Just how long have you been cooking today? Aren't you supposed to rest?"

Jay laughed. "I'm fine, I promise. I didn't precook the noodles, I just used extra sauce in the layers. I mixed the cheese layers sitting at the table, and the sauce was from the stuff we made a while ago and froze. I really only stood to brown the meat and put it in the oven."

Bailey gave Jay a hug and kiss. "Okay, as long as you didn't over do it. I'm glad you're feeling better."

Bailey went in to their room to change clothes, feeling the need to shed her work clothes as soon as possible. She was glad Jay hadn't gone back to the office yet. She didn't want to tell Jay and have her upset or worried, but it felt like there might be some backlash building from their outing as a couple after all. She had spoken to Sharon about it today, but there really wasn't anything to be done yet. Once things became flagrant, Bailey could go to HR or directly to the Board of Directors, but neither woman thought it would do any good. Until things got worse, or Jay talked about going to the office, Bailey didn't want to worry her.

After washing her face and hands and then blotting them dry with a thick and fluffy towel, Bailey felt better and was glad to be home. She went back out and saw that Jay was settled on the couch, so she grabbed plates to set the table.

"Honey, want me to make a salad?" Bailey called into the other room.

"Check the fridge," Jay called back.

Sitting in the refrigerator was a gorgeous salad, two kinds of lettuce, lots of veggies, and a bottle of Jay's homemade dressing. Bailey went into the living room and leaned over the back of the couch to embrace Jay.

"You are the most wonderful live-in lover ever!" she proclaimed.

"Have you lived with many?" Jay asked playfully as she cocked an eyebrow at the other woman.

Bailey chuckled and gave her a quick hug. "Of course not you lug, I've been holding out for the best."

She dropped a kiss on the top of Jay's head and went back to finish setting up for dinner. Bailey decided to whip up some garlic bread with some leftover Italian bread. Once it was ready, she carried the food to the table and called to Jay to join her as she went back for the bread. Jay was in place at the table by the time Bailey returned with the warm bread.

"Great idea for the bread. Thanks for doing that," Jay said as she flashed Bailey a smile filled with tenderness.

"You are quite welcome, thanks for the rest of dinner. After we finish, I'll take dish duty since you did most of the cooking."

Jay agreed and they ate while discussing their day and some work related issues, but Bailey kept quiet about her uneasiness at work.

* * *

"You wanted to talk to me?" asked Jay when she got Sharon on the phone.

"Thanks for calling. Jay, I didn't want to call and disturb you. That's why I sent the e-mail. I figured you'd get it when you were ready."

"Is there a problem in the department? Bailey hasn't mentioned anything to me."

"Well, it's not so much a problem within the department, as within the company. I think Bailey hasn't wanted to worry you so she hasn't mentioned it."

"Now you have me a little nervous. What's going on?" Jay asked.

"I'm hearing rumors, murmurs, about the two of you and your situation. Some people are saying you shouldn't work in the same part of the company, some are saying things that are more negative about you two personally," Sharon explained.

"I see, would there be anything I could do if I came into the office? Someone I could address this to in person?" Jay asked.

Sharon thought for a moment. "You could bring it up to the HR VP. She might listen to you. She and I have gone rounds when I've wanted to let someone go and didn't have enough documentation, but you have a good relationship with her. Bring up the concept of discrimination and allowing a hostile work environment, and she might listen. Just remember, there is no company or state policy protecting you from being fired for being a lesbian. Technically, they could pull out the morals clause in the company handbook and use it on you."

Jay grimaced. "I can't believe they would go that far. It would be kind of a stretch since nothing has ever taken place on company property, or on company time. I mean, hell, I have cancer and I'm still working part time from home, just weeks after major surgery. What more do these people want from us?"

Sharon heard the exasperation in Jay's voice and tried to calm her down. "Look, I know it stinks, but nothing overt has happened yet. So far it's been subtle stuff that could be read two ways."

"Can you give me an example?"

"There was a committee formed and instead of asking Bailey to represent your department, they went to your Team A leader and asked him to join the committee. Now, it could be that they knew Bailey would want to spend more time helping you instead of sitting on a committee."

"Or?" Jay asked.

Sharon sighed. "Or it could be a way to shut you both out because someone didn't approve of two executives dating in the same department."

"So, they want to play that way? We'll see about that!" Jay grumbled.

"Jay, I mostly wanted to talk to you so you would know what Bailey is dealing with, not so you could get involved. Promise me you will continue to work only part time and only from home. I don't want you to try to come in before you are ready!"

Jay was taken aback by the obvious emotion in Sharon's voice. She hadn't realized Sharon cared that much, and she was touched.

"Fine, for now I agree, and I'll find a way to bring it up to Bailey so we can talk it over. Thanks for the heads up, Sharon, that was really good of you." Jay paused then made a decision she hoped Bailey would agree with later. "Sharon, are you doing anything Friday night?"

Taken slightly off balance at the new direction the conversation had taken, Sharon stuttered. "No... a... not really. I was going to stay home and relax this weekend. Did you need something? I'm happy to help you guys out if you need me."

"No, it's nothing like that. We're having a friend over for dinner, and I thought you might want to join us. Nothing fancy, jeans are the fashion requirement, and then we'll pull out a board game or something." Riley was going to be over, and she hoped that with three bankers, she wouldn't be too bored, but she felt as if she owed Sharon a little more than just a thank-you on the phone.

"If you're sure, then I'll be there. Do you need me to bring anything?"

"Just you. We've got it handled. Oh, and of course you can bring someone if you would like. I don't know if you're dating anyone."

Sharon smiled wistfully. "Just me, no one in my life right now. Thanks, I'll see you on Friday, Jay." After they hung up, Sharon wondered if the woman she met at the hospital would be there but shook her head clear of the silly thoughts she was having. *There was no way that tall, athletic woman would want anything to do with an older, out of shape banker.* With a sigh, she went back to her computer and her paper pushing.

* * *

When Bailey got home, she saw that Jay was waiting for her. She had a bottle of wine on the coffee table, since the ban on alcohol had been lifted for now, and she smelled a pizza staying warm in the oven. She leaned down to kiss Jay and then kissed her again to thank her. Jay slipped her tongue between her lover's lips, and Bailey was more than willing to extend her thank-you kiss.

When they broke apart, Bailey looked at Jay appreciatively, "What was that for?"

"Because I love you."

"And?"

"Does there have to be an 'and'? Maybe I just missed you."

Bailey knew she was seeing something else in Jay's warm brown eyes. "Uh huh, it's possible, but I suspect something else is afoot here." Bailey gave her a hug. "I don't mind though, anytime you want to bring something up, feel free to start with a kiss like that one. Do you want to talk now or later?"

Jay laughed, happy that her lover knew her so well even as it disconcerted her a bit. "Let me get the pizza while you change. We can talk after we eat."

Once the pizza was demolished, and about half the wine gone, Jay brought up work. "Anything going on there I should know about?"

Bailey looked to the left a little before answering. "No, I think we're doing well."

Jay's face grew grim. "Bailey McIntyre! I cannot believe you would sit there and lie to me! Why haven't you told me about the bullshit going on there? I deserve to know, and you shouldn't have to deal with it alone." Jay was a little worked up, but she felt she had the right to defend her lover, and it felt as if it was being denied to her.

"Sharon called you?" Bailey asked, looking at the floor.

"Not exactly, she e-mailed asking me to call when I could. She didn't want to tell me, but she suspected that you hadn't since I hadn't called before now."

Bailey got up and poured a little more wine. "I really like this Yellow Tail Merlot. I'm glad we picked it up."

"Stop avoiding me, Bail, this isn't how you and I do things. Talk to me, please?"

When Jay said "please" Bailey knew she had to talk it over with her lover. She couldn't resist her, and she knew that Jay was right. This isn't how they did things. They shared pretty much everything.

"Okay, I'll make you a deal, I'll tell you about it, but you can't go in there trying to fix it. I just want you to focus on you healing enough to start the rest of the treatments and getting through those. That should be all you worry about for now."

Jay understood a little more about why Bailey had kept her concerns from her. She was afraid the stress would be bad for her recovery. Bailey was afraid. The sudden realization hit Jay, and she made a promise to herself to be on the lookout for signs of fear from Bailey so she could reassure her in the future.

Jay went to Bailey and took her hand; she moved her over to the sofa, and pulled her down on her lap. Cradling her against her chest, Jay spoke very calmly to her. "Bail, I won't let anything compromise my treatments, I promise. I will fight this with everything I have in me so that I can spend a long life with you. I will not leave you, not if I have any say at all in the matter. But you can't use this disease as an excuse to keep things from me. I'm not fragile, I won't break, and I can control my temper enough to not charge in there to knock heads. I promise. Please trust in that and talk to me."

Bailey leaned into her, hearing Jay's strong heartbeat inside her chest. She sniffled a little, trying her best not to cry, but it was futile. "I'm so sorry. I'm supposed to be strong for you now, and here I am crying all over you."

Jay held her close and rubbed her back gently, trying to soothe her lover. She repeated over and over again that she loved her, and that it was good to cry. Jay had been waiting for Bailey to let go about all this, and she knew it was crucial for Bailey to cry so she could start dealing with the changes in their lives because of the cancer. Finally, Bailey's tears quieted, and she dried her now red and swollen eyes with a tissue that Jay handed her.

"I'm sorry, Jay. You shouldn't have to take care of me now."

Jay turned her head so that her brown eyes could look into Bailey's green ones. "I don't recall that part of our relationship being discussed. I thought we were supposed to be here for each other, not just one for the other. There are no rules that say you can't be human and grieve the loss of a part of our lives. We should still be in the honeymoon phase of our relationship, but instead we've had to deal with life threatening illness and hassles at work. I grant you, we instigated the outing of our relationship, but it's still hard to deal with. Am I right?"

Bailey nodded slowly and snuggled into Jay's chest. "It has been hard there since I've been back. I don't understand it. We've never done anything improper at work, and you aren't in my chain of command. Yet, there's all this underlying tension going on in the office that I don't understand. I knew it would be hard being in a conservative business at times, but this is beyond my expectations."

Jay continued to hold her while she listened and rocked her gently. Her left side was starting to tingle a bit, but she didn't care. She needed this closeness with Bailey while they discussed the situation.

"How do you want to handle it, Bail? Honestly, you could quit. I can keep working from home and stay on the insurance plan, and we'd be fine. You could find something else in the field with no problem if that is what you want to do."

Bailey shook her head emphatically. "No way am I letting them win that easily! I think I'm going to continue as I have been but with a few not so subtle changes."

Jay could almost see the wheels turning and saw the devilish glint in her lover's eyes.

"I think I'm going to put a picture of you on my desk, maybe one of both of us together. We have a couple of them from that thing at your folks' house right before this all happened. Other people have pictures of their significant others on their desks. Why not me? I'm also not going to beat around the bush if people bring up your name or wonder how you're doing. There is no reason why I can't discuss you without fear of crossing some weird line."

Jay marveled at the strength Bailey had found after letting go of her tears and stress. This woman was amazing, and she realized yet again how much she loved her. "I'm fine with it, honey. Do whatever you need to do to make it bearable. Is there anything I can do to help? Is there anyone you want me to talk to about anything?"

"No, I need to do this on my own, I think. When you get back to work in the office, things will be strange enough. It will be so much worse if my girlfriend has to fight my battles."

Jay nodded in agreement and decided Bailey had it under control for now. "Speaking of work, I may have forgotten to mention this, but I asked Sharon over for Friday night. She seems to be reaching out. It's subtle and took me until today to catch on, but I think she misses having lesbian friends. I don't think she's dated in years. She's been so afraid of exposure at work."

"Hey, I'm fine with it. She's been trying to help us out so the least we can do is entertain her for one evening. Now, let me up. I'm going to go take a shower before I get ready for bed. I'd ask you to join me, but I know your scar is still raw."

In truth, Jay had been reluctant to be fully undressed in front of Bailey since her surgery. She knew it made no sense. Bailey had taken care of her while the wound was fresh and had seen it as it healed, but she didn't feel comfortable in her own skin. She sure didn't feel beautiful or sexy, mostly she felt damaged, angry and sad. She stood up, kissed Bailey, and started tidying up the living room and kitchen from their dinner before turning off the lights and heading into their bedroom.

She looked around, noticing again the pictures Bailey had put up on the walls, pictures of them together as they grew up. It seemed as if they had known each other forever, and yet they still learned new things all the time. Grabbing her sleep clothes, she changed from her sweats into shorts and an old tie-dyed T-shirt before going into the bathroom to brush her teeth. In another hit on her self-esteem, she put in her fluoride trays after brushing her teeth. She'd been told to sleep with them in as long as she could into her radiation, then brush or swab the fluoride on her teeth if her mouth became too sensitive for the trays. Looking in the mirror, she grimaced at her image and turned away quickly. Going into the bedroom, she turned out the main lights, leaving just Bailey's bedside table lamp on for her to see by when she came in the room. She heard the shower stop, and then she heard Bailey getting ready for bed. Jay rolled onto her right side, the closest to a comfortable position she could sleep in so far, and willed herself to sleep so she wouldn't have to face Bailey's beautiful face and body in bed.

CHAPTER 15

*I*T WAS ALMOST three weeks since Jay's second surgery, and in another week, she had to go back to Fox Chase for her radiation set up. She would also have a meeting with the chemotherapy doctor. Since Sharon and Riley were coming over, Jay and Bailey had decided to cook a bit of an elaborate dinner while Jay was able to enjoy it. Jay decided to make a glazed corned beef, while Bailey had chosen to make bubble and squeak, a more English dish, but also a popular Irish dish. They were also steaming asparagus with a little lemon, parsley and white wine just before they sat down, but it was all prepped and ready to go.

While the meat simmered, Jay and Bailey had tidied up the condo. As they worked, Jay was reminded yet again, of how lucky she felt to have Bailey back in her life. Just as she was about to say something, Bailey came over to her and gave her a hug.

"What was that for?" asked Jay.

"I was watching as you dusted, and I had one of those surreal moments. I just couldn't believe that we're actually living together, doing things like a regular couple after all we went through before. I feel blessed to have you in my life, Jay, and I wanted to let you know that."

"Baby, you have to remember, we are a regular couple. Well, as regular as two absolutely weird people can be, and we're both lucky. We lost some time, but we're together now, and that is all that matters. I love you." Jay pulled her close for a kiss, reveling in the feel of Bailey's body as it molded to her own. Bailey swatted Jay's bottom as they broke apart to continue their chores.

Jay relaxed while Bailey took care of her part of the meal.

"The Bubble and Squeak is ready to go. I'll put it in the oven when you pull out the meat to rest."

"Great, I cleared off the table. Want to help me set it?" Jay asked.

They worked together setting the table and chose some light music, mostly some Bonnie Raitt and Ella Fitzgerald for the CD changer. After making sure things were relatively picked up, they changed their clothes, and then sat down to relax and cuddle until someone showed up. When the bell rang, Bailey went to answer the door. She came back with a smiling Riley who was carrying a mile high apple pie and a block of Irish cheddar cheese.

"I thought I'd handle dessert tonight. I hope you don't mind, but I do know how you love apple pie with cheddar." It was something Jay and Bailey had grown up with, heating up a slice of pie and melting a small amount of cheddar over it, mixing the sweet of the pie with the sharpness of the cheddar. Jay grinned at her and rose to give her a quick hug as Bailey relieved her of her burden and her jacket. She brought her into the living room and motioned for her to sit down and get comfortable.

"Thanks, Rye, that was sweet of you. We actually got some French Vanilla Ice cream for dessert so that goes well with the pie if any heathens want it that way."

Rye grinned back, knowing she was the heathen in question. "Hey, you know me! I don't turn down quality ice cream. So, what's this about a fourth tonight? You guys aren't playing matchmaker, are you?" She mock glared at both of them as Bailey returned carrying beers for all of them.

"Actually, we really aren't, Rye. I invited my boss, Sharon, over. It feels like she's been trying to help us out and get a little closer, but she isn't sure how to do it. She's been out of circulation for a while since she's been playing it straight at work for so long."

Rye sat up a little straighter at Jay's comments, and Bailey gave her a look.

"Is it all right with you, Rye? We didn't think to ask you first." Bailey wondered if something had happened when they ran into each other at the hospital.

"Uh, nope, it's totally cool. If she's helping you two out, then she's good people as far as I'm concerned."

Bailey went to baste the meat for the last time and left the other two talking about some video game. Just as she left the kitchen, the doorbell rang again.

Bailey answered the door, and Riley suddenly jumped up and said something about the restroom as she dashed out. Jay, a bit startled, simply sat there for a second before getting up and going into the hallway to greet Sharon. Jay took Sharon's coat and hung it up, and then took her into the living room while Bailey went to get her a drink. Jay was a little uncomfortable having Sharon in her home, but she had invited her and made the best of it. Bailey came in and handed Sharon the beer she had requested and sat down next to Jay on the couch. Bailey was just starting to say something when Riley came back in the room.

Jay was surprised to see Riley's hair down. She was sure it had been in a ponytail when she arrived. She looked closer at Riley, *was that lip gloss?*

Jay was about to tease her, but as if Bailey had read her mind/ "Jay, can you help me in the kitchen for a minute?"

"I can help if you need it, Bailey," offered Riley.

"Why don't you just keep Sharon company while we finish things in the kitchen. We won't be very long. Thanks, Rye!"

Bailey tugged Jay towards the kitchen, leaving the two other women in the living room. Jay grumbled at her. "What was that for? Did you see, Rye? What was with the lip gloss?"

Bailey looked at her in disbelief. "Are you really that dense, Jay? Riley likes Sharon. And, from the way Sharon kept adjusting her collar and smoothing her hair, I think she likes Riley too. Why didn't you tell me they met at the hospital?"

"I don't know, because I was in pain and on medication? It just never occurred to me." Jay shrugged and turned towards the oven to pull the beef out and slide in the casserole Bailey had prepared.

* * *

Riley's palms were sweating a little as she grabbed her beer, and sat down on the corner of the couch closest to the leather chair where Sharon sat. She wasn't sure how to start a conversation but thankfully, Sharon took care of that for her.

"So, I'm told you're a golf pro? And you were on the tour? That must have been amazing."

Riley was surprised that Sharon would have enough interest in her to find anything out about her. "Uh, yeah, I mean yes, I played on the LPGA circuit for a while, but I wasn't in the top rankings by any means. I work up at the same club that Jay and her parents belong to in Bucks. That's how we met actually."

Sharon nodded and smiled. "Do you give private lessons?" Suddenly flustered, as she realized that that could have come across as a serious flirtation, Sharon blushed. "I mean um, for golf. Is it group or private lessons? I've been thinking of taking up the game, but I'll need some lessons to get started."

Riley blushed also. "Sure, I mean, we offer group and private lessons at the club. We can do special groups if you put your own together or general sessions. The private lessons are good too of course." Riley stopped. She knew she was babbling like a brook and couldn't seem to help herself.

Sharon took a sip of her beer to cool down. She suddenly felt a little warm. "Great, maybe I'll get the information from you and join. I live sort of between the city and Jay's folks."

"That would be great. I'd be happy to show you around any time," Jay said with a nod and a smile. "We do stay open during the off season, but it's a lot quieter then of course."

"So, you just moved back here not too long ago? May I ask why?"

"I wanted to spend more time with my family. I felt like I was missing out on more than I was gaining by being on tour. It isn't as if I was a top player or anything. I was middle of the pack most of the time. Nothing spectacular but not a washout either. What about you? Are you close with your family?"

Sharon felt a twinge of discomfort at talking about herself. She had spent so much of her life hiding her true self that it had become second nature. Something about the woman in front of her made her want to open up though so she decided to try. "Actually, I'm the middle child out of three, but I'm the only one that stuck around the Philadelphia area. At first, I stayed because my parents were still here, and I wanted to be here to look out for them. Then I stayed because it was my home, and I had started to advance in my career."

Riley felt herself relaxing as Sharon talked. She enjoyed the sound of her voice as well as the fact that she was opening up. "Do they still live around here?"

Sharon shook her head. "They actually moved to Florida several years ago. They seem happy down there, and my younger brother is close by in case they need help. I go down to visit about once a year, depending on things at the office."

"Do they know you're gay?"

Sharon smiled at that question, knowing that Riley knew of the closet she lived in a work. "Yes, they know. I think they knew before I did to be honest. They have never had a problem with who I dated unless they simply didn't like her. My mother keeps trying to pair me up with the daughters of her Florida friends now. She seems to forget that I don't live in Florida."

Riley chuckled in appreciation. "My sister does the same thing to me. It was easier to avoid when I was on tour, but now I find myself dodging blind dates set up by my sister. So, what do you like to do for fun?"

Sharon blinked at her. "Fun? I don't know. I guess I garden when I can. I enjoy keeping my yard up, but most of it is done by the landscaping service I hired. I pretty much work, come home, eat something, work out, and go to bed. I watch some TV or read if I have down time."

Riley had to ask, even though she thought she knew the answer. "So, there's no one special to spend your time with?"

Sharon smiled, but it seemed slightly sad to Riley. "No, there hasn't been anyone in a very long time."

Riley nodded, deciding not to push for more details. "Yeah, me either. Life on the tour was fun but not conducive to long-term relationships.

Sharon was amazed to find herself opening up to Riley. "It gets lonely sometimes being so high up in the company. I have a lot of obligations. Most women feel slighted by the time I spend at work, but I enjoy what I do. My last girlfriend had major issues with my remaining in the closet at work. She felt it was dishonest and helped keep the community in minority status. Pointing out that the GLBT population is numerically a minority was apparently not the right way to go."

Riley let out a chuckle. "Tell me you didn't actually say that to her? No wonder you guys didn't last!"

Sharon joined the laughter. "Yeah well, I wasn't too bright, but what I said was true. We are a minority, and as long as the patriarchy is in charge, I'm not sure coming out in a conservative company is the best move. The truth is I've admired Jay for having the strength to do it. And Bailey, she's been out her whole time with us too. They even managed to come out as a couple and so far, things have been just fine. I wish..."

Riley leaned forward, putting her hand on Sharon's arm. "What do you wish?"

Sharon released a long sigh. "Sometimes I wish it were different, that I was different. I'm lonely, and as I get older, I recognize that the eligible pool of women shrinks. But I won't settle. I want what my parents have. They are best friends and partners in life. They've been together since high school, and he still buys her flowers for no reason. She still bakes apple turnovers for him every Sunday morning. I want that, and failing that, I prefer to be alone. Anything else would feel like settling. Enough of that, I'm rambling. I'm sorry."

Riley put her hand back on Sharon's arm and waited until Sharon was looking at her. "Never, ever apologize to me for sharing your feelings. If you need a friend to talk to, I'm happy to be here for you. I understand that not every employer is happy with diversity. Besides, who you date doesn't have to be a matter for the workplace. As a high level manager, I expect it is hard to make friends at work without the appearance of favoritism. You can talk to me whenever you need to, just call."

Just then, Jay and Bailey came back in the room.

"Dinner is served! Let's get everyone to the table. More to drink for anyone before we sit down?" asked Bailey. After filling drink orders, Bailey joined everyone at the table and started passing food around. She gave Jay a meaningful look, and Jay shrugged, but asked Sharon how things were at the office.

"You can talk about it in front of Rye. She's the best friend I have outside of Bailey."

"It's been pretty steady with no increase in comments. If anything, things seem to be calming down. I don't suspect that will change until or unless, Bailey has to miss more work when you start treatments," Sharon said as she glanced up from her plate.

Riley looked on, still confused how the three of them worked for such a company with such a conservative corporate culture. "So, is Bailey going to lose her position over this? I mean, can they really force her out just for taking care of Jay while she's sick?"

Sharon shrugged but looked troubled. "Unfortunately, she doesn't qualify for protection under the Family Medical Leave Act. No one has ever pushed for it before, and she could get separated for excessive absenteeism if someone wants to push it. Honestly, I'm part of the problem. If more of us would speak out at work, then maybe this kind of thing wouldn't happen. I'm just afraid to admit anything now. Either way I'm perceived as a liar instead of a private person."

"I've never heard you lie about dating someone or anything. You simply keep to yourself, you don't discuss anything personal, and as far as I know you haven't dated in years," Jay defended Sharon.

"That's true, I suppose," Sharon replied with a nod. "Not a much better statement of who I've been though, is it?"

"We each have to live how we see fit. No one else has to live inside our skin after all. If this has been working for you, then that's just how it is, to hell with anyone else. If you decide it no longer works, then you can change it." Riley spoke up.

Sharon smiled at her gratefully.

"We didn't purposely try to change the corporate culture. It was only out of necessity's sake that we said anything at all. It wasn't about hiding so much as being discreet about dating my former boss," Bailey added.

"I see your point," said Riley. "I don't go out of my way to discuss things with the club members or my co-workers, but if one asked me directly I wouldn't change pronouns or names either."

The women moved the conversation to other things, and in the process found out that they all enjoyed some of the same music, which prompted Jay to turn on the stereo. Riley got everyone laughing with stories of some of her golf students and LPGA players on tour. Bailey told stories about living through some nasty hurricanes in Florida, and Jay was telling them an anecdote about her and Bailey when they were growing up, when the telephone rang. Jay and Bailey looked at each other, and then Bailey went to answer the phone. While she was out of the room, Jay made use of the chance to talk to Sharon.

"Seriously, have you heard anything that suggests she might have a hard time taking time off?"

Sharon responded in the negative, and Jay let it drop.

Bailey returned just a few moments later. "It was your Dad, Jay. He's going out of town and wanted to let us know he might not be back in time for dinner tomorrow night."

Jay nodded and mentioned that they had plans with her parents for tomorrow before going back to her conversation with Riley about the last book they had both read.

After dessert, they went back into the living room to talk, and Bailey suggested they play a game. Riley laughed and said they couldn't play Monopoly; she refused to play any money games with three bankers. They all laughed and decided she was right, so they chose a trivia game and played as they continued to talk. By the end of the evening, Jay was surprised at all the things she had learned about Sharon and was genuinely glad to have invited her. Before long Sharon announced that it was late, and she was tired from work so she was going to head out. Riley quickly jumped up and said she was ready to go as well, so she might as well walk Sharon out. Bailey had to bite her lip to keep from laughing, and Jay continued to look baffled by Riley's behavior.

As they got ready for bed, Jay asked Bailey what was going on with Riley, and she burst out laughing.

"Honey, sometimes you are so thick! I love you but, damn woman! Riley is into Sharon!"

"What? Riley's into Sharon, our boss? You've got to be kidding me. Please tell me you're kidding me?" pleaded Jay.

"Why? What's the big deal if they like each other? Frankly, I think Sharon is mellowing since everything with us has been going on. Maybe they could be good for each other."

Jay shrugged as she finished changing for bed. "I don't know, maybe." She sounded skeptical, but she really did want Riley to be happy. If Sharon did it for her, then so be it. She stretched out in bed and waited for Bailey to finish getting ready. As soon as she came to bed, Jay snuggled up behind her and nuzzled her neck. "I love you. You know that, right?"

"Of course, honey, I love you too! Are you okay?"

"I'm great! I just want to make sure that you know it every day."

Bailey leaned back and gave her a kiss that showed Jay just how much she understood. They settled back in and snuggled as they drifted off to sleep.

* * *

Just over a week later, Jay was getting ready to go to her radiation set up appointment, and meet with Dr. Goldman again about her course of chemotherapy. Jay was driving up on her own today, and she was happy to be out and about. She had developed a case of cabin fever and knew it would only get worse. Jay knew it wouldn't be long before she might not be able to do any driving for a while. She listened to music on the way, good and loud stuff that she listened to when she was younger, the Clash, The Ramones, and of course, the B-52s. When she arrived, she decided she was ready to face this head on, and she would give it her best effort. Soon she heard Dr. Goldman's nurse calling her name. They went through the usual check of weight and vitals. Once the nurse was done with her questions, she left the room and came back several minutes later with Dr. Goldman and one of his residents.

"Feeling okay after your surgery?" he asked as he checked the area of the scar for himself and then listened to Jay's lungs and heart. She was waiting nervously for him to get to the part of their visit to do with the chemo. She had read up on it a lot in the past month and was frightened of the side effects.

"Jay, what we've decided on is this if you agree. Three days of chemotherapy, then three weeks off between rounds. We'll use Cisplatin and Thiophosphoamide. I've prepared handouts for you on both medications, and I will warn you now, it's a heavy hitting dose of each. This is an aggressive cancer, and since it was in two lymph nodes, I want to go after it as hard as we can now."

Jay tried to absorb the information, grateful for the handouts to give Bailey later. She glanced through them, saw all the side effects, and wondered which of them she would have.

"I'm going to have a port put in so that we won't have to start IVs on you each time. The number of IVs would increase venous scarring, and I've found it is much easier on the patient to go with the port. I was thinking this Thursday for the port placement if you can get a ride. It is implanted while you are under twilight anesthesia. Not quite out of it entirely, but out enough that you probably won't realize what is going on. Obviously, we can't have you drive home after that, but it is done as an outpatient."

Feeling almost numb at this point, Jay simply nodded. Her face slightly more pale than usual, and her mouth a thin line, as she struggled to keep from crying. Dr. Goldman asked her if she understood everything so far and she nodded.

"You won't get both medicines each day of treatment, the Thiophosphoamide is only done once per round as it's very strong stuff. The Cisplatin is going to go in each of the three days, so your first treatment of each round will be the longest of the week. Does a Wednesday through Friday schedule work for you? That way your partner will be home over the weekend with you when you will be at your weakest."

Again, Jay nodded mutely and waited for him to continue.

"Jay, I'm not going to lie to you. We really only have one chance to beat this kind of cancer. If it does reoccur, especially if it travels before it comes back, then we have lost. We can continue to treat it, but we won't get a cure. This is the only chance for a full cure. That is why I want to go with this course of treatment. Do you have questions?"

Feeling overwhelmed by it all, Jay felt tears pool in her eyes, but she fought to maintain some form of composure as she responded to the doctor. "No, I understand about the medications and side effects. I've read up on the treatments and on port use, so I'm ready. I'm terrified, but I'm ready. I think the fear of the unknown is my worst problem with this right now. I hate being sick though. I'll get something for that won't I?"

Dr. Goldman nodded and tried to reassure her. "Of course, we have medicine we'll prescribe. Jay, by acting as quickly as you did, you gave yourself the best chance of successful treatment. Now, we're going to do our part to give you the happy outcome we all want for you. I wish I had a guarantee I could make, but it doesn't exist. I plan to start your first round of treatment next Wednesday."

"That soon? But I thought I would have radiation first?"

He shook his head. "We're going to start the same week. By doubling up on the treatments, we hope to basically beat the cancer into submission."

* * *

After seeing the doctor, Jay headed to the basement of the cancer center. She stepped off the elevator into a small alcove with a reception desk off to her left. Hanging on the wall was a ship's bell so she went to read the plaque beneath it.

"Ring when your treatment is over."

"You like it? We thought it was a nice take on the Naval tradition of ringing an officer off the ship when they retired or left the service of a particular ship." The woman speaking was dressed in scrubs and had a clipboard under one arm.

"Uh yeah. Isn't it tempting fate though? Kind of like challenging the cancer to come back?" asked Jay.

"Some look at it that way, but some look at it as the prize to strive for during treatments. It might be a small goal but baby steps get you to the finish line just as surely as sprinting." She smiled and held out her hand. "I'm Janie, one of the radiology techs down here. Are you here for treatment or set up?"

"Setup I guess. Where do I go?"

"I'll show you, I'm heading that way with this chart."

As they walked deeper into the facility, Janie showed Jay around and dropped her off in the waiting area for setup. After showing her where to change her shirt for a gown, Janie left her alone in the waiting area.

Again, waiting in the chairs, she became self-conscious of her scars. Thankfully, no one was around her, and her discomfort eased. *Damn,* she thought, *I'm sitting in a cancer center worried about my scars! There are people much more disfigured than I am. What the hell am I thinking?* Shaking off her wave of self-pity, Jay waited until a tech came back for her and brought her into the simulation room.

"Jay, I'm Dylan, one of the techs that will help you through your radiation treatment. If you have any questions during your setup or treatment, make sure to ask us. Now, are you ready to get started?

Jay nodded, too afraid to speak lest she lose her breakfast. Dylan introduced the other techs and then directed Jay towards a low table that was covered by a thin sheet.

The technicians marked the area where the treatment would be concentrated with three tattooed dots and then moved along to make mold of Jay's face to ensure that she would be in the right position for the entire length of the treatments. Dr. Zach had come in person to ensure that everything was as it should be, and as Jay left, she felt better knowing that she was in caring hands.

* * *

Bailey was struggling to maintain her composure at work. She had spent almost an hour minutes on the phone with a new lender, trying to decipher a credit report on a customer before making a decision on a loan application. Unfortunately, the new lender was not looking closely enough at the details, and Bailey developed a headache as the person on the phone tried to convince her it was a good risk. Today, she just couldn't take much more. Resting her head back against her chair, she stretched and tried to loosen her neck and shoulders.

Bailey decided to go for a cup of tea in the kitchen before tackling her next series of reports. She was a little behind after spending the previous day teaching a loan class to some new customer service representatives from various branches. While waiting for the tea to steep, she leaned against the counter and let her mind drift a bit. The reality was that her head and heart were with Jay right now. She knew how hard things were on her lover, but she didn't know what to do to alleviate any of the stress for either of them.

Bailey was terrified of all that Jay would have to endure while still knowing that she might still lose the bigger battle.

Sighing, she turned to remove her tea bag and added some sugar to her tea. Knowing what the problem was didn't help her solve it, and it was keeping her distracted from her work.

Bailey sighed and headed back to her office. As she passed Sharon's office, she heard her name called.

"Bailey, can you come in here a minute, please?"

"Should I grab any files?" Bailey asked as she stuck her head in the door.

"No, just come on in and shut the door."

Bailey complied and sat in one of the chairs. Sharon came around the desk, an unusual move for her, and sat down next to Bailey.

"How are you doing, Bailey? I'm getting the feeling that you might need some help."

Bailey grimaced a bit and refrained from the sarcastic comments that came to mind. "I'm doing well, all things considered, but thanks for asking."

Sharon looked closely at Bailey, easily reading the stress in her face. "Listen, I can help out with some more of the workload, and I'm going to bring in two of our more experienced branch level lenders to help out for now."

"That's not a bad idea. Will the chain shift to include them before a call to the main office?"

"Exactly, we'll call it "Experienced Lender Level," and include a slight raise for completing the new program."

"Sounds like a good plan." Bailey started to get a little more enthused as she realized that the extra help would be in place just in time for her to be able to help more with Jay's transportation for treatments, and to care for her around the house. They talked a bit more about the program and agreed to get started with it the following week.

Sharon gave Bailey a quick look and continued in a soft voice. "Thanks again for having me over the other night. I had a lot of fun. Please remember, if you two need anything, let me know. I really do want to help out if I can." Bailey thanked her and left for her own office and the pile of work waiting for her.

CHAPTER 16

$\mathcal{R}$ILEY GLANCED AT her watch and grumbled under her breath as she finished with her customer. She was running late for her next private lesson, and she hated being late. Leaving the Pro Shop, she grabbed her clubs and clipboard and headed for the driving range where she was to meet her newest student. *Strange,* she thought as she flipped through the clipboard's forms, *there isn't a name filled in, just a time and a request for me specifically.* She shrugged mentally and kept walking, taking note of the grounds crew and nodding to a few late season golfers headed for the first tee. Starting a new student in mid-autumn was unusual, but not unheard of, and Riley was glad for the extra work. When she didn't have enough to keep her occupied, her thoughts wandered to Jay and her situation.

Truthfully, her thoughts also wandered to Sharon, and that wasn't overly productive either. Other than at Jay and Bailey's, there was little chance that she'd run into her again. All that talk about taking up golf was surely just Sharon's way of showing polite interest in someone she had to socialize with for the evening. Pushing her thoughts away, she nodded hello to the clerk at the driving range and looked around for her student.

Standing off to one side, with an obviously brand new set of clubs, was Sharon. Riley stopped short and let out a nervous breath when she saw her. Sharon offered a smile that warmed Riley to her toes, and she approached her with a timid smile.

"I hope you don't mind. I asked them to leave my name off the form. I wanted to surprise you today." Sharon offered a shy half smile to Riley.

"Um, no, no problem at all. I just figured it was a clerical error or something. So, um, I guess you decided to take up golf?"

Riley tried not to blush as she stated the obvious, but she was flustered to find the woman she had just been thinking about in front of her. *Oh God, I'm going to spend an hour with her! I can't behave like a blithering idiot the whole time!*

Sharon simply nodded and smiled shyly at Riley, admiring the slight blush that crept over the other woman's face. She also admired her long legs, lean build, and self-assured, athletic look. Realizing where her mind was headed, and it wasn't to a golf lesson, Sharon gave herself a mental shake. "So, what should I do, Coach?"

Riley seemed to falter, then she quickly regained her composure. "Well, I need to find out some information such as have you ever played golf before?"

Sharon nodded. "Yes, but it was years ago as a teenager. I haven't picked up a club since I turned twenty."

"All right then, it will all come back to you. Let's do some stretching, and then we'll see what you remember as far as grip and swing."

Riley showed her some basic stretches to loosen up and then grabbed a bucket of golf balls. Riley led Sharon to one end of the range and got set up. Riley was quaking inside, but she fought to keep her hands steady as she reviewed with Sharon the proper way to hold her club. After explaining the principles behind a good golf swing, Riley demonstrated in slow motion and broke it down for her student. Finally, she teed up a ball and showed Sharon the proper way to address the ball before she drove her first shot. It went about two hundred and twenty-five yards, *not too bad for my first shot in several hours,* thought Riley as she encouraged Sharon to step up to the tee. Riley felt her heart speed up as she examined the other woman.

She was dressed casually in khakis, sneakers, and a light colored polo shirt, and she looked trim and in decent shape. Focusing her attention back onto Sharon's address and swing, she watched as the older woman took her first tentative swing. Predictably, she missed the ball entirely, hitting the Astroturf pad the tee sat upon.

Sharon groaned in frustration, but that groan made Riley's insides twist up.

Riley walked over to the other woman to give some gentle pointers. "Don't lift your head until you finish your swing. You were in such a hurry to watch the ball fly that you forgot to watch the ball get hit."

She demonstrated the twisting of the waist and the levelness of her shoulders, then she had Sharon take a few practice swings before addressing the ball again. Stepping back, she watched Sharon square her shoulders and saw her take a deep breath before attempting her swing. This time, Sharon's club connected with the ball, and it flew out about a hundred yards with a nice natural fade to it. Sharon had a delighted smile on her face that caused Riley to break into a grin as well.

"Did you see that? I actually hit the ball, and it went mostly straight!" Sharon enthusiastically shouted.

Riley burst out laughing at her enthusiasm and congratulated her. Riley teed up another ball for her student. "Go ahead, do it again!" Riley challenged.

Sharon addressed the ball and took a swing at it sending it out about ninety yards but straighter. Riley pointed out that she had dropped her shoulder a bit and lifted her head too early, common mistakes for most golfers. They continued the lesson with Sharon learning a little about most of the clubs in her bag, and Riley admiring the way Sharon tackled the learning process of the game.

At the end of the lesson, Riley asked Sharon if she planned to schedule more lessons. Sharon nodded emphatically, and Riley chuckled. They set up another time and date for a lesson, and walked back to the clubhouse together, each carrying their golf bags over their shoulders. "Do you have plans after this? I mean, are you headed back to the office or anything?" Riley asked Sharon when they arrived back at the Pro Shop.

Sharon shook her head. "No, I took a half day. I decided to do something for myself for a change."

Riley took a deep breath. "Would you like to have a late lunch or an early dinner with me?"

Sharon was a bit surprised but nodded happily. "I'd love to! Did you have a place in mind or did you want to eat here?"

"Not here. I know a great steakhouse near here though, if you like steak." Sharon agreed, and they decided to have Riley drive so they could ride together.

* * *

Jay answered the phone, a little surprised to see Riley's number on her caller ID. Riley was usually one of those early to bed people, and it was almost nine thirty at night. Noticing the time, she was a bit surprised to realize that she hadn't heard from her lover in a while either. Riley was excited, talking about a dinner date she had earlier in the night.

"What? Who was it and when did you meet her? Why didn't I know about this?" Jay was full of questions about this mystery date.

"Well, actually, you know her, and I met her after your second operation. She's a new student of mine at the club too."

"Okay, so who is it since I know her?" Jay was silent for a minute, and then it hit her. "Oh my GOD! You mean Sharon? Sharon, as in my boss? Bailey's boss? That Sharon? When did you two...?" Jay paused at a loss for words. She didn't know that Sharon was interested in dating anyone again.

Before she could ponder that detail, Riley was speaking again. "I know she's your boss, and I'd totally understand if you didn't want me to date her, Jay, but I have to tell you, I really like her."

Jay took a slow breath, thinking quickly. "Hey, you're a grown up and so is she, date whomever you like. I'm just worried about you, Rye. She hasn't dated, as far as I know, in a long time."

"I know, buddy, we talked about it and her situation at dinner tonight. She was my new lesson this afternoon, and I'm telling you, there is just something about her that gets me stirred up. I don't understand it, but it feels good. So, I asked her out to dinner, kind of casually, and we really talked."

"And?" Jay was concerned but admitted to some curiosity too.

"And, I really like her. I understand why she's remained so closeted for so long. She was sort of scared into it. She's the youngest of a large family, and her folks are kind of old school. The fear of failing in her family's eyes was pretty intense."

Jay remembered that concert from so long ago. It had seemed as if Sharon was slightly paranoid about the possibility of being outed. "Okay, so based on this, what are you thinking about, Rye? Is this just a fling for you or her? I doubt she'd risk her closet coming open for a fling. She hasn't done it yet as far as I know."

"I don't know how to explain it, but I can talk to her, Jay. She seems to get me, you know? We're totally opposite, from different worlds and in careers that couldn't be more dissimilar, but we seem to have a lot to talk about."

Jay was surprised, but she kept it to herself this time. "Hey, Rye, if you're happy, then I'm happy for you. It's not as if you need my permission to date anyone. Just be careful, okay? Don't rush into anything."

Rye had one more question. "You know how we all hang out sometimes? Would it be okay if she were with me? I don't want things to be weird since she is your boss, but you guys are my closest friends. I just want to make sure it's cool to have her mixed in, you know?"

Jay gave the question some consideration as she formed an answer. "It's cool, Rye. I mean, I did invite her over that night, and it went better than I thought. She seems different lately. Maybe she's getting mellower. I'm sure Bail will be fine with it too."

"Awesome, thanks, Jay. So, both of us can come over tomorrow night? I still want to see you before you start treatment. And remember, I'm serious about helping with rides. I don't want you driving yourself when you're sick or worn out."

"You got it. We'll see you both tomorrow night then." Jay said and then paused. "Hey Rye, I'm glad for you, you know that right?"

"We're cool, Jay, I know you're just being protective, but even though it's scary, I think she might be worth it."

"All right, buddy, be good then, and we'll see you tomorrow."

After hanging up with Riley, Jay decided to track Bailey down, but before she could dial, the door opened, and her lover walked in looking worn out.

"Hey, honey, where have you been? I was starting to get worried." As Jay went to hug her lover and give her a kiss hello, Bailey gave her a tired smile and gratefully leaned into Jay.

"I'm sorry, I should have called, but I lost track of time. When I realized how late it was, I decided not to call in case you were sleeping."

They walked into the living room, and Bailey sank gratefully onto the couch. Jay sat next to her and raised her arm so Bailey could snuggle in against her.

"What's going on, Bail? Do you need to talk? I know we have a lot going on, but I'm still here for you, you know?"

Burrowing into the warmth of Jay's body, all Bailey could think about was going to bed and blocking out the world for a little while. She voiced that to Jay, and after extracting a promise from Bailey that they would talk in the morning, the two women went off to bed.

* * *

Bailey awoke the next morning and felt the arms of her lover wrapped around her. She let herself relax into the warmth and safety of Jay's arms, trying to block out the fears and anger running through her head. There was no answer to her fears other than time, patience, and faith, but she wished for some magic solution. She felt Jay stir behind her, and rolled over to find those beautiful brown eyes looking at her with nothing but love shining in them. Bailey was overwhelmed and buried her face in Jay's neck.

"What's wrong, honey? What can I do?" Jay was perplexed by Bailey's recent behavior. Bailey started crying softly against Jay's neck, and she burrowed in tighter.

"Please, just hold me, and promise you will fight this with everything you have in you. Please don't give up on us, Jay, please."

Bailey started crying in earnest, tears flowing freely down her face, and Jay turned so they could face each other.

"I promise you, Bailey. I love you with all that I am. I will do my damnedest to stay here with you. I'll be the best patient ever and take whatever treatment they throw at me. I can't promise not to complain at times, but I'll do it all, so that we can spend the next fifty years together."

Bailey's tears had started to ease as Jay talked with her. Bailey hugged her close. "I'm sorry I'm so messed up. You're the one going through the hard stuff. I'll try to keep myself under control."

Jay shook her head. "Don't say that, sweetie! We're both going through this, just like you told me. I get that now, and you need to remember it too. We just need to tell each other when we're scared, or angry, or whatever else we are. I promise to do my best to get you through this, and you will get me through it. We're going to be fine and stronger than ever. Remember, fire forges iron ore into steel and makes it much stronger, just like we'll be after walking through our fire together."

Bailey nodded and smiled then wrapped her body around Jay's. "I'm still not willing to let you go right now. Are you okay with some cuddles this morning?"

"This morning and any other you wish," Jay replied as she settled back into her pillow and tried to silently give Bailey the strength and love she needed.

* * *

During breakfast, Jay recounted her conversation with Riley the night before and verified that Bailey was okay with Sharon coming over again. They decided to do a quick and easy dinner that night, just a basic chicken stir-fry with brown rice that Bailey would handle. They had everything they needed on hand, so they could let dinner preparations wait for a while.

This was the last weekend before treatments started for Jay, and she was plenty nervous. She decided to ask Bailey to go for a walk with her so they could talk. Jay seemed to think better when she could move around, and she wanted to get out while she could, not certain how the treatments would affect her mobility.

They cleaned up from breakfast and headed out to walk around Old City. The two women did some window-shopping as they walked through the artist refuge of the city. They talked about the possible side effects of the treatments, likely timing of those affects, and whatever else they could think of that bothered them about the upcoming treatments. There was no skirting the issue anymore, the time was almost upon them, and there were things to be said before it started.

They reminisced about their time growing up together, and they talked more about their time apart. Mostly, they tried to reassure each other that they would get through this horrible nightmare they were living in. As they approached their street again, they both felt better after having the conversation they had avoided for so long. Each of them was afraid. It was natural, but they were both fighters, and they wouldn't give in willingly.

CHAPTER 17

RILEY WAS PACING as she waited for Sharon to pick her up. She had planned on picking Sharon up on her way to Jay and Bailey's, but her Jeep decided to act up today. Now it was sitting at the dealer's, waiting for a mechanic on Monday. Sharon had offered to drive rather than have Riley get a rental for the weekend. Riley was nervous about Sharon coming over, but she didn't know what else to do, other than pace. Her duplex was clean and organized, everything put away, and not overly cluttered with lots of memorabilia from her golf touring days.

Riley admitted the truth to herself, she was nervous about what Sharon thought because Sharon mattered to her. That hadn't happened in a long time, and she wasn't entirely sure she was happy about it happening now. Riley simply knew that she had to see where it led, or she would always wonder. One of the things life on the tour taught her was that you couldn't go back and relive a moment. You had to go for it, or live with the regret of not trying at all.

A car pulled up in front, and a door slammed. Riley opened the door for Sharon, smiling as she came up the walk. "Come on in. We have some time. Don't we?"

Sharon nodded and stepped inside. As Riley shut the front door, Sharon looked around. "You have a great place, Riley."

Riley blushed and thanked her before offering her a drink.

"I'm fine, thanks. If you're ready, we can head out. Traffic shouldn't be too bad, but you never know."

Riley knew the truth of that statement all too well. I-95 had a tendency to back up in certain places for no discernible reason, then all of a sudden it flowed smoothly again. It was just one of the quirks of the area, and one that people that were new to the area had to get used to quickly. Riley grabbed her jacket, and they headed out to Sharon's car. Sharon unlocked it by remote but stepped up to open Riley's door and waited to shut it behind her before going around the front of the car to her own door.

Sharon made sure their seatbelts were fastened, and then grinned at Riley as she started the car, heading to the city for their dinner. On the way in, they talked about music and books mostly, with each woman slipping in a few personal details. The talk turned to Jay and Bailey's situation, and what they could do to help. Sharon surprised Riley when she mentioned something she had been thinking about at work.

"I'm thinking about coming out at work soon. What do you think, Riley?" Sharon glanced over to gauge Riley's reaction.

Riley smiled at her companion. "I have to admit, I think it would be great for you to do it, but why now? How does this help them or you?"

"It's not as much about any of us as it is about other gays and lesbians in the company. As an officer and senior manager, I've been neglecting those employees who are not represented. Look at the mess we had trying to get Bailey time off to take care of Jay! And the real battle hasn't even been fought yet on either front. I know I'll run into opposition when I give her time off or permission to work from home during Jay's chemotherapy. By coming out myself, maybe I can point out that I know the unfairness of the system and perhaps become a voice for change. All we need is to show that there are gays and lesbians in important places in the company. We all deserve the same treatment that any other staff member would receive if their partner were gravely ill."

"Wow, sounds like you've given it a lot of thought, Sharon. Hey, whatever you feel is the right thing to do, I'll support that a hundred percent. Are you sure your career isn't at risk though?"

Sharon took a minute to merge into traffic before answering. "It might be, but frankly, I dare them to fire me. I'll slap a lawsuit on them so fast their heads will spin. Besides, like Jay and Bailey, I've also made some good investments, and I've lived a fairly indulgence free life. I've buried myself in my job for so long that there wasn't time, or anyone with which to spend the money I worked so hard to earn."

Sharon hesitated before she continued. "Besides, I've lived in fear of my parents disappointment for far too long. I told them last night, and they were relieved I finally told them. I've wasted so much time, and I think most of it was fear from within. I've seen Jay and Bailey living openly at work, and other than some issues because of the chain of command and departmental concerns, there hasn't been a bit of issue. It's all been in my head."

"Well, I have to say I'm impressed. I didn't expect that kind of support for them, but I'm glad they have you in their corner too. I don't know how things were for you at work when you started there. Maybe back then it was best for you to stay hidden. I think you're right though, you don't need to anymore." Riley turned in her seat and looked more closely at Sharon. Her semi short blond hair shone in the fading sun, around her eyes was the start of faint lines, and she seemed more relaxed than she had been when they first met. "I may not have mentioned it earlier, but you look great tonight."

Sharon blushed slightly, but her face also lit up at the compliment. "Riley, I'm just wearing jeans and a sweater. It's not like it's a designer outfit." Sharon tried to downplay the compliment, but the truth was she was thrilled to have received it. She was very attracted to Riley which was part of why she decided to come out at work. She didn't want to play pronoun games, or go stag to events if she had someone she wanted to bring as a date. Now that she had someone that she might want to keep in her life, it was worth the risk at work.

"Thanks for the support, Riley. It means a lot that you think it's a good idea. I'm tired of hiding from myself. I haven't had a life outside of work for so long that it just didn't seem to matter to me."

"Does this mean you might want more of a life outside of work?" asked Riley with a bit of hesitation and hope.

"Most definitely, I do now."

* * *

On the ride home, they sat in relative silence, other than a soft music station playing some old hits from the eighties. They both thought about the evening and how devoted their friends were to each other, especially in the face of Jay's illness. Sharon thought about how boldly Bailey had stood up at work to make sure she would be available to care of Jay and still tried to pull a full load at work. Riley thought about how brave both women were and prayed that she could be as brave for them as they were for each other. As if by consensus, they both shook off the gloomy thoughts and decided it was time for a different kind of talk.

Riley brought it up first. "Sharon, I wanted to let you know, I'm having a lot of fun getting to know you. I know we're from different backgrounds and all, but I want you to know that I really like you."

Sharon felt the thrill of butterflies in her stomach and was happy to hear that they seemed to feel the same way. "Riley, I really like you too. You've been like a breath of fresh air in my life, reminding me of the important things I have neglected for far too long. I would really like to continue to see you if you're open to it too."

It was all Riley could do to smother a shout of happiness. Instead she allowed a big grin to spread across her face, letting her dimples show. "I'd really like that too. I think it's good that we're taking things somewhat slow. I'm not into the whole U-Haul thing. It is one reason I don't date much. That and women seem to think that because I'm a jock I don't have a brain too."

"Really? But you're so well read and are up on all the current technology changes, how could they not see your intelligence? That and your good heart are what interested me first. Of course, I do like those dimples too." Sharon was amazed that she was being so open, and flirtatious on top of it, but for some reason she felt safe with Riley. Sharon made the choice and decided to trust her instincts.

When they got back to Riley's house, Sharon shut the car off, and they sat there for a moment listening to the tick of the engine cooling. Riley turned to her, and they both started to speak at the same time before both dissolved in laughter. Riley finally took the lead. "Would you like to come in for a cup of tea? No strings, I just like spending time with you."

Sharon declined. "It's getting late. Are you free for brunch tomorrow instead? I know a great place not that far from here."

"That sounds great. Pick me up around ten?"

"I'll be here."

Riley leaned over and gave Sharon a quick, but gentle kiss. She then turned swiftly, and let herself out of the car and into her house, offering a quick wave goodbye as she vanished inside.

Both women had the same thought, "Amazing!"

* * *

Jay's first two radiation sessions went well, and she had driven herself to and from the cancer center. Bailey had taken off Wednesday to spend the day with her for her first chemotherapy appointment. First, she went to the lab to get blood work drawn and then to the radiation unit for her treatment. She showed Bailey where it was before she left her in the waiting room while she went into one of the changing rooms. She was able to leave her jeans on, just as in the simulation, and then went into the waiting room and sat with Bailey.

"This part won't take too long. This seems like the easiest part of all the stuff they're throwing at me so far." Just then, her favorite tech came out for her. "Hey, Dylan, this is my partner, Bailey. Bailey, this is Dylan, radiation tech extraordinaire."

Dylan smiled at both women. "Bailey, you're welcome to join us if you'd like. You can see what goes on with Jay."

Bailey nodded. "You don't mind, Jay?"

"Course not. Come on in and meet my mask."

Bailey followed them past the several inches thick door, down a short hallway, and into a slightly chilly room with a large machine that extended over the table that Jay would lie on. Dylan spread a sheet on the table, and Jay climbed on, laying her head on the plastic tray. As he got the mask from its cubbyhole, Dylan explained it to Bailey.

"So, this helps keep her in alignment, but she can breathe?"

"Yup! Now, we have to adjust her. Jay, slide up and to your right a bit. Good."

Two other techs came in to help with the adjustments and alignment. After they turned out the lights, cross hairs lit up from the machine so the techs could line up the cross hairs with the marks on the mask, and Jay's little blue tattoo dots. Then it was time to leave the room, and Jay received her ten-minute dose of radiation.

When they came back in, they lowered the table and released Jay's face from the clamps. She hopped off, smiled, and thanked the techs, promising to see them tomorrow. Jay went off to change and then met Bailey, and they went off to her doctor's appointment with Dr. Goldman.

With lab time, and waiting time, plus the time for infusion, this process would eat up most of her Wednesday each round. After seeing Dr. Goldman, they headed over to the infusion area and signed in. Too nervous to deal with much else, Jay held hands with Bailey and prayed that this would go well. If there was one thing Jay hated, it was losing control of her body. The cancer was a big enough loss of control, but the idea of uncontrollable vomiting and nausea was almost unbearable to her. They had given her a prescription for two anti-nausea medications which she had been told to take, needed or not, throughout the days of her treatment and for the next few days after each round. By trying to stay ahead of the nausea, she might beat it or at least minimize it.

Jay was called into the infusion room, and Bailey went with her, carrying Jay's backpack with her sweatshirt jacket, paperback, iPod, and headphones. They also did the ritual weigh in, and then got her settled in a chair that reclined and offered her a blanket and pillow.

Jay responded politely yet with evident tension. "No thanks, I just want to get this started."

Before long the tubes were hooked up and the treatment began.

"I'm scared, Bail. I don't want to do this!" Jay started to panic, her eyes darting from the IV to the door.

Bailey took Jay's hand in her's and tried to soothe her. "I'm here Jay, and I'm going to take care of you. I know you're scared, Jay. What can I do for you? Whatever you need, baby, I'm here."

Jay saw the sincerity in her green eyes. "I know, but I'm just so scared. Why am I going through this? I thought I was ready, but I'm not!"

"Neither of us is ready, but I don't want to risk your life. I promise, I'll do everything I can to help."

An hour into the treatment Jay nodded off. Bailey was relieved that her partner was finally able to get some rest though she was concerned about the timing of it.

Bailey spoke to the nurse when she came around to check things. "Is it normal for her to fall asleep during this?"

Shelly finished tucking a thin blanket in around Jay as she answered. "Actually, the combination of all three anti-nausea and anti-anxiety medications is probably what made her sleepy now. As treatment progresses, she'll probably sleep through without the medications. A lot of our patents on a heavy regimen like this spend more time asleep than awake during their treatments."

Bailey decided that if she had to go through this, then sleeping through it would be best. She tried to read a book but found herself watching Jay sleep, as if some primal need caused her to guard her lover.

* * *

Saturday morning Bailey was trying to interest Jay in any food or drink, but she was too nauseated to even hear about food. Jay's mother had been the transportation for treatments the last two days and had stayed with Jay until either Bailey got home or Riley got there. Jay was miserable. So far, the medications were keeping her from being sick, but she was still nauseated all the time. Jay was able to sip gingerale, and Bailey had stocked up, hoping to get some liquids into her at least. The doctors had warned them about dehydration lowering her immune system further, so she was doing her best to tempt Jay. Jay moaned and gently turned over, clutching a pillow to her stomach. There was no relief in sight, she could hardly choke down her medications without gagging, and had managed only a few bites of saltine crackers now and then.

"All this and I get to lose my hair too! How did I get signed up for such fun?" Jay was grumpy, and no one blamed her. This was already taking a huge toll on her, and it was only the first week of treatment. Bailey figured they would cope as best they could, and she would try to find foods that Jay could tolerate to keep her strength up.

Riley had offered to come by and help on Sunday, but Bailey decided against it. She didn't want to take advantage of Riley, and she wanted some time alone with her lover. Bailey wanted to spend the weekend taking care of the condo and the basic chores of dusting and laundry. She tried to keep cooking to a minimum so Jay wouldn't have to smell food cooking, so she had planned mostly cold meals of salads and sandwiches for herself for the weekend. Jay slept a lot of the time, and Bailey spent time watching her sleep. Bailey found herself wishing she could make things better. She felt frustrated by her lack of ability to make this better for Jay.

* * *

By the second week of radiation, Jay was able to eat more, but now her mouth and neck were starting to show the signs of the radiation. No matter how much lotion she rubbed on her neck and shoulder, the skin was dry and reddened. The inside of her mouth was starting to feel as if it had sunburn. The cheek lining was ulcerated as if she had eaten something too hot and held it in her cheek.

Riley and Jay's mother were providing most of her transportation with Bailey's mother filling in a day here and there as well. Jay was too worn out to do the drive for the radiation. She wasn't really even checking her e-mail for work at this point, and she didn't care. The pain medication for her mouth had her too tired to do much but sleep. Jay was praying for an end to the radiation even though she still thought it better than the sickness of chemotherapy.

The weekend after week two, Bailey had to cover part of the weekend shift, so Riley decided to crash at their place to be on hand just in case. She and Sharon had continued to take things slowly, but they were learning to trust each other more, and Sharon found herself getting ready to confront the issue of partner benefits at work and come out herself in the process. She was joining Riley for a few hours at Jay's to discuss it with her while Jay napped. When Sharon arrived, Bailey had just left, and Riley whispered that Jay was crashed on the couch. They crept past her and into the guest room where they could talk softly without disturbing the sleeping woman.

Sharon stepped into Riley's arms for a firm hug and a light kiss across her lips. They stayed like that a moment before sitting on the edge of the bed to talk. Riley kept the door cracked so they would hear Jay if she awoke and needed anything.

"Riley, my bosses have been asking about Bailey's time off. They really want to keep her in the office while Jay is sick."

"She hasn't taken any days off since Jay's first day of chemo. Why the hassles now?"

"I don't know, but I know Bailey plans on going to the first day of each round of chemo. That is only three more days, spaced well apart, why should it matter how she uses her time off? I don't know why but something is going on that I'm not privy to yet."

"Do you think it will be a problem? I know Bailey doesn't want anyone else there for the long days."

"I don't know, but I set up a meeting with the company's state President and HR for Monday. I'm planning to let them know exactly what I think of the treatment Bailey has received. I'm also going to come out to them."

"Really? Are you sure about this? You can't take it back once the words are out there. I'm proud of you for wanting to help them, but is this going to hurt you?"

Riley was a little surprised to find out the meeting was already scheduled. The truth was, Riley still had a hard time comprehending that it was that big a deal. She believed that Sharon and some others perceived it as such, but she had questions in her head about it. This would be the true test. Would Sharon be reprimanded, shut out of things, or worse? Would she be able to protect Bailey and Jay at work?

"I know it is a bit of a gamble, but I think that I've proven my worth for long enough that I might be able to pull it off. If I don't, then at least I was honest and struck a blow for change within the company. I really feel like I need to do this now."

"Then I'm with you a hundred percent!"

The women heard Jay start to stir and waited a moment before going in to check on her.

"Oh, hi, Sharon, didn't realize you had gotten here. I must have been out again, huh?"

Sharon nodded and smiled gently. "I think your nap was needed, Jay. You still look worn out. Can I get you anything to drink or eat? Is there anything I can do to make you more comfortable?"

"I could try some more gingerale, I guess. I'll need some to take the next dose of meds anyway. Thanks. Hey, Rye, could you give me a hand? I get dizzy when I stand up, but I have got to go to the restroom."

Riley stood next to Jay as she got herself into a sitting position, and she nodded. Riley gave her a hand getting to her feet. She swayed a bit then seemed to regain her balance.

"Thanks, Rye, I should be good from here."

Riley looked a bit worried but let her go on her own, knowing that Jay needed every ounce of independence that she could get now. They both understood that she would lose it before this was all over.

* * *

Riley had been surprised when her phone rang Monday morning. It was Sharon asking to meet with her for lunch. Today was the day she was scheduled to come out to her boss, and she needed a little moral support. Riley was more than happy to see her, so they arranged to meet at a small bistro not that far from Sharon's office. Riley was early and had already gotten a table by the time Sharon arrived, looking tense. Unsure of how to greet her given that she had no idea if anyone Sharon did business with was in the restaurant, she smiled awkwardly as she stood and waved Sharon to the table. Sharon collapsed in her chair with a sigh of relief.

"Thanks for meeting me on such short notice, Rye. I just needed to see you today."

"Anytime, though I must admit, I'm feeling a bit awkward. We don't usually hang out near where you do business, and I'm not sure how to act."

Sharon was somewhat surprised by Riley's reaction. "Act like you, the woman that brought me back into the world of the living. I know we've been taking things very slowly, but I hope you know how much you've changed my life for the better," Sharon responded.

It was Riley's turn to be surprised by Sharon's admission, and she wasn't sure what to say next. "Sharon, I know we haven't known each other that long, but I'm very attracted to you. I'm pretty sure you feel the same way." Riley paused as she recognized that she had admitted more than she intended, but decided to finish. "I care about you, and taking things slowly has been good for both of us. I hope you know you've been good for me too."

Okay here goes nothing, or everything. Sharon thought as she gave Riley a grin. "Good! Since we can agree on that much, you were the first person I wanted to tell this to, and I couldn't wait."

Riley made a go-on motion, and waited silently.

"The HR vice president moved the meeting to right before lunch. I didn't know she was going to do that when I called you this morning, and I didn't have a chance to call you back and let you know. I did it! I came out to my boss and the vice president of HR and they were both speechless."

Riley could feel her jaw drop open, and she knew she was staring but she couldn't formulate words.

"My boss surprised me today. He said that he was sorry that I'd felt the need to hide for so long. Then he told me that his son had come out to him about four years ago, and his attitude has changed since getting to know his son and his son's partner better. Can you believe it? All that angst, and it wasn't that big a deal! How will I tell Jay? It's my fault she's felt awkward with me at work. I'm the one who warned her about being open."

Riley started to see that Sharon was upset with herself about warning Jay about being open. "Shar, you can't blame yourself for that, you thought you were protecting her, and it was her choice to follow or not follow that warning. Besides some of the backlash Bailey experienced when their relationship was made public was homophobic in nature."

"Yes, but apparently HR has been investigating the problems and has already filed warnings against the major troublemakers. I wasn't informed because they thought I might be one of the homophobic troublemakers in question." After a minute, Sharon continued ruefully. "I guess I did a little too good a job of playing straight."

Riley sat back in her seat, totally in shock about all she had just been told. Sharon's job, as well as those of Jay and Bailey, was apparently quite safe, and HR was taking steps to improve life for gays and lesbians. Sharon told her there was even talk of partnership benefits, including insurance and FMLA, for situations like the one affecting their friends. In the meantime, Sharon had been told to make sure Bailey had the time she needed to care for Jay, and the help she needed to keep the department up to speed.

"All this because his son is gay?" Riley was a little skeptical about the motives of the Sharon's boss since this was all so sudden.

Sharon revealed that the company had been the subject of a civil lawsuit in another state for not giving domestic partner benefits, and they were trying to be proactive now.

"Of course the whole thing is going to take a year or two to implement, but at least it is in the works. The general staff won't hear anything about it for quite sometime, which is unfortunate, but they don't want to announce anything without the plans ready to roll out."

Riley was blown away that everything had gone so easily. "So, what do you think, is it all for real? I mean no consequences, and suddenly you can just be open?"

"I think that's a bit optimistic," replied Sharon. "I do think it's a huge leap forward, and it tells me that I was too cautious in the past. Maybe all it really takes is enough people saying it out loud. It may be a lot of smoke being blown around. The benefits might not happen unless the state's laws change, but my boss seemed to think they would happen sooner rather than later." Suddenly, Sharon looked at her watch and realized she had a meeting to get back for soon. "Can we meet later? I'd like to see you tonight if you're free."

"Sure, I'll be at Jay's. I'm headed over soon so that when Jay's mom gets her home she can take off, and I'll stay with her."

"Okay, I'll call you when I'm leaving work. Maybe I can pick you up, and we can go out for dinner or something."

They hugged goodbye at the doorway, and Riley headed to Jay's still in a daze from her hug with the other woman.

CHAPTER 18

$\mathcal{T}$HE FIRST DAY OF Jay's second round of chemo was cold, so Bailey made sure to bundle her up and get the car warmed up well before she brought Jay outside. Jay was more tired than Bailey had ever seen her, and she was having a near impossible time getting and keeping anything inside of her. Her mouth and neck were so raw from the radiation that a bad bout of coughing could tear open scabs on her neck and make her bleed. It had become physically painful for Bailey to watch as her strong and sensitive lover became weaker and more dependent as they battled this disease. Jay had asked Bailey to buzz her hair as she couldn't tolerate showers on her burns, and washing it had become a problem. Jay slept most of the way to the cancer center, and when they arrived, Bailey dropped her off at the main entrance so that Jay wouldn't have to walk as much and went to park the car,.

They went to the lab first, and then down to radiation for her treatment. Jay had worn a loose shirt with a lower neckline so she didn't have to change before radiation this time. When the tech came out for her, he motioned Bailey to follow as before.

This time, when they went into the control room for the treatment, he asked about Jay. "So, how is Jay really doing? When I ask her, she tries to be as cheerful as possible and says she's fine. I can see that she isn't. Is there anything you need? If there is any way I can help, please let me know."

Bailey smiled. "Thanks, she's trying to put up a tough front, but I know she's hurting. Just keep kidding around with her. I know she appreciates the humor."

"She's been one of my most memorable patients. She comes in and keeps a smile on her face, no matter how sick or tired she is feeling. Last week she brought in a trick light bulb and pulled it out when we got her on the table. She stuck it in her mouth and told us we were turning her into Uncle Fester, and then she made it glow." He smiled at the memory and checked the progress of the treatment. "If you guys need anything from us down here, please let us know. She's been really brave and we all admire her fighting this as hard as she has been."

Bailey smiled and felt the tears welling up in her eyes. It was comforting that others saw Jay the way she did, brave and strong, trying so hard not to let the cancer and the treatment steal her sense of humor and fun. Bailey thanked him and the other techs and promised they would check back after Jay's treatments were over. She only had seven more, and she would be done with the radiation portion.

When Jay was done, they went to see the oncologist before getting the infusion done. When Jay did her weigh in, no one was surprised to find that she had lost close to ten pounds.

Trying to make light of it, Jay joked. "I finally got rid of that bulge around my middle that I've been fighting for years." It hurt to talk, but she was still making jokes.

Bailey fell a little more in love with her each time she saw her take another shot at the cancer, refusing to let it get all of her. The doctor and his staff met with them and discussed her lab results.

"I'm not really happy with some of the numbers this time. I'm going to order an extra bag of fluids for today and Friday. It will add some time to the treatments, but it should make you feel better too."

Jay just nodded slightly, too much movement hurt, and she was starting to feel worn out again. "I'm also going to have them give you a shot to boost your red blood cell count. Your count is a little lower than I would like it to be going into treatment, but we'll fight it with the medication."

By now, Jay knew what to expect so she waited patiently as the nurse set up her chair and all the paraphernalia. Jay had brought her own fleece blanket as she found the room a little cold, and the room temperature fluids going into her body temperature system chilled her as well. She waited until they had her set up, and then put on her iPod and dozed off. Bailey kept watch again as Jay slept and worried even more about her lover as she watched the poison drip into her body.

* * *

"Jay, we're here." Riley tried to wake Jay up gently as they got to Fox Chase for her last radiation treatment on Friday. She would have made it through a major part of her treatment after this last day. Riley looked compassionately at her friend, noting the increased burn damage and the start of hair loss. Her heart twisted, and she wished once more for a magic wand with which she could heal Jay, but she knew it was futile. Gently, she unlatched Jay's seatbelt and went around to open her door.

"Jay, buddy, it's time to get up, we're here." Jay slowly opened her eyes and promptly grabbed for her bucket that was a constant companion now. Riley held Jay's head as her friend was sick, and she tried to hide her fear. When Jay was finished, Riley gave her some water to rinse her mouth and took the bucket from her. She helped Jay out of the car and into one of the wheelchairs by the main entrance. With a quick stop by the first bathroom they found, Riley cleaned out the bucket and gave it back to Jay before taking her down to radiation.

As soon as they got to the treatment waiting room, one of the nurses came over and spoke to Jay. "How are you today, Jay? Any better than yesterday?"

Jay mumbled something, and Riley filled the nurse in on the last twenty-four hours. Jay hadn't kept anything down at all, including her medication that morning. The nurse said she would be right back and went to consult with Dr. Zach.

Dr. Zach came in and sat down next to Jay. "So, I hear you're having some increased problems today, Jay."

Jay looked up at him with an expression on her face that could only mean "Duh!"

"I'm glad to see you still have some humor left in you. I'm going to pre-treat you with an IV dose of anti-nausea medication before we put you on the table today. I want to make sure you will be safe. This way we should be able to finish the treatment without stopping, and you will feel better at the same time."

Jay nodded and smiled very weakly. "Thanks, Doc, I really don't feel too good. It got much worse this morning, and my hair started coming out two days ago."

He patted her knee and promised that he would do his best to make her feel better. He also prescribed Marinol for her, a liquid capsulated version of THC, the active ingredient in marijuana. He hoped it would help her beat some of the nausea she was facing.

After the IV medication, Jay was brought into her treatment and the techs locked her into place for the last time. They turned on a radio station they knew she liked, and after the treatment was over, they gave her the mask to take home. Everyone wished her well and reminded her to visit when she felt better. With that, Jay's time with radiation treatment was done, but she declined to ring the bell on her way out.

"No sense tempting fate," was all she said to Riley as they left.

* * *

Sirens, Jay knew she heard sirens. Not that unusual in the city, but they seemed really close. Suddenly, nausea wracked her body, and she felt herself vomiting again and again. All she knew was pain as her body tried to turn itself inside out. As the spasms eased, she felt someone turn her over and wipe her face with a cool, damp cloth. Sounds faded again as she lost her tenuous grasp on the world around her.

Bailey sat in the front of the ambulance as it made its way from their condo to University Hospital. She had called 911 after she found Jay unresponsive on the bathroom floor after another bout of vomiting and diarrhea. She prayed for Jay to wake up, and when the EMTs arrived, Jay's eyes did open for a moment. Then she had another round of dry heaves and passed out again. Now, they sped to the hospital, and all Bailey could do was pray and tamp down her panic and fear.

When they got to the hospital, the EMT crew directed Bailey to registration to sign Jay in and give her history to the staff. Thankfully, she had grabbed their big cancer notebook that had reports on her tests, surgeries, treatments, medications, and listed her doctors' names and contact information. After she finished the registration process, Bailey called Jay's parents and asked them to call her own for her. She also called Riley and asked her to let Sharon know that she didn't think she would be in to work tomorrow, or until things were stable.

"No problem, Bail, she's here with me, I'll tell her, and then we're coming down to be with you." Bailey, too numb to really hear anything, just mumbled something and hung up.

Finally, a nurse said she could go back to Jay and sit with her. Jay was hooked up via her port to an IV with a second bag piggy backed to the first. Bailey checked the labels and realized it was normal saline, and the piggyback was Compazine to deal with the nausea. She had learned a lot recently, more than she ever wanted to know, about medicine and its procedures. Bailey knew the staff wanted to introduce hydration as quickly as possible and give Jay's body a chance to settle down.

Just then, a nurse came in and started asking questions about Jay's recent history, and she verified her medication list and allergies. "The doctor will be in shortly."

"Can you tell me anything yet?"

"Right now she is resting, but Jay is running a fever which indicates that an infection has taken hold. We're working on hydration and getting her cooled down. Blood work has been drawn and sent to the lab for rapid analysis to determine what we're fighting. In the meantime, a broad-spectrum antibiotic will most likely be given soon."

"Thank you. Can she hear me?"

The nurse smiled reassuringly. "Yes, she isn't unconscious, just worn out. You can talk to her or just keep her company."

As the nurse left the room, Bailey reached for Jay's hand, so pale on the stark white sheets of the hospital gurney. She smoothed back the wisps of hair from Jay's face as she tried to will strength into her lover.

"Please fight this, Jay, please get better," she whispered. Bailey lost track of time, and she sat there holding Jay's hand and pleading with the Goddess for the medical staff to fix Jay.

The curtain parted, and an average sized man in his late twenties walked in wearing a lab coat and carrying Jay's chart. A nurse in scrubs was with him and proceeded to retake Jay's vital signs for him. The man introduced himself, with a slight Pakistani accent, as one of the attending physicians and asked Bailey if she wanted to remain as he examined Jay.

She nodded firmly. "I'm not leaving her."

He nodded and set the chart aside, washed his hands, and snapped on a pair of examination gloves. The doctor did a quick physical exam, listened to the nurse's report on vital signs, and read through the lab report that had just come back.

"Your relationship to the patient? I need to know before I can discuss my findings," the doctor asked.

"I'm her lover, we live together, and I'm her primary care giver," Bailey answered, her tone practically daring him to refuse her information. Instead he nodded and motioned to the chair next to the bed as he pulled up a stool and sat.

"Here's what I found. Jay has at least one infection going on, and her blood levels are seriously lower than the normal ranges. Her resistance to infection is almost zero, her red blood cells are excessively low as well, and she is severely dehydrated. You did the right thing by getting her in here."

Bailey swallowed hard, her gaze drifting to Jay. "You can fix this, right? You'll give her some medication and fluid, and she'll be okay, right?"

The doctor ran a hand over his face before responding. "I'm not going to lie to you, this is serious stuff. We're going to admit her to a special part of ICU where the room will have a type of air system that pushes out all the air and pumps in sterile air. It is an isolation room with positive pressure. There will also be precautions in place that must be followed. You and all visitors, including staff, will have to wear gloves, masks, and gowns."

Bailey noticed that as he spoke, the nurse had come back and put a surgical type mask on Jay.

"That is for her protection until we can get her upstairs. Her body is without any reserves to fight off infection, and her counts are so low that we have to rebuild them," the doctor explained. "I'm going to order some packed red blood cells and platelets to be infused into her as well as additional fluids. We've already started antibiotics, and we'll keep giving her more of those. Do you have questions?"

Bailey was too numb to ask anything else. She just thanked him and went back to hold Jay's hand. The nurse made her wash her hands and put on gloves before she would allow Bailey near Jay again. Bailey simply sat next to Jay, willing her to fight back and beat this latest challenge.

* * *

"There she is. I see her!" Riley pulled Sharon behind her as she sped through the halls of the hospital, looking for the ICU waiting room and Bailey. Laura and Steve were on the same elevator car and followed on Riley's heels. She rushed over to the smaller woman and enveloped her in a big hug.

"What's going on Bail? How is she?" Riley's eyes rested on her with compassion, recognizing that the smaller woman was terrified. Bailey filled them in on everything she knew, and then repeated it when her parents arrived.

"They won't let me in to see her yet. They needed to get all of her treatments started, and they made me wait out here for now. She did wake up a bit before we left the emergency room, but she was really out of it."

Laura took her daughter's lover into her arms for a hug, and then kissed her forehead. "Thank you, Bailey, you may have saved her life by getting her here so quickly."

Everyone sat and waited. Bailey found herself bookended by their mothers with Riley standing behind her keeping a hand on her shoulder to steady her. No one spoke until an ICU nurse came into the room. She asked Bailey if she was allowed to speak frankly in front of everyone waiting. Bailey assured her that it was fine. She introduced the nurse to everyone and explained that they were Jay's family and friends. When the nurse realized that Jay's parents were there, she looked confused about to whom she should address the information, and Jay's father caught the look immediately.

"I know we're technically next of kin, but Bailey has every right to make decisions and receive all information. We'll sign a form if we have to so that it is understood clearly."

The nurse thanked him and arranged for Jay's parents to sign a power of attorney form waiving confidentiality and allowing Bailey full rights in decisions and information. Bailey eyes began to tear up when she saw how Jay's family stuck up for them. The nurse filled them in on Jay's condition and the procedures in place for visitation.

"There can be no more than two at a time in the room, but I'll look the other way when it comes to Bailey. I won't count her as one of the two," explained the nurse.

"Thank you, I don't want to leave her alone." Bailey tried to keep the tremor out of her voice and was grateful for the support of her mother standing beside her.

"I feel that having a spouse in the room eases the patient's fear and enables the patient to heal faster. Plus, it keeps the spouse calmer," the nurse explained.

Everyone thanked her, and Jay's parents followed Bailey and the nurse to the area outside of Jay's room to get ready to go visit.

Everyone had to scrub at the sink, put on a disposable yellow gown, a surgical style mask, and gloves. Only then, could they go through the special door that kept the air from the hospital from entering Jay's room. Bailey went right over to Jay, grasping her hand and whispering to her lover that she was with her again.

"Jay, your mom and dad are here too. My folks are in the waiting room with Rye and Sharon. Come on, sweetie, wake up and show me those big brown eyes."

Jay moaned a little, and finally, her eyes fluttered open. Her eyes glittered with fever, and her skin was pale. A big bag of reddish fluid hung on one IV pole, and Bailey decided that it was the packed red blood cells the doctor had mentioned.

Laura and Steve leaned into view and spoke softly to Jay, letting her know they loved her, and that they were counting on her to fight this and get better. Jay's eyes darted around the room, slightly unfocused, and she didn't respond to anything they said. When Bailey removed her hand from Jay's, to allow Laura better access, Jay reached out and grabbed Bailey's hand back with her own.

A smile played across Laura's face. "Even now she knows better than to let you go again."

Bailey remained focused on Jay but nodded slowly. "I'm here baby, I'm here. I'm not going anywhere. Just rest and get better." Jay's eyes fluttered closed again, but her hand remained tightly wrapped around Bailey's.

* * *

The next day found Bailey still in her seat next to Jay. The nurses had let her stay in the room overnight. Jay's breathing was getting worse, and she didn't look any better. Yesterday, they had found two more infections after the infectious disease specialist had ordered cultures taken from several areas. Jay's neck wound was infected, her intestinal tract had an infection, and there was another one that they hadn't located.

Bailey used the call button to get a nurse in about Jay's breathing, and he decided to put her on oxygen. He monitored her oxygen levels, determined that the levels were coming up, and left the room again. Riley surprised Bailey by coming in a little later and taking up watch on the other side of the bed. They didn't really talk, they just sat and watched Jay as she struggled to breathe, and they both prayed for her to get better.

The room's telephone rang, causing both women to jump, before Bailey reached for it. Jay's mother was on the phone asking for an update. She told Bailey she'd be in soon and asked if she could bring anything for her. Bailey responded in the negative and rang off. Riley was aching for both of her friends, but she had no idea how to help. She went to Bailey and gave her a hug from behind, offering what support she could.

* * *

Sharon hung up the telephone at her desk and wanted to pull her hair out. Riley had just called with an update about Jay. She was on oxygen, and she hadn't woken up in a while. Riley sounded terrified, and if she was that afraid, Sharon could only imagine how Bailey must feel. With a groan she stretched and then stood behind her desk to stare out the window. Sharon decided that she could at least do something to help, even if she was stuck in her office for the day. She called her assistant in and explained what she wanted done. He took notes and promised to get it done right away. He left her office, and Sharon sat back down and started going through the loans, thankful that she had gotten the staff of Experienced Lenders up and running before all hell had broken loose. At least she had field help while Bailey and Jay went through this crisis.

* * *

A nurse stuck her head in Jay's room and asked Bailey and Riley to come with her for a moment. They were puzzled, but they followed her back to the ICU waiting room. Sharon's assistant was there with bags of food from a deli. He set them down on a small table and greeted Bailey with a sympathetic smile.

"How are you holding up?" he asked gently. She shrugged, still not sure why he was there. "Sharon asked me to make sure you two ate. I brought some stuff from the deli that you usually order from, and there's some drinks in that other bag." Bailey felt her eyes well up as she realized that Sharon had helped them again, and she was overwhelmed by both her, and her assistant's unexpected help.

"Thanks, John, and please thank her for me as well. That was kind and generous of you both."

He ducked his head and replied that it had been no bother at all and told her to call if she needed anything else. He made sure she had his cell number before he left.

Riley suggested they take advantage and eat before going back in the room. They tore into the food, and Bailey hadn't realized how hungry she was until she was eating. After they finished, Riley cleaned up so Bailey could get back to Jay. Riley sat another moment, grateful for Sharon's kindness, and decided to thank her in person later. She pushed herself out of the chair and started gathering the trash.

* * *

Laura and Steve came into Jay's room midday on Wednesday to find Jay looking worse and Bailey in tears. They gave her a hug and got an update. It had been a rough night for Jay. Her blood counts were still in the basement, and her breathing had gotten worse. In addition, her fever hadn't broken yet, and she was hardly ever awake. When Jay was awake, she was very unaware of the goings on around her, but she did seem to realize that Bailey was there with her. Bailey refused to leave at all. Laura tried to get her to go with her for some food, and Bailey finally gave in when Steve promised to sit with Jay until they returned.

As they sat in the cafeteria, Bailey picked at her salad listlessly, and Laura watched her with worry in her eyes.

"Bailey, you can't keep doing this to yourself. Jay is my daughter, and I love her more than my own life, but you can't destroy yourself. There is nothing to be gained by you getting sick now too. When is the last time you slept?" Laura pinned her with her gaze, and Bailey had no choice but to answer.

"I slept some last night and this morning. They brought that reclining chair in for me, so I was fine. I just can't leave her. What if she needs me, and I'm not there? She doesn't really know what's going on right now, but she knows me and seems comforted that I'm there for her."

Laura understood, but she didn't want the younger woman to destroy her own health. Bailey was like a second daughter to her, and the thought of them both being ill caused Laura physical pain. For now though, she decided to let it rest as long as Bailey made a promise.

"Promise me that you will remember to eat now and then and get some rest. Jay will need you healthy and strong for her when she is well enough to be awake more often. She will never forgive either of us if she wakes up and finds out that something happened to you."

"I promise, but I need to get back to her now, please."

The two women walked back to the ICU in silence.

That evening Jay awoke and sat up suddenly. She looked around in a panic and realized she was hooked up to all sorts of things, but she felt like she couldn't breathe.

Bailey went to her quickly, "What's wrong, baby? What can I do?"

She leaned over and hit the call bell rapidly as she tried to figure out what was wrong. Jay was breathing fast and shallow and her skin was clammy. Bailey realized that her lover was having more problems breathing. She raised the head of the bed so that it kept Jay almost fully upright, and grabbed the oxygen mask from the head of her bed. She put it on Jay and turned the knob until she heard the hiss of it flowing. Bailey hit the call bell again and kept a close eye on Jay. Within minutes of the mask going on, her color improved a bit, and she had calmed down.

Finally, a nurse arrived and asked impatiently what they needed. Bailey hadn't seen her before and wasn't impressed. She explained what had happened and asked that Jay's doctor be contacted.

"I'm not going to wake up the doctor when the patient appears to be stable."

Bailey fought hard to control her temper and not raise her voice. "She is on a mask now, one that I had to put on her because you didn't answer your call bell. How is that stable? If you don't get a doctor up here, I will, and trust me, you do not want to have me go find a doctor!"

"Fine, I will page someone, but I'm going to make sure to tell them you insisted that I wake up the on-call person."

She turned on her heel and marched out.

Bailey held Jay's hand again and asked God and Goddess for strength to see them both through this crisis. Within five minutes, a woman entered the ICU room. Bailey stood up but did not let go of Jay's hand.

"What happened? I was simply told that you insisted I be woken up. By the way, it is fine that you did. Even if there is nothing wrong, I would rather be safe than sorry."

Bailey told the resident about Jay sitting upright and gasping for air and her subsequent actions.

She quickly assessed Jay's breathing, mental status, and oxygen saturation before she spoke again. "You did the right thing, both as far as putting on her mask and calling for me. I'm going to order a portable chest x-ray. I think we found her missing infection. It looks like she has a small case of pneumonia brewing."

"How can she handle anything else? She looks so fragile and pale already."

"Like I said, you did the right things. Being upright is certainly helping, as is the oxygen. As soon as I get the results from the x-ray, I'll come back and brief you. Is there anything else I can do for now?"

"Yes," as Bailey glared at the nurse behind the doctor. "Can you see that this nurse is removed from caring for my partner? I'd like a different nurse please, this one refused to believe me that Jay needed help."

The doctor looked at the nurse. "Certainly, consider it done, and I will speak to her, as well as her supervisor, at once. Sloppy care is not something we tolerate here."

With that, the doctor and nurse left the room, and Bailey held Jay's hand as she sat near her. Her lover was sleeping a little more peacefully now, and her breathing seemed a lot better. She agreed to leave the room during the x-ray but returned right away. She decided against calling anyone, it was late, and she didn't want to worry their families since things were handled. Riley was coming in the morning and that would be soon enough to let people know about the pneumonia.

* * *

"Bail?" One word, croaked out from a dry mouth and throat, and it was the sweetest sound Bailey had ever heard.

She smiled down at Jay and whispered to her. "I'm here baby, I'm here. You've been pretty sick, sweetie, but you're getting better now."

She fed her a few ice chips to get Jay's mouth moistened and rang the bell to let the nurse know she was awake.

"What time is it?" asked Jay slowly.

"It's about four in the afternoon on Thursday."

Jay looked surprised, the last thing she knew it was the Saturday after her last radiation appointment. She didn't really remember much since then.

"What happened? Why don't I remember?"

Jay appeared more than a little anxious, so Bailey worked to soothe her quickly. She sat next to her on the edge of the bed and pulled her closer, letting one hand rub small circles in the small of her back.

"I had to call an ambulance on Sunday. You collapsed, and I couldn't get you to wake up. You were throwing up and having diarrhea, and we couldn't get it to stop. It turns out that you've had very low blood counts and three infections. They put in a lot of red blood cells, platelets, and fluid, plus a lot of antibiotics to get you feeling better."

Jay leaned into Bailey, still astonished that she didn't remember much of anything of the past several days. "Was Dad here? I think I remember him talking to me, but I don't know what he said. Rye was here too, right?"

Bailey nodded and gave Jay a gentle kiss on her cheek. "Your folks were here a lot, and your dad sat with you when your mom took me to get something to eat downstairs. Riley has been here a lot, and Sharon has been coming by when she gets off from work. She even sent over food a few times so that Riley and I could eat without leaving the floor."

Jay was getting tired again, and the nurse had come in so Bailey moved away and let the nurse check her. Once Jay dropped off again, Bailey started making phone calls to let everyone know that the worst was over. The fever had broken, the counts were coming up, and Jay was a lot more aware. Bailey wept softly when she hung up the phone. She was so damned grateful that Jay was coming back to her. She just kept staring at her lover in wonder. She had been so afraid for so long it seemed, and now she was coming back.

* * *

"I won't do it! I'm done! No more, no way, no how!"

Jay was not shouting, but she was getting loud, and very firm, as she announced that she was done with chemo treatments.

"Dude, you still have two more rounds. You can't quit now."

Riley was adamant about this point. She was at the condo hanging out with Jay while she rested, and Bailey went back to work. She had been in the hospital for ten days, and home for five more days. No one wanted to leave her alone yet since she was still weak, so Riley had offered to hang out during the days.

"I can stop treatment whenever I damn well please! I'm not letting them put more of that poison in me! They almost killed me! The cancer must have died by now, and I'm not letting them get near me again with that crap!"

- 217 -

Riley didn't want Jay getting too worked up so she decided to try a new approach. "Okay, dude, how about this? We do some research and figure it out. We talk to your docs and Bailey about whatever we find. If everyone can come to a consensus, I'll back you a hundred percent. If it looks like chemo is the best way to be sure, I will fight you to keep going."

Jay smiled since she knew she could win this one. Recently she had joined an online support group for people with Merkel Cell Carcinoma, or MCC as they referred to it online. It was a Google group run by, and for, survivors and their caregivers. People from all over the world used the group to trade information and treatments, trying to give everyone the support and options for the best chance of survival.

Jay logged on to her laptop and pulled up the group's website. Through the links page, she brought up a few research articles by a prominent researcher and care provider for MCC patients. He monitored this Google group and several of his patients were members who had nothing but praise for this man. His research seemed to indicate that surgery and intense radiation treatment to the localized site was the best chance of fighting a recurrence of this aggressive disease.

"Here, read these and tell me if you think they make sense." Jay pushed the laptop across the coffee table to Riley and leaned back while her friend read the reports.

Riley's eyebrows rose as she read, and Jay heard her click to another website to look something else up. Finally, after about an hour and a half, Riley leaned back and blew out a big breath.

"So, still think I have to do chemo?"

Riley didn't know what to think, but the points brought up did make some sense to her. The problem was there wasn't a lot of research since the cancer was so rare, and there was even less research dealing with someone of Jay's age.

"I don't know Jay. I just don't know what to think about it. All I know is that none of us wants to risk your life. What if this stuff is wrong? What if the chemo could prevent it from spreading and you don't finish the treatment?"

Jay acknowledged the legitimate fears her friend expressed. "Yeah, but what if it kills me? I can't go back, Rye, I'm afraid." Jay said that last part very softly as if it pained her to admit to her fear.

"Hey, it's okay, Jay," Riley moved to sit closer to her friend and hoped she could find some words to comfort her now. "We're all afraid, but you and Bailey have the most reason of all to be scared. I just want to make sure you do this for the right reasons. If you stop treatment, you have to be sure it's because you think it's the right move, not because you are afraid of getting sick from it again."

Jay knew she was right, but she also thought the research made some good points. "I'll print it out and take it to the cancer center with me next week and let them look it over. I also promise to listen to them and to Bailey. However, if I decide to stop treatment after that, will you support me?"

Riley gave her a hug and held her for an extra minute. "I'll always have your back, no matter what, Jay. You never have to ask again. I'm always going to be here and support you. I just want you to beat this thing, and I don't care how it happens."

Jay was grateful yet again for having found such a good friend in Riley. One thing she had learned was what a true friend Riley was, always there during the toughest times. She also took comfort knowing that if anything did happen to her, Rye would make sure Bailey was okay.

CHAPTER 19

SHARON LEFT HER office after one more glance around to make sure she hadn't forgotten anything. She needed to hurry though, she and Riley were having dinner soon, and she wanted to change before Riley came over. Things were going really well between them, and Sharon felt a lot less nervous about things now. In fact, she was starting to think it was time to move things along a bit. Up until this point, they hadn't done more than a little kissing and cuddling, and Sharon thought it was time that Riley stopped being quite so chivalrous. They spent a decent amount of time together, considering their schedules, but they had both been content to let things develop slowly, building trust and intimacy before leaping into bed.

Tonight, Riley was coming over for a quiet dinner, and Sharon had decided it would be a good time to talk about their relationship a little bit more. When she got home, she pulled out the chicken to warm up and went for a quick shower to rinse off her day before changing into jeans and a sweater.

When she got back into the kitchen, Sharon washed and dried the chicken breasts and seasoned them to roast with some vegetables for their dinner. She checked the bread machine that she had set before leaving for work that morning. The dough was ready, so she pulled it out to shape and rise before going to set the table. By the time the doorbell rang, the dinner was almost finished, the bread had just gone in the oven, and the wine was chilled and ready.

Sharon opened the door and grinned up at Riley. They were close in height, but Sharon still had to tilt her head to look into Riley's eyes. She pulled the younger woman inside and gave her a hug, sliding her hands under Riley's winter jacket before taking it from her with a quick kiss. She hung up the jacket as

Riley removed her boots, so she wouldn't track wintry sludge into Sharon's home.

"Something smells amazing. Please tell me that's our dinner." Riley realized she was hungry, and the wonderful smells of freshly baking bread and roasted chicken were overwhelming her senses.

"Yes, dear, dinner is almost ready," joked Sharon as she led them into the eat-in kitchen. Sharon poured them both a glass of wine and brought one over to Riley before joining her in the alcove that was outfitted with a small love seat and had been turned into a little reading nook.

Riley felt her heart jump a little when Sharon called her "dear," even though it she knew Sharon had said it jokingly. She was finding herself rather invested in this relationship. Riley was a little nervous about that since neither of them had dated anyone seriously in several years. But she had pushed aside her fear when she recognized that they both wanted to go slowly. When Sharon settled in next to her, Riley put an arm around her. As Sharon snuggled in to her body a little, Riley couldn't help but think about how right it felt to hold Sharon and listen to her talk about her day.

When Riley interrupted to ask a question, Sharon smiled as she realized that Riley was not only listening but was interested in hearing her out.

Sharon checked on dinner and announced that it would be ready in about ten minutes. She pulled the chicken out to rest, tenting it in foil to keep it warm, and set it on top of the stove. Rejoining Riley, she asked how Jay was doing, and what the results of today's visit to the cancer center were. This had been the visit that Jay was going to talk to everyone about her chemo treatments.

Riley ran a hand through her hair and took another sip of her wine. "She really doesn't want to do any more chemo, but Dr. Goldman wasn't all that impressed with the study she showed him. There isn't any evidence that doing the chemo hurts her chances, but there is no evidence that it helps either. He wants to be aggressive and play it safe by covering all their bases, and she just doesn't want to be sick anymore. The whole mess just sucks."

Sharon could see that Rye was hurting for her friend and didn't know what to do, so she just leaned against her and gave her a hug. "You're doing everything you can, you know." Sharon looked in her eyes. "You've been amazing, but you have to let her decide. She's the only one who has to go through it. She and Bailey will figure it out and do what they think is best, honey."

Riley looked a little surprised, and then she smiled. "Hey, that's the first time you called me that."

Sharon looked a little flustered. "I'm sorry, it just slipped out. Is it all right?" she asked a little shyly.

"It's perfect," Riley said kissing the tip of her nose.

Just then, the timer went off, and Sharon jumped up to save the bread. They let their conversation drop and got dinner on the table together. They sat down to eat and switched to casual topics during dinner.

When they finished and cleared the table, they took their wine glasses into the living room. Sharon turned on her gas fireplace and put on a relaxing mix of Celtic music. They snuggled together on the couch, and Sharon turned to Riley, ready to speak her mind about their relationship. Riley turned to her and started to say something, just as Sharon started to speak. They laughed and both indicated the other should go before Sharon got frustrated and took charge.

"I'm going to start. We've been seeing each other for a little while now, and I thought we should talk about it. I just want to make sure we're on the same page."

Riley felt a knot of fear form in her stomach. She thought about it and was confused, because hadn't Sharon just called her "honey?" *Was she about to end things because she was growing attached?* That didn't jibe with the woman she was getting to know, so she took a deep breath, and tried to listen carefully.

"I'm really glad we met, Rye. I've been attracted to you since that day in the hospital. Watching you with Jay and Bailey has just made you all the more attractive. You've become such a good friend to me and so much more." Sharon paused, then took another sip of wine before setting her glass down. "I want to take things to the next level, I want us to be exclusive, and I want us to become a little more..."

At that, she stalled out, but Riley was smiling from ear to ear. "Sharon, I want that too. I haven't been seeing anyone else, and I want us to go forward. I think we have something pretty amazing going, and I'd like to see where it leads."

Riley leaned forward and kissed Sharon's mouth gently at first, then growing in boldness. She slipped her tongue inside Sharon's mouth and found that Sharon's tongue was ready and waiting for her. They deepened their kiss, and Riley felt Sharon's hands moving restlessly over her shirt.

Riley slid down further on the couch, bringing Sharon's legs up to join her, and stretching out partially on top of her. Sharon moaned deep in her throat, and her hips started moving against Riley as they continued to kiss. Riley slipped one hand under Sharon's sweater and gasped at the warmth of her bare skin. She let her hand drift upwards until she brushed against the satin of Sharon's bra and gently cupped her breast.

Sharon pulled away enough to look at Riley's face. Riley looked back. "Is this too soon? Too fast?"

Sharon shook her head but bit her lip. "I'm sorry. I want this, but I'm worried."

"Worried? Why?"

Sharon bent her head down and blushed. "I'm just not as young as you or the women you met on the golf tour. I'm worried about if you'll think I'm sexy enough."

Riley's first thought was to laugh because she had been twisted up in knots with wanting Sharon from the first time they met. *She has no idea just how desirable she is.* Riley stifled the urge to laugh and decided to just be honest. "You are partially right. You are about six years older than me. You are also right that I slept with some younger women on the tour. But Sharon, I have never, ever, wanted a woman the way I want you right now. You are so sexy that I think my heart might beat out of my chest if I don't get to touch you soon."

Sharon saw nothing but the truth, love, and desire shining in Riley's eyes. She pulled Riley back down to her mouth, stopping after a searing kiss to thank her. "That was what I needed to hear. I'm sorry, I'm just a bit insecure. I know you want this too. I know it isn't just a game. Please, don't stop."

Riley started kissing a line down Sharon's neck to her cleavage. She spread kisses as far as she could reach without removing Sharon's clothes.

Sharon arched up into her then, pulling her lips away from Riley she gasped. "Take it off, please take it off."

Riley groaned and lifted up enough to slide Sharon's sweater over her head and unclasp her bra before sliding that off as well. Riley quickly pulled off her own sweater and bra before settling back down on Sharon with one jean clad thigh between Sharon's legs.

They started exploring each other's skin, gasping when their hard nipples rubbed against each other for the first time. Sharon urged Riley on as she kissed her way down Sharon's neck and to her breasts. Taking one firm nipple in her mouth, she licked and sucked gently, as Sharon arched into her moaning her name. Sharon ran her hands up and down Riley's back and then grabbed her ass, pulling her more tightly against her as they moved together. Riley could hardly believe this was happening, and she was so turned on that she worried she wouldn't be able to hold out for long. She paused for a second to calm her libido a bit, but Sharon had other ideas.

"Oh God, don't stop, please don't stop. I want to feel all of you against me, please Riley."

With a growl, Riley moved to the other breast, feasting on it as she moved her hand down to cup the warmth between Sharon's thighs. She reached to undo the jeans that barred her way, but Sharon gasped when she felt the hand move away from her. Riley returned to cup her and squeezed gently. Sharon's hips bucked and drove harder as her breathing became more erratic.

"Oh God, Riley, don't stop, you're going to make me come," she cried out.

Riley redoubled her efforts, moving into her more forcefully, and paying attention to both breasts. She knew there was no way she had time to get into Sharon's jeans this first time, but she knew there would be plenty of more chances that night. Suddenly, Sharon stiffened and groaned as she came in Riley's arms. Riley slowed, easing the pressure as she felt the shock waves slow down.

Sharon smiled into the eyes of her lover. "I can't believe I came that fast. I'd say I'm sorry, but I don't want to lie."

Riley grinned. "It is totally fine with me, there's plenty more where that came from. I didn't even get to the really good stuff yet." Riley stood, offered her hand to Sharon, and helped her up. "Let's go get more comfortable. I know you have to have a bed around here some place."

Sharon laughed and pulled her along, up the stairs and into her bedroom. She stood Riley before her bed and lowered her gaze to the top of Riley's jeans. She bit her lip and slowly worked the buttons to open Riley's fly. Sharon started pushing the material down, taking Riley's panties with it. Riley helped her, stepping out of her jeans and turning back to Sharon. Sharon quickly stripped off her remaining clothes, and the two women fell into each other's arms and onto the large bed. Riley was amazed at the passionate woman in her arms. She knew Sharon had many different sides, but this was one she had kept hidden quite well, until now. They kissed deeply before Sharon made her way down Riley's body with her mouth following her hands.

When she reached the triangle of hair between Riley's legs, she paused. "Is this all right? I really want to taste you, please?"

Riley moaned and nodded, throwing her head back as Sharon lightly kissed her way down and found her clit with her tongue. Sharon licked her way through the wet, swollen folds before going back to her clit while she slid first one, then two fingers into Riley. Sharon moaned softly as she felt her fingers slide into the moist heat, and she started to move in time with Riley's thrusting hips. She felt herself growing wet and hard as she made love to Riley, but pushed it aside as she reveled in the joy of her lover. She felt the muscles tighten around her fingers and started sucking on Riley's clit harder and moving her fingers faster. Riley let out a groan and came hard, shaking and shuddering for a full minute before the tremors eased. Sharon slipped out of her and slid up the bed to embrace Riley.

"Was it worth the wait?" she asked.

Riley started laughing before she could respond. "Well worth it. Want me to prove it again?"

"Umm hmm," grinned Sharon as they continued their explorations for the majority of the night.

* * *

Jay glanced up from her laptop when Riley came in the room. "Hey, buddy, when did you get here?" she asked.

"A few minutes ago I guess. I heard you working in here, so I made us some tea," she said passing over a mug to Jay.

"Thanks," she took an appreciative sip before setting it on the coaster. "Are you feeling okay? You look a little tired today. I'm fine if you need to head out and grab some sleep, or you could crash here in the guest room."

"Nah, I'm fine, but I'm glad to see you feeling so much better. You're not over doing it, are you? No one expects you to do much work right now."

Jay shook her head and reached for her tea again. "I'm mostly just catching up on e-mail and such. I'm taking it slow, I promise." She looked up at her friend and decided to come clean. "I'm just trying to get some stuff done while I have the benefit of feeling better before I go back for chemo in a week."

Riley looked at her in shocked surprise. "I thought you were dead set against it? What happened?"

Jay filled her in on the discussion she had with some of the members of her support group, and her radiation doctor. A few people had pointed out that even if she was prepared to live or die by her choices, they asked her one good question time and time again.

"The question most people asked me was how would I feel if I have a recurrence and didn't finish my chemotherapy treatment?"

"And?"

"The truth is I think I'd be fine, but I thought about how Bailey would feel if I didn't do it. The guilt of making Bailey wonder if chemo could have saved me is too much to live with. I never want her, or anyone I love to question the choice. If I have a recurrence I don't want any of you wondering if you could have saved me by forcing me into chemo."

"So, you're doing it for us? For Bailey and the rest of us?" Riley couldn't believe what she was hearing. She had been certain that Jay was going to stop treatment.

"Yeah. Basically, you all mean too much to me to let you have that kind of guilt if I don't win in the end. Plus, the doc agreed to change chemo drugs to a slightly less caustic drug, added in a shot for red blood cell production, and another for white blood cell production."

"Why didn't they do those shots before now?" Riley wondered if that was why Jay had gotten so sick.

"Based on my age and health after the first round they decided to hold off. But, he also assured me that my condition was more a result of the combined effects of the radiation and the chemo together. Since I'm done with radiation, I'll be in better shape to withstand the chemo. The new regimen should mean less nausea, though much more fatigue. I decided I could use more sleep anyway, so that isn't as big a deal as getting sick and being nauseated all the time."

Riley was glad to hear that she had decided to go forward with treatment. As much as she was willing to support any choice Jay made, this one was what she felt most comfortable with for the long term.

"So, Rye, tell me, why are you looking so tired anyway? Are you sure you feel okay?"

Riley blushed, something Jay didn't think was possible, and it let her know something was seriously going on.

"C'mon, spill it, dude, I wanna know, and you can't deny a sick woman her wishes." Jay grinned knowing that playing on her illness was a totally dirty trick. She suspected the reason for Riley's exhaustion from the blush, and she wanted to find out if she was right.

"I just didn't get much sleep last night is all. No big deal really."

"Uh huh, and I'm not bald either," retorted Jay. Most of her hair had fallen out, and Bailey had shaved what little remained when Jay told her it actually hurt to lay her head on the dying hair that hadn't fallen out yet. Jay wore a headscarf or knit cap when she went outside to keep warm.

Finally, Riley admitted that she had spent the night with Sharon, and Jay hooted.

"I knew it! I knew it! You've totally fallen for her, haven't you? Admit it!"

Riley gave her a bashful look. "Yeah, I really have, I guess. She's so different from other women I've dated. She's not what I would have considered my type, but I can't stop thinking about her. We just mesh so well that it scares me a little. Last night just kind of happened when we started talking about how things were going, and where we thought we might be headed."

Jay chuckled. "So, you were headed to bed?" She smirked as her friend blushed even more then let her off the hook. "Rye, I'm happy for you. You deserve to be happy and so does she. Sharon's come a long way in a short time, and I think you had something to do with that change. You're both good people, and I hope you're happy together."

Riley ducked her head and grinned and then decided it was time to change topics. She started talking about some changes at the club as far as staffing, and some renovations planned for the course next season. Soon, Jay was sleepy and went off to take a nap, and Riley stretched out on the couch to do the same.

* * *

The next couple of months went by in kind of a blur for Jay and Bailey. Jay had two more rounds of chemotherapy with almost four weeks between sessions to give her counts a better chance to recover. Bailey was busy at work, and at home, taking care of things for Jay. Mostly Jay slept a lot. The doctors had been serious when they warned of a lot of fatigue, but she still thought it better than being sick all the time. Her mouth had mostly healed, and she could eat relatively normal foods as long as they were bland and easy to digest. Her mouth was still sensitive from the burns, but her neck was healing. It looked much better than it had during her time in the ICU. All in all life had settled down, at least a little bit, for them.

The last days of Jay's treatment were literally a blank for her. She knew that Riley had been the one to take her to and from, and hang out with her, but she honestly didn't remember going to treatment, or anything else from that Thursday and Friday. It was not a big loss to her way of thinking, not remembering treatment didn't seem that bad of a deal.

Bailey was still worried about her and kept a close watch to make sure Jay didn't over do things and ate a healthy diet. Bailey had switched over most of their food to organic products and had looked for cancer fighting foods to incorporate into their diet. Riley found a book, of course, and brought it over, along with a quart of pomegranate juice since that was supposed to contain immune system boosting agents.

Sharon and Riley had gotten more comfortable as a couple and were hanging out with Jay and Bailey about once a week or so to help out and keep them both company. Riley had even donated her hair to Locks of Love, the organization that makes human hair wigs for cancer patients. Now she really looked like a lesbian golfer, she joked, with that short golf pro haircut. Jay was touched that her friend had done that, especially since Jay really missed her own hair. It had never been a source of much vanity, but she found that her head was cold most of the time. She had taken to wearing bandanas around the condo to stay warm. She even slept with something on her head, or she woke up freezing during the night.

Bailey spent most of her time at home watching Jay sleep. She was so happy that the treatments were over but terrified that they hadn't worked. She was less afraid though since she had joined Jay's online group and talked to other caregivers. Everyone seemed to say the same thing. Having a great support network was a key to survival for all concerned. It was all about finding strength in numbers and knowing there were others going through the same struggle – that you weren't alone.

CHAPTER 20

*A*BOUT THREE WEEKS after Jay's last treatment, she was able to start slowly doing more work from home. She had been keeping up with e-mail, other than the week right after treatments when all she did was sleep. She picked up some of the load from Bailey and Sharon, and she hoped to get back to her full duties soon. But she understood that she needed more time to heal and rest before she could tackle things like a full day in the office. Things were starting to look up after close to eight months of surgeries, treatments, hospitalizations, and illness.

According to the LiveStrong website, all cancer survivors become survivors the moment they are diagnosed. Jay was really only starting to understand that concept. She realized finally that the whole time she had been going through this battle for her life; she was showing the skills of surviving against the odds.

Jay finished her musings when she heard the door slam, announcing Bailey's arrival home and the start of a three-day weekend. They had decided to go away just to get away from all things cancer related. Their bags were packed and ready. All they needed was Bailey to get changed, and they could hit the road. They planned to take advantage of the early spring that seemed to be happening and head to the Pocono Mountains. Jay's family had a cabin up there, and they were going to spend the weekend enjoying the solitude and relaxing.

"Hey, baby, are you ready to head out soon?" Bailey asked as she joined Jay in the living room.

"You bet! I'm ready to blow this place anytime you are! Of course, I'm curing cabin fever by actually going to a cabin, but what the hell, let's get on the road!"

Bailey took a playful swat at Jay as she went past on her way to the bedroom to change clothes for the drive. Jay grabbed her jacket and felt in the inner pocket again to make sure that Bailey's present was still there. She had gone out with Riley the week before to make the purchase, and it had been burning a hole in her pocket ever since.

Bailey came out of their room with their bag and grabbed Jay for a kiss. "Let's get this show on the road, woman! I can't wait to see trees, grass, and mountains!"

* * *

The drive up was uneventful, and Jay even took a turn at the wheel for a while to give Bailey a break. Close to four hours later, they reached the cabin and unloaded the groceries they had stopped for in the last little town. Bailey brought in their bag, and Jay brought in some firewood for the huge stone fireplace in the great room. It was a two-story log cabin, built by one of those companies that builds it off site, takes it apart, and rebuilds it where the owner wants it. There was a great front porch, and a back deck that looked out on a small lake about half a mile away. The cabin had open space, lots of exposed beams, and huge glass windows. It felt like you were still in the middle of the outdoors while warm and snug inside.

Jay got the fire going while Bailey pulled together a light snack for them. They had stopped for dinner just before they got their groceries. However, that was a while ago, and Jay's appetite had changed to more of a grazing pattern, many smaller meals throughout the day, rather than two or three larger meals.

After settling in, they relaxed on the couch in front of the fire and listened to soft music as they talked. Finally, after letting the fire burn down, Jay banked it, and they headed up to their bedroom. They decided to take a quick shower to wash off the grime of the road before going to bed. Jay still felt self-conscious about her scars, so she waited for Bailey to finish before heading in for her own shower. She knew logically that Bailey had seen her scars. Hell, she had treated her scars!

However, between the scars and other damage from the surgery, pain and tingling from damaged nerves and muscles, and her hair loss, Jay felt less than attractive. She was also so tired that while the idea of sex with her lover was enticing, she was worn out at the very thought of using that much energy. She found it easier to avoid situations where she might get carried away and then disappoint Bailey.

* * *

The sun was up and so was Bailey. She knew something was going on with Jay, but she wasn't sure what it was yet. She was still acting a bit off, not sharing showers anymore, not wanting to cuddle as much, and she was certainly not interested in much physical activity. Bailey understood her lover must have issues with her changed body image and with her energy levels, but she missed that feeling of closeness that they had shared. It wasn't about the sex, though she missed that as well, it was the lack of any real physical intimacy.

Bailey was afraid of causing Jay pain in her injured side, while Jay seemed afraid of something that Bailey couldn't name yet. She certainly planned to find out about it this weekend. She went outside and turned on the hot tub that was on the back deck, checked the chemical levels, and adjusted them. There was a property manager who kept up with things for the vacation homes in the area. He had gotten the place ready when they had called to let him know they would be using the cabin this weekend.

Bailey sneaked upstairs quietly and slid back into bed next to Jay. She rested her head lightly on the other woman's stomach, and started drawing random designs on her skin with one hand.

Slowly, Jay stirred and gazed down at her. "Having fun?" she asked.

Bailey shifted up the bed so she was lying on her side facing Jay. "As a matter of fact, I was thinking of ways we could have fun. For example, remember the hot tub? I just made sure it's working, and as we speak it's warming up and ready to relax us."

Jay grinned at her lover. "Give me ten minutes, and I'll be there."

"I'll give you twelve if you forget your bathing suit," returned Bailey with a devilish grin.

Jay chuckled. "We'll see, you evil woman! Now get out of here and let me get up and get ready."

Bailey agreed to meet her on the deck, saying that she would take care of breakfast while Jay got herself together.

Jay stared at her reflection in the bathroom mirror, trying to figure out why Bailey would still be attracted to her. She just didn't see a reason. All Jay saw was the scars running up and down her neck, staple marks that looked like railroad tracks, the smaller scar from the port, which had just been removed the week before, and the scars from her drains.

Jay grimaced as she continued to look at her reflection. *My neck is lopsided from the muscles they had to remove. The scars are red and hideous. And of course, who was the fool who said that bald is beautiful?* With a sigh, she readied herself to go outside, slathering on water resistant sunblock, even though the hot tub was in a shaded area. She had been warned about sun damage on her already damaged and sensitive skin, so she invested in a large amount of sunblock and used it daily, even for car trips or hanging out by the windows during the day.

She pulled on a long T-shirt to walk through the house in. Isolated or not, she just didn't feel comfortable traipsing around naked. When she went out on the rear deck, she found the small table had been set up with chunks of fruit, fresh orange juice, and croissants. She also found her beautiful Bailey, luxuriating in the warmth and bubbles of the hot tub with her eyes closed. Her heart clenched at the sight, and she felt a stirring of desire for her lover. She was surprised but also afraid of starting something she wouldn't be able to finish, so she pushed the desire aside for now. She slid the shirt off and slipped into the water to rest adjacent to Bailey in the water.

Bailey opened her eyes when she heard the door open but quickly shut them again. She was afraid of scaring Jay off. She leaned back and remembered her talk from the previous day with Riley.

"I don't know what else to do Riley! She keeps pushing me away!"

"Bail, you know she loves you, right? I think she just isn't really secure right now."

Exasperated, Bailey threw her hands in the air and started pacing. "What? Not secure? I moved states, took a lot of risk to come back and ask for another chance. I stood by her and watched her almost die! What more can I do to prove that I love her?"

Rye just sat and watched her friend pace. "Listen, I think you two need to sit and talk some things out. I don't think she doubts your love, just her worthiness of you and that love. I think she's also afraid to be happy."

Bailey turned a puzzled look on Riley and stood still for a moment. "What do you mean?"

"Think about it, Bail. She had been surviving until you came back into her life. Everything started to come together in her life, and then she was diagnosed. Now she has physical and emotional scars that need to heal. Maybe she's afraid that if she is too happy, the cancer will come back. I read about it in one of those cancer books I bought. Sometimes the survivor is afraid to trust in their health returning."

With a sigh, Bailey flopped back down onto Riley's couch. "What do you think? She tells you stuff, right? What is it that she needs from me? I just want my life with Jay back."

Riley paused and then made a suggestion. "Just be patient, Bail. Try to show her that you're aware of the changes, but that you aren't afraid of them. She'll come around. I know she will. She misses things too."

Bailey stood again and pulled Riley up from her seat. "Thanks, Rye. I'm sorry to dump on you, but I appreciate your friendship more than you know."

Riley chuckled. "Trust me on this one. Don't push. She's on her way back to you... it might take a little while, but you will get her back fully."

Bailey knew that Jay had gotten sensitive about her looks and couldn't seem to understand that she found her every bit as beautiful now as she had before the cancer. Even more so in fact because the scars were badges of honor and courage in her eyes. They showed her that Jay loved her enough to fight for her life, even when giving up was so much easier. She felt Jay enter the tub and kept her eyes closed until Jay was settled in the water. She opened her eyes lazily and looked over to find Jay watching her.

For a moment, she could have sworn she saw a hint of desire. Feeling encouraged, Bailey moved a little to be closer to Jay on the bench. Jay moved so that her right arm could drape around Bailey and hold her close while they relaxed into the water.

"That feels so good on my bad shoulder," Jay said, as she let the water work its magic. "Maybe we should get a whirlpool tub for the condo. Or, maybe we should move out of the city and buy a house. Perhaps up in Chestnut Hill or Mt. Airy," she suggested. As she said it, she watched Bailey for a reaction about buying a house together. Bailey looked at her, her green eyes bright with excitement.

"Really? You would be willing to leave the condo? We could get a real house with a yard, and a basement and stuff? Could we get a dog too? I love dogs!"

Jay laughed at Bailey's burst of enthusiasm. "So, I guess that's a yes? Let's give a call to a realtor when we get home and see what we can find. If we don't find anything we like in Chestnut Hill or Mt. Airy, we can always look at Media, it's close enough to work, and either area has a good lesbian population and a Trader Joes."

"Well, as long as we have a Trader Joes," Bailey joked but looked at Jay with adoration. "I can't believe it, Jay, I've wanted to own a house for so long, but it never seemed like a good time. Then when you got sick, I didn't let myself think past each day. I think we should do it! And I really do want a dog. What do you think of the name Bob?"

Jay laughed again, starting to feel her fears lessen. "I take it we're getting a male dog?"

"I don't care if it's a male or female. I just like the name Bob."

Jay shook her head but grinned at her lover and agreed to let her name the dog whatever she wanted, as long as she also cleaned up Bob's accidents while he or she was getting house trained.

As Jay leaned back and relaxed, Bailey decided it was time to reassure Jay about her desire for her. She started trailing her hand up and down Jay's stomach and side as she leaned against her lover; enjoying the feeling of the muscles as they shifted and tightened in response to her touch. She leaned down and captured a nipple in her mouth, licking it to attention, and swirling her tongue around it as she sucked gently. Jay started to protest, and Bailey shushed her.

"Jay, I know your body is different now, and I know you don't have as much energy. I get it, but I miss you so much. Just lie there and let me make you feel good. Please, just let me love you."

Jay hid her face as she started to turn red, and her eyes welled up with tears. "How can you want me when I'm so scarred? I'm not the woman I was when you fell in love with me!"

Bailey straddled Jay's hips and pulled her chin around with one hand, so they were looking into each other's eyes, green into brown.

"Jay, the woman I fell in love with has been through a fierce battle and come out with scars that show her courage and faith. These scars are a part of you and that's fine with me. It is a constant reminder of all you went through to give us a chance at a long life together." She leaned forward and gently kissed Jay's lips.

"Baby, I love the person you are inside and outside. But, as long as the inner you is there, the outside doesn't matter. Would you love me less if I were scarred in a car accident?"

Jay shook her head, slowly understanding that Bailey meant it, she still considered her sexually attractive.

"Does that mean you accept that I still find you unbelievably hot and desirable?" asked Bailey.

Jay chuckled. "I get your point, and I'll try to feel less self-conscious about my scars around you. Be prepared to remind me now and then."

"Let me remind you right now," murmured Bailey as she leaned in for a kiss.

Jay leaned back, and she let herself believe in the strength of their love for one another. She felt Bailey's mouth as she kissed and licked her way over her body and felt her body responding. She gave herself over to the feelings Bailey was stirring up and reached out for Bailey. As Bailey rode her thigh, she entered Jay with two fingers and used her thumb to stimulate her clit. Jay positioned her fingers at Bailey's entrance so that as she moved against her thigh, she would move along Jay's fingers. Their mouths met in a frantic kiss before Bailey threw her head back and screamed Jay's name. With the evidence of Bailey's passion, Jay fell over the edge, holding Bailey tightly against her as she shook and trembled.

Eventually, they had to leave the hot tub or risk turning into soup, but they had already decided to use it again later. They wrapped themselves in the big bath sheets that Bailey had set out earlier and sat to enjoy their light breakfast. They traded looks and started laughing.

"What if any of the other cabins had people in them? Do you think they heard us?" Bailey wondered.

Jay chuckled and pointed out that if they were occupied, and they had been overheard, then the other couples either got some good ideas of how to spend their morning or got jealous of the lucky woman screaming in ecstasy.

After lazing around a bit, they headed upstairs to get dressed and go for a drive down to the lake. Normally, Jay would have hiked the meager mile or so, but between getting there, walking around or hanging out, and then hiking back, it would have been too much exertion for her. They drove down to the dock and left the car in the parking area while they walked along the water's edge, holding hands and talking softly about their plans for a house.

Feeling emboldened by their lovemaking, Jay decided to test the waters a bit further and see how far she could take things in one day. "Um, Bail, if we're going to buy a house together, maybe we should see a lawyer about some paperwork. You know like wills, living wills, that kind of thing. I was thinking that it would have helped you when I was sick if you had my power of attorney, but we didn't think to do that in advance. Maybe we should get all that stuff done. What do you think?"

Bailey felt her heart thumping in her chest. Part of her was thrilled with the idea of legal documents binding them together, and part of her was terrified because she thought that Jay might be doing it to protect her in case the cancer came back. Bailey didn't want to think about that happening so she hesitated.

Jay read her response incorrectly and started to recant the idea as just a silly thought until Bailey stopped her. She took Jay's hand and led her to an outcropping of rocks not far from the water and pulled her down to sit.

Looking her right in the eyes, Bailey took Jay's hands in her own. "Honey, please don't think I'm not interested in doing the paperwork to legalize our lives. I was just afraid that you were doing it because of the cancer. Like you might have been trying to protect me just in case, and I got scared. It has absolutely nothing to do with how I feel about you or us. I would be happy to see a lawyer and do the whole thing. Wills, living wills, power of attorney, partnership agreements, whatever we need."

Jay took a tremulous breath and let it out slowly. "Are you sure, baby? I don't want to rush you. I know we haven't been together that long officially, but – "

Bailey interrupted her with her emerald eyes flashing. "Jay Conway, we've known each other most of our lives! How are we rushing anything? If I hadn't been so stupid, we'd be married and in a house already, celebrating our fourteenth anniversary or something." Suddenly, she stopped, realizing what she had said in her moment of ire.

Jay on the other hand, took the chance. Jay looked at Bailey for a moment with love pouring from her eyes. She motioned for Bailey to stay where she was but pulled her hands away for a moment to reach in her pocket for something. She knelt by the rocks and took Bailey's left hand in her right one. Bailey looked shocked, but didn't say or do anything, afraid to break the moment, and afraid she might be wrong.

Jay looked up at her and with a slight tremor in her voice, she started speaking. "Bailey, you're right. We've known each other a very long time, and if things had gone differently, we might have been all the things you just said. The truth is we both had some growing up to do before we were ready for the intensity of our feelings. I've always known you were the woman I should be with, but I wasn't ready to be the woman you needed. I am now. I'm ready to live my life with you, and beside you, for the rest of our time here."

She opened the box that had been concealed in her left hand. "I know we have a lot of challenges to overcome, but if the past year has taught me anything, it is that we can handle whatever comes our way by sticking together. Bailey, will you marry me? Please?" Jay's voice shook as she asked the all-important question.

Bailey's eyes welled up with tears, and she was overwhelmed with emotions as she realized what Jay had said and asked. She knelt down next to Jay and kissed her gently on her lips. "I would like nothing more than to marry you, my love. You have no idea how long I've been hoping to hear that from you."

They flung themselves into each other's arms and embraced tightly before Jay pulled back and took the ring from its box. She slipped it on Bailey's left hand ring finger, and they both looked down at it. Only then did Bailey register the design of the ring on her hand. It was an Irish Claddagh ring, but it was different from many she had seen. It was made of platinum with a small green stone held by the traditional hands. The band had a design of Celtic knot work that connected one hand to the other. She looked up at Jay with a question in her eyes.

"I got it because the emerald reminded me of your eyes," she said softly. "As soon as I saw it, I knew it was the perfect ring for you." Bailey was overcome with emotion and kissed Jay with all of her passion and love. Jay returned her kiss with fervor until she realized they were in a rather public place.

"What do you say we take this back to the cabin?" suggested Jay, with a twinkle in her eyes. Suddenly, she wasn't too worried about being bald or scarred. All that mattered was being with the woman she had loved since she was much younger and still naïve about the world.

EPILOGUE

16 months later

SHE SAW A FEW clouds in the sky and instantly worried. *A perfectly sunny day was too much to hope for,* thought Jay, as she glanced out the window of the second bedroom. The home that she and Bailey had found in Chestnut Hill last year was perfect for them. It allowed a couple of guest rooms and space for them to have a workout room, a shared office, and good amount of storage. The second bedroom had become Jay's dressing area for the events of the day.

Riley sat on the edge of the queen size bed as she bent over to tie her shoes. Looking up at Jay, she grinned and asked a question she already knew the answer to a long time ago. "So, you sure we should just be friends? Maybe we didn't give ourselves enough of a chance? What do you say we ditch this shindig and go on a date?"

Jay started laughing before Riley could even finish her question. Wiping her eyes, Jay leaned over and gave Riley a big hug. "Thanks, Rye, I can always count on you for support and laughter! I don't know if I would be holding it together if it weren't for you."

It was Riley's turn to laugh. "Jay, you held it together for a long time before I met you. I suspect you would do just fine without me. Rest assured though, I'm not going anywhere. Remember, as long as you cook, I'll be around to eat." She smirked at Jay, knowing there was little the other woman liked as much as an appreciative audience for her cooking.

There was a knock at the door, and Laura stuck her head inside. "Jay, are you ready? It's almost time for things to get underway."

Jay smiled at her mother and nodded her head. "I'm ready, Mom. Let's get this thing started!"

Laura chuckled at Jay's enthusiasm. "I'll go down and let everyone know to get seated. Get ready to join us and start the next phase of your life, honey. I just want you to know how proud I am of you! I love you, and I wish you nothing but a long life of health and happiness."

"Thanks, Mom, I know, and I love you too! Now, I'm keeping someone very important waiting, so let's get going."

After Laura left the room, Jay looked at Riley as she let out a long, slow breath of air. "Let's go, man, I'm ready for this show to end and the rest of my life to start."

Riley clapped her hand on Jay's right shoulder and nodded. They walked out into the hallway, headed down the stairs, and out the back door into the spacious back yard. The guests were settling in the chairs rented for the occasion inside the large white tent. Jay had insisted on the tent to prevent rain from ruining this special day. Cautious as always, but it also served to keep the sun from shining directly upon her and the guests.

Then the back door opened, and Bailey came out of the house, looking radiant and lovely as always. She joined Jay in the open space inside the tent, clasping her hand as she did so. The Wiccan priestess that Bailey had studied with was there, waiting at the small table serving as an altar for the event. Jay, Bailey, and Riley stood quietly as the door opened again, and Scott, Jay's longtime personal assistant came out with Sharon. Scott was carrying a small bundle in his arms as he and Sharon joined the women under the tent.

The Priestess spoke, her voice ringing out, loud and clear in the calm spring day. "Ladies and gentlemen, we are gathered here today for a truly blessed event. The creation of a family. Just over a year ago, we rejoiced in the joining of Bailey and Jay in matrimony. Today, we bring into this family a new member of this strong household."

She held her arms out and accepted the small bundle from Scott. "This is Brigid Regina Conway-McIntyre. Her name comes from the Celtic High Goddess Bríghid and the Celtic word for Queenly. I think that growing up surrounded by such strength and love, she is destined to live up to her name. Who stands for her as God and Goddess parents?"

Riley and Sharon clasped hands and stepped forward, as did Scott. Each in turn took the baby in their arms and promised to help her grow to be a strong, healthy, well-cared for adult. The Priestess took the baby back and handed her to her tearful parents.

"Remember, children are a gift whose future is determined by how well you do your job as parents. Love her and each other well, be firm, but show compassion. Be her example and let her make mistakes. May the God and Goddess bless you all."

Bailey looked at Jay, her eyes brimming with tears. "Jay, I love you and Brigid, thank you for this today. It was perfect!"

Jay kissed the soft fuzzy head of their daughter before kissing her wife. "Honey, this is just the start. Did you forget we have a celebration planned? Let's show this daughter of ours how the Irish throw a party!"

As Jay escorted her wife and daughter, she realized how blessed they truly were. When she and Bailey had gotten married, Bailey's High Priestess had flown in to do the ceremony, just as she had today. Scott had run things at the office in her absence, so well in fact, that she had arranged for a promotion for him. She was flabbergasted when he turned it down. He announced that he was very happy working where he was as her assistant. So, Jay created a new position for him, a management position that kept them working together, with him as her right hand still, but with more money and authority behind him.

When Jay told him of her marriage to Bailey, he had asked if they wanted kids. The truth was Jay hadn't really thought about it because of the cancer. They decided they did, and Bailey would try to conceive after they were married and settled in the new house. That was when Scott offered to be their donor. He willingly signed away parental rights and agreed to help them inseminate again if they wanted more children. Thankfully, the pregnancy had been uneventful and led to this amazing day, their daughter's introduction to her family and her parents' friends.

The new family led the way out of the tent, followed by the godparents, the pastor, and finally, the guests. As they walked, Riley and Sharon held hands and smiled at each other.

"So, what do you think, Sharon? Ready for this new responsibility of ours?" Riley gave her a teasing grin as she asked, but there was something else behind her question.

"I think that I can handle one small kid, honey. I do run a rather large division every day. What's one more small person? Besides, you have to help too!"

Riley smiled softly as she held the hand of the woman she loved. She swung their hands and decided to hold off on the talk she had planned until later that night. For now, this day was about Brigid, and welcoming her to the clan. Everything else could wait until later.

The End

Recipes From Strength In Numbers

Jay's French Toast

2 large eggs or equivalent in egg product per person
1/2 tsp of vanilla extract (real please) per person
dash of kosher salt and a few grinds of white pepper
1 tsp melted butter or margarine product (soy works well)
a splash of orange juice (to taste)
freshly ground nutmeg and cinnamon (to taste)
Day old Brioche or Challah, sliced about an inch thick

- Whip eggs and add in melted butter then the rest of the ingredients. I find if works best if I can let it rest a few minutes to blend.
- Allow each slice of bread to soak for a few seconds either fully submerged or turning to fully coat. Allow to drain before cooking.
- Heat a skillet or griddle to med high (until water droplets will dance not evaporate immediately). Spray lightly with some sort of cooking spray before adding the bread to cook. Brown lightly on each side and cook until the center is no longer mushy.
- Serve with syrup or powdered sugar. Goes well with scrambled eggs with dill.

Bailey's Salmon Pasta Salad

I actually got this from a friend I used to cook with years ago. Truly, this is Penny's Salmon Pasta Salad

8 ounces elbow macaroni or other medium pasta shape -- uncooked
1/4 cup low-sodium chicken broth
1/2 tsp all-purpose flour
3 tbl non-fat sour cream or plain yogurt
1/2 teaspoon dried dill weed
1 can (6 1/8-ounce size) skinless, boneless salmon (or equivalent cooked salmon
1/2 cup frozen peas
1/2 cup diced roasted red peppers -- very coarsely chopped
Freshly ground pepper -- to taste

- Prepare pasta according to package directions; drain and set aside.
- In a small bowl, combine chicken broth and flour. Whisk until flour is fully dissolved.
- Add sour cream and dill and whisk until smooth.
- Pour the sauce into a large skillet over medium-low heat. Add the flaked salmon, peas, red peppers and ground pepper.
- Warm just until heated through, stirring once or twice.
- Add the pasta to the skillet and stir gently until coated with sauce.
- Refrigerate and serve chilled.

Glazed Corned Beef

Actually, this is a slightly altered version of my mother's recipe. Those times when I was able to request a meal, more often than not glazed corned beef was my choice!

1 corned beef (flat or point work for this dish, just pay attention when slicing)
1 small can frozen orange juice
brown sugar
Dry mustard powder

- Boil the corned beef according to package directions, usually about 2-3 hours.
- Score the meat in a diamond pattern, fat side up after placing it in a roasting pan.
- Mix frozen orange juice (might have to partially thaw) with brown sugar until it forms a thick paste. Add in dry mustard to taste. I use a good 2 tsp usually. Coat meat and make sure to get the paste into the scored pattern. Roast at 350° F for about an hour or until meat is fully cooked. Glaze at least once more during cooking.

Bailey's Bubble and Squeak

Wonderful when using leftovers, but Bailey has to make it from scratch to go with Jay's corned beef.

1 med-lg russet per person, baked in skin
roasted garlic (can be done while potatoes bake)
a handful of shredded or chopped green cabbage (or brussel
   sprouts work well) per potato
sliced onion if desired
milk/cream
butter or margarine
Kosher or sea salt/ white pepper

- Scoop soft insides out of potato jackets into a mixing bowl. Add enough butter/milk/cream to turn into a decent mashed potato. (baking the potatoes eliminates much of the hard work).
- Sautee cabbage and onion until translucent and combine into potato mixture along with the roasted garlic
- Salt and pepper to taste
- Mix and pour into a greased baking dish. I tend to spray the top with cooking spray to help it brown. Bake at 350° F until brown and cabbage is cooked through.

About The Author

JEANINE WAS BORN and raised a New Englander and is still trying to find her way back home. In the interim she and her family reside in the Philadelphia, PA area. Her wife, their son, and the family dog have all been amazingly supportive during this venture into writing. Currently, Jeanine works as an Emergency Medical Technician in a hospital setting but has worked in hospitalities, emergency medical services, home care, and strangely the financial sector. She has plans to continue to write and occasionally to win a game on the Wii.

More can be found at:
http://JeanineHoffman.com

Book Back Summary

*J*AY HAS LIVED for her work the past five years. Suddenly, her past reenters her life just as she is questioning the future she faces. As she starts to think about how she is spending her life, two women enter her life and make her consider her present and future.

Bailey left home in a hurry thirteen years ago and has only recently discovered that too much was left unresolved in her past. She quits her job, moves back in with her parents, and struggles to reclaim the past she derailed all those year ago.

Riley has recently quit the LPGA tour in favor of spending more time back in Pennsylvania with her family. She decided that a mediocre golf career didn't take the place of watching her nephew grow up, and made the decision to become a golf instructor at a local golf club.

Sharon has hidden in a professional closet for so long that she can no longer see the light of day. Her career is solidly on track, but she despairs of ever having a personal life again. Can she combine life in a conservative company and a happy home life? She hasn't found a way but might be willing to try one more time.

When a crisis hits one of the women, no one is sure how to react or handle it. All four prepare to do battle with both the crisis and their own issues. Life is about to turn upside down for a lot of people but, there is *strength in numbers*.

* * *

*T*hank You for Purchasing and Reading
Strength in Numbers.
L-Book ePublisher, LLC

Breinigsville, PA USA
11 June 2010
239696BV00004B/1/P